SECOND CHANCE
on the
Shore

Coastal Dreams Book One

ALEXA ASTON

USA TODAY BESTSELLING AUTHOR

HOUSTON

Carson Andrews kissed his wife as he entered the kitchen, his morning jog behind him. He headed straight for his stainless steel water bottle, drinking its entire contents before coming up for air.

"I'll get Lily up while you're in the shower," Angie said. "Once she's dressed and fed, I'll drop you off at school."

He stole another quick kiss and left the kitchen, stripping off his T-shirt as he headed to their bedroom. Turning on the shower, he shed the rest of his clothes, putting them in the laundry basket in the closet, just as his wife had trained him to do. He stepped into the shower and adjusted the temperature before washing his hair and lathering his body. And the entire time, he couldn't help but think just how good his life finally was.

It hadn't always been that way. His parents and younger brother had died in a car accident when Carson was twelve. He hadn't been with them because he was spending the night with a friend, and the guilt had about eaten him whole. His only living relative was his dad's sister, Jayne, a maiden aunt who neither wanted to raise an almost-teenage boy nor spend any time with him. Carson had learned early that while he may have a roof over his head, he was definitely on his own. He'd dived into school, and basketball had become his refuge. His aunt had never come to a single game he played in, nor had she attended either his high school or college graduations. By the time his small wedding with Angie rolled around, he didn't even bother sending her an invitation, knowing she wouldn't RSVP, much less show up.

Surprisingly, Aunt Jayne had left him her house and everything inside it when she passed a year after his wedding. He and Angie had taken a few months to get the house into shape to sell. They sold most of the furniture, which had netted a tidy profit because almost everything was a valuable antique. They pulled up the carpets and had the floors re-sanded, making the wood gleam. After they painted the inside themselves and had a painting crew take care of the outside, they had put it on the market and sold it within four days. Taking the money from the sale of the house, they had bought a place of their own and owned it, free and clear, thankful they had no mortgage to pay.

Angie had grown up in foster care, so they knew they were starting from scratch in building their family. Lily had come along twenty-two months ago and was the apple of their eyes. She had the blond, curly hair of her mother, as well as Angie's clear, blue eyes. She ran more than she walked and jabbered constantly. He wasn't as fully fluent in Lily-speak as Angie was, but Carson was starting to pick up more and more on what his daughter said. He and Angie were both ready to try number two. Maybe spring break would be a good time for them to start.

As he toweled off and dressed for the day, he was eager for his upcoming spring break to begin once school was out this afternoon, probably more so than the students he taught and coached. Basketball season was over, and the Andrews were headed to East Texas and the piney woods of Tyler State Park. He'd reserved a cabin through Wednesday at noon. That would give them the weekend, plus a few extra days to rent canoes on the lake, fish, and hike. Lily loved being outside, and they enjoyed pointing out various wildlife to her. Carson wanted to take her fishing, hoping to catch a few catfish or bass. Knowing his daughter's tender heart, most likely he'd toss anything they hooked back into the lake.

He returned to the kitchen, seeing Lily in her high chair. Cheerios were her favorite food, and they were scattered about the tray. She also had slices of bananas and a yogurt for breakfast.

"How's my favorite girl?" he asked, leaning down and kissing her cheek.

"More milk, Daddy," she said, handing him her sippy cup.

Carson filled it and placed the lid atop it, giving it back to Lily.

"Kank oo."

"You are welcome," he replied, smoothing her hair.

Turning to Angie, he asked, "Do you have Binky's things ready?"

The beagle heard his name and stood. He'd been sitting under Lily's high chair, hoping for Cheerios to fall.

"Already put his bag in the car, along with his blanket and lovey. Diaper bag is there, too."

Binky was the newest addition to their household. They had adopted him two weeks ago at a community fair. They would drop him off at the vet's this morning since he'd just turned a year old. The adoption agency said that was when he should be neutered. Binky would stay at the adjacent kennel, recovering from his surgery until they returned Wednesday afternoon, getting rest and quiet.

"Finish up, baby girl," Angie said. "It's time to drop off Binky and Daddy."

Carson wet a rag and cleaned Lily's face and hands before taking her to the car and buckling her into her car seat. He got in the passenger seat as Angie opened the back door for Binky. The dog immediately jumped up and sat next to Lily, who began stroking his fur. He was glad they had decided to adopt the beagle. Already, the two were inseparable. Lily was also learning how to be gentle with Binky. Their daughter was the one who had named the dog Binky, after her pacifier. Angie had said they could get a dog if Lily would give up her binky. The toddler had tossed it aside the moment she'd laid eyes on the beagle and hadn't asked for it once, not even at bedtime.

They reached the vet's office, and Carson snapped on Binky's leash and led him inside. He handed over the bag of Binky's things, and the vet tech who took Binky in hand said they could call after three to see how the beagle was doing. He thanked the guy and kissed Binky's head before returning to the car.

Usually, he drove himself to work, but he needed new brakes on his truck, something he'd deal with once they got back to Houston. Angie had offered to drop him off at school, and they would take her SUV to Tyler State Park. She'd taken the day off from the hospital in order to pack and run several errands, including picking up food and snacks for the cabin. Once she dropped him at school, she would take Lily to the daycare at the hospital so she could get more done. Lily was in a big "helping Mama" stage, and it took Angie three times as long to do anything if Lily assisted her.

She drove past the front of the high school and to the field house in back, where his office was located.

Carson leaned over and gave her a goodbye kiss. "Hope you get lots done. See you this afternoon."

"I'll pick up Lily first. When we get you, we can head straight out of Houston."

Angie handed him his lunch, and he waved goodbye as she drove off.

His day was busy. He worked on his athletic budget in his office before heading into the main building to teach his three World Geography classes. He would have preferred to teach history, since he had a passion for it, but when he'd been hired straight out of college, the geography slot had been the open one. By the time another US History vacancy had appeared in the department, Carson had already been teaching geography for two years and decided to pass on making a switch. He already had lesson plans and activities for geography, and he'd come to enjoy teaching freshmen, something many veteran teachers avoided doing.

He ate lunch with a few of the other coaches in the break room inside the field house. The soccer and baseball coaches wouldn't really get a spring break since their teams had games scheduled. He was thankful to have some time away from Houston with his family. Basketball season always drained him, with long days and nights, plus weekend tournaments. He would recharge his batteries during his time off and enjoy spending time with his family. He hated shorting them, but that was the life of a coach during season.

Carson returned to working on his budget, which was due two days after he returned from spring break. He texted Angie twice, just checking in, but she didn't reply to either text. He knew she was getting her hair cut and thought she might be in the chair and not able to reply to him.

He glanced at his watch and saw school let out in fifteen minutes. It would be a zoo in the parking lot, and he'd told Angie to park two blocks away to avoid the traffic. He decided to slip out now before the bell sounded and the chaos began. Knowing his wife, she would already be waiting for him.

Then the phone on his desk rang. Reluctantly, Carson answered it, not wanting to get tied up when he was ready to duck out the door. "Hello?"

"I need you to come to my office right away," Joel Campbell said.

"Could we do this over the phone?" he asked, not wanting to leave the field house, cross the parking lot, and wind his way to the front office where the principal was. Even if Joel only spent two minutes with him, by the time he trekked back, school would be letting out.

"No. This needs to be in person, Carson."

"Be right there."

He hung up without protesting, wondering what his principal might want. Grabbing his cell, he texted Angie that he would be a few minutes late to the car because Joel needed to see him.

As he headed to see his boss, he worried that maybe Joel was firing him. That couldn't be. Joel was easygoing, despite being the leader of a large, inner city high school campus. Besides, Carson's varsity team had won district this year and made it to the second round of the playoffs. He wouldn't be let go because of that. If anyone fired him, it would be the athletic director, but he'd given Carson no signs of trouble on the horizon.

"Stop worrying," he said under his breath, passing noisy classrooms with teenagers ready to bolt for the door the moment the bell sounded.

He entered the secretary's office and saw her frowning. Carson called her name and she looked up, clearly distracted. Even upset. A woman sat in one of the two chairs designated for visitors, and he wondered if she had anything to do with the situation.

Before he could ask her if things were all right, the secretary said, "Go right in, Carson."

He did as instructed, tapping lightly on the closed door before entering. Joel was already rising to meet him. Carson spied another man also coming to his feet, dressed in a brown suit and having nondescript features.

"Close the door," Joel instructed.

After doing so, he faced his principal. "What's going on?"

"Have a seat, Carson," Joel said, his voice strained.

A feeling of dread filled him. "No. I think I'll stand."

Looking pained, the principal said, "This is Detective Kazinski. If you'll excuse me."

Joel slipped from the office, leaving Carson alone with the stranger.

"What the hell is going on?" he demanded. Then fear filled him, and he anxiously asked, "Lily? Angie?"

"Your daughter is fine, Mr. Andrews," the police detective assured him. "She's with Child Protective Services, and you will be reunited with her soon."

"What?" he exploded. "Why were they called in? My wife and I are excellent parents, Detective Kazinski. If someone's filed a complaint against us, they're just plain wrong. Yes, Lily has a bad bruise on her shin now. She fell. But she didn't break anything. She's never been mistreated. We love her."

Sympathy filled the man's face. "I'm sure you are a great dad, Mr. Andrews. I'm here to notify you of your wife's passing."

"Passing?" he croaked, a thousand thoughts swirling in his mind. "Wait. Angie is...*dead*?"

"I'm afraid so, Mr. Andrews."

"No," he said, shaking his head back and forth in disbelief.

"No. She dropped me off at school this morning. She took Lily to daycare. We're going to Tyler State Park for spring break. She's waiting for me in the car."

Frantically, he pulled his cell from his pocket. Instead of texting, he called Angie. "Pick up. Pick up," he urged, even as his stomach knotted painfully.

Kazinski reached and removed the phone from his hands, ending the call. "Please sit, Mr. Andrews."

"I...can't." He swallowed hard, his brain still racing.

Somehow, the detective eased Carson into a chair and took one next to him.

"Mrs. Andrews was at a gas station a few blocks from here. A man carjacked her. Witnesses say she was shouting, running alongside the car as it sped away. Telling the man that her baby was in the car." Kazinski paused. "He shot her and drove off." Pausing, the detective added, "She died on the way to the hospital."

"No," he whispered. "No."

Carson felt cold inside. Dead. Unfeeling. He couldn't imagine his life without Angie's laughter. Her teasing. Her lattice apple pies and pot roasts. Singing off key in the shower. Covering Lily's face with kisses and tucking her into bed.

He met the detective's gaze. "She's really gone," he said dully, reality setting in.

Kazinski nodded. "Yes, she is."

"Lily?" he said suddenly.

"Apparently, your daughter was crying hysterically after hearing the gunshot. The carjacker stopped a few blocks from the gas station. A witness saw him trying to unbuckle her from the car seat. He couldn't figure it out and got frustrated. Ran off. The witness crossed the street and found Lily inside the vehicle and called 911. That's why she's with Child Protective Services."

"I need her. Now," he said, an urgency rushing through him. It was as if he couldn't believe his little girl might still be alive unless he held her in his arms.

"Let me run through a few things with you," the detective said.

Carson tried to listen to what he had to say, but everything jumbled. It was as if the cop spoke Greek to him.

Kazinski handed over his card. "Here's my number. I'll be in touch with you. We've already caught the guy. He confessed right away. He's being assigned an attorney. There's the possibility of a trial."

"And my wife?" he asked, feeling broken.

"A colleague of mine is waiting outside. She's going to walk you through a few things. How to claim Mrs. Andrews' body. How to get your car back."

Carson felt as if he were underwater, drowning, no one rushing to save him. Numbly, he watched Detective Kazinski leave Joel's office. He returned with the woman who'd been seated outside.

"May I offer you my condolences, Mr. Andrews?"

They kept calling him Mr. Andrews. He was Coach Andrews. No one ever addressed him as Mr. Andrews. He almost laughed, hysteria rising within him, thinking of something meaningless at such an awful time.

She introduced herself, but he didn't care what her name was. He listened, trying to pay attention to what was being said.

"Here's a packet with information you'll find helpful," she told him. "I've placed my card inside. If you have difficulty with anything, just give me a call, and I'll help you cut through the red tape if I can."

Carson couldn't help but think of how much he had to do. Claim Angie's body. Call a funeral home. Plan a service.

And try to wrap his head around living a life without his wife.

"I need to see my daughter," he said firmly.

"She's in a car outside," Detective Kazinski assured him. "We can go see her now. Just try to stay composed, Mr. Andrews. She's been through a lot. You don't want to scare her."

They left the office, and he saw Joel come to his feet, stepping toward him.

"Whatever you need, Carson. Just let me know. You don't have to come back to school after spring break. Take all the time you need."

"I'll let you know," he said stiffly.

The principal's secretary looked up at him, tears in her eyes. "I'm sorry, Carson."

"Thanks," he whispered, knowing he would hear that over and over in the next days and weeks. But sorry didn't mean anything.

The bell had obviously rung while he was inside Joel's office, but he didn't recall hearing it. A few scattered students were still in the halls, but most had vacated the building as quickly as possible. Same for the teachers.

He accompanied the police outside to a black sedan. The back door opened, and a woman climbed out.

"Mr. Andrews?"

"Yes."

She smiled brightly. "Lily is such a love."

He had no time for niceties. Carson got into the backseat, finding his daughter in a car seat. Her eyes were swollen from crying. She clung to Ralph Rabbit, a stuffed animal that was her most treasured possession. It had been the only thing Angie had from her childhood, and she had passed it down to their daughter.

"Hi, sweetheart."

"Mama? Where's Mama? Loud noise, Daddy. Hurt my ears."

"I know, sweetie. I know. We're going to go home now."

Carson glanced up, seeing the woman who'd exited the car standing nearby.

"We need a ride home. I don't have my car here at school."

All he could think of was if only Angie hadn't taken him to work today. If she hadn't stopped for gas in this dicey neighborhood. If she'd taken Lily straight to daycare in her car and let him drop off Binky at the vet's.

But all the *what-ifs* in the world would never change the one, final truth.

Angie was dead. She was never coming home again.

Buckling his seatbelt, he closed the car door as the woman climbed behind the wheel. Carson gave her their address and sighed, his eyes filling with tears. He placed a hand on Lily's plump thigh, the one Angie would put her lips to and blow against it, making a god-awful noise that never failed to make their daughter laugh.

He leaned down and did so now, his heart shattering as he heard Lily's joyful giggle at the sound. He would have to be strong. Protect Lily. Be both mother and father to this precious child.

"Daddy sad?" she asked, cocking her head as she studied him.

"Daddy is sad," he agreed. "But Lily makes me very, very happy."

Carson clung to his sanity now—and the hope that his little girl might be the shining light in the darkness which now surrounded him.

Chapter One

Mila Perry was done with dating.

Especially when it came to coaches.

"Thanks anyway," she told her sister-in-law. "I'm just not going to date for a while." She grinned. "Maybe forever."

Cecily shook her head. "You don't mean that, Mila. And I know you want kids. You're so good with Bobby and Gina."

Cecily referred to her two children with Michael. Cecily was more sister than sister-in-law to Mila, especially since she and Mila's brother had been dating since sophomore year of high school.

"I have plenty of kids at school. Being around hormonal teenagers makes me question if I ever really do want to have kids of my own."

Both women laughed, and Mila added, "Seriously, Cecily. I haven't had great luck in the dating department. You and Michael are lucky to be high school sweethearts. You married and have two gorgeous kids. You're so happy that if I didn't love you as much as I did, I would be insanely jealous of you."

She had dated a guy seriously for two years when she first

got out of college and landed a volleyball coaching job in San Antonio. Mark had been the whole package. Smart. Funny. Handsome. But just as every other coach, he wanted to move up in the ranks. Middle school coaches maneuvered to land a job in high school. Assistant coaches dreamed of becoming head coaches and running their own programs. Mark had been an assistant football coach at a San Antonio high school which had a terrific football program, winning district championships and regularly making it deep into the playoffs. The head coach was constantly having to replace members of his staff because other districts throughout Texas plucked from his staff on a regular basis, offering them positions as offensive or defensive coordinators or even head coaching slots.

That's where Mark was now, in a small town about thirty miles north of Dallas, in charge of his own program. It had broken Mila's heart when they parted, but Mark wasn't ready to put a ring on her finger. Even she knew it would be foolish to try and follow him to a new district, especially since the district which had hired him already had a volleyball coach. She wasn't willing to give up coaching the sport she loved to coach something different, much less be stuck in a school district she didn't want to be in if she and Mark didn't move forward in their relationship.

When the opportunity came, she left her assistant coaching position for a head job here in Driftwood Bay. Of course, she had thought she would never return to her small hometown on the Texas coast, especially because her dad was now the superintendent of the school district. Still, when the chance presented itself, with her former volleyball coach asking Mila to interview for the position she was retiring from, Coach had said Mila's four years of seasoning at a large San Antonio high school, along with her years of playing volleyball through the college level at Texas State in San Marcos, made Mila more than qualified.

She had interviewed with Jon Earl Horton, the district's head football coach and athletic director, and was offered the job on the spot. True, there was likely talk somewhere in town of nepotism and her not earning the job but being given the vacant position because of who her dad was, but Mila hoped she had squelched that with three winning seasons under her belt, the most recent one culminating in a district championship.

This past school year, she had dipped her toe into the dating pool again, the first time she had gone out with anyone since she'd returned to Driftwood Bay, accepting a date with the Pirates' head basketball coach. Sam was a true competitor who hated losing and also fun to be around. She enjoyed going to his games and watching him coach from the stands. They had dated for six months—and then Sam got the call to interview for a new position in a district two division levels larger than Driftwood Bay. He was out the door so fast that he barely had time to say goodbye to Mila.

That had been a month ago, causing her to swear off men.

"I know you were upset when Sam took the new job," Cecily began. "It doesn't mean you have to give up on dating, though. And Chris is a really great guy. Plus, he's not going anywhere. He's happy at the hospital."

Chris was the nurse Cecily was trying to convince Mila to go out with. Her sister-in-law drove twenty miles each way to work at a hospital in Corpus Christi. While twenty miles didn't seem all that far, it was enough of a distance to give Mila second —and third—thoughts about going out with Chris, much less beginning a relationship with him.

"I think you have a lot in common. He's athletic. Plays on the hospital's coed softball team. He likes all kinds of sports. Is big into music. One very early marriage behind him which didn't last but a year. No kids." Cecily paused. "Plus, he's really cute. But don't tell Michael I said that."

Mila shook her head. "Despite your glowing review of Chris, I'm going to pass. Nurse my heart and try to put the pieces back together again. That means no dating for a while. Give me until November, after volleyball season ends, then I'll think about it."

Cecily sighed. "I get where you're coming from, Mila. It was rough when Michael and I broke up for that six months when I was in nursing school. The long distance relationship was hard to manage, especially with as much as I needed to study, coupled with his firefighter's schedule. We got through it, though. You shouldn't let being burned twice keep you from going out."

"I appreciate your support, Cec. You know that. Maybe I'll feel differently in six months, and you and Michael can double date with Chris and me. For now, though? I'm going to revel in being single again. It's summer. I have a couple of weeks off before I need to run my camp and think about lesson plans and volleyball again. I plan to enjoy having some time to myself, and I don't mind taking Bobby and Gina off your hands some. I can come and stay here for a weekend. They'll be near all their toys, and you and Michael could do a little getaway."

"We just may take you up on that," her sister-in-law said eagerly. "Let me see what Michael's shifts look like for the month of June. I can always have someone cover one of mine."

She finished her coffee and set down the mug. "It was good visiting. I've got to swing by the ad building and school now. Text me if you can work out a getaway."

"Will do."

Mila went to her Jeep and drove the short distance to the school administration building, which conveniently sat directly across from the high school. She was looking for a new volleyball and track coach for the middle school program and hoped she would be able to find one quickly so she could enjoy the next couple of weeks. When she left admin, she would go across the street and speak with Jon Earl about interviewing three candidates she liked.

She dropped off a flash drive of curriculum she had been working on the past few days for US History, updating it to match some changes the state had recently made. The secretary thanked her and said she would print out copies for Pamela, the director of Social Studies and ELA, to review. Then Pamela walked by, a stack of folders in her hands.

"Have a few minutes to talk?" she asked.

"Sure."

Mila followed Pamela into her office. They talked for half an hour about those changes, as well as debriefing about the past school year. Mila had always received excellent feedback from both her evaluator at the high school, as well as Pamela, and the older woman liked to bounce ideas off Mila, especially where change was concerned.

"I'll look over your updates and see if anything needs to be tweaked," the director said. "I doubt it because you're so efficient in everything you do, Mila. If you ever want to get out of coaching, I think you'd make a fine administrator."

"Actually, I've been giving that some thought, Pamela," she admitted. "You're the first person I'm sharing this with. While coaching is in my blood, the hours can be insane. I'm thinking about applying to Texas A&M in Corpus and starting on my masters in educational administration. I can do the entire coursework online, which really appeals to me because of my hectic schedule. It would certainly give me options regarding my career."

She hesitated. "Please keep this between us. If Dad got wind of this, he'd be all over it, pushing me to go into admin."

Pamela smiled. "Bill Perry would love to have you in the district as an administrator, but I'll definitely keep quiet about it. Let me know if you need a rec for the program. You know I'm happy to write a glowing letter for you."

"I appreciate you saying that. I'll be looking at everything in-depth, now that school is out. I'll get back to you if I need a rec letter. Thanks."

Mila told Pamela goodbye and glanced at her watch. Jon Earl would have left school by now for lunch, so she thought she might stop by her dad's office and see if he wanted to grab lunch on the square with her. Then she could talk to Jon Earl about the open position.

She went down the long corridor and stopped at the desk outside his office, greeting Sandy, his longtime secretary, who kept her dad in line and on top of things. He had inherited Sandy when he took the principal's job at the middle school and had asked her to go with him when he moved up to serve in the same position at Driftwood Bay High School. Sandy had accompanied him again when Dad came to the ad building, working his way up to being the district's superintendent. Like Cecily, Sandy was family to Mila.

"Hey, girl," Sandy greeted, sympathy in her eyes. "I hear things went south, with Sam leaving."

She nodded. "We'd only been going out for six months. It wasn't that serious," she said, trying to convince herself as much as Sandy.

"You know, I have a cousin who just recently divorced. He lives in Rockport." Sandy smiled hopefully.

Mila laughed. "Thanks—but no thanks. I'm going to enjoy the single life for a while. Is Dad available for lunch?"

Sandy consulted the desk calendar. "He will be as soon as he finishes up with the new basketball coach."

"He's already hired one?"

Sandy nodded. "He's coming from Houston. Jon Earl really likes this guy. I'm not sure why a coach would take a step back from a big school to here, but your daddy said he'll be a great addition to the district."

Before Mila could ask anything else about the new coach taking Sam's place, the door opened. She saw her dad standing there, offering his hand.

"We're glad to have you as a Driftwood Bay Pirate, Carson. I'll have HR print out the paperwork. If you can come back around one or later, everything will be ready for you to sign."

"Thank you for this opportunity, Dr. Perry," the new hire said, shaking her dad's hand.

Mila studied his profile for a moment, drawn in by how hot the new coach was. Like take-your-breath-away hot. She silently reminded herself not to look for a wedding ring on his finger, however. She was done with dating for now.

Both men turned, and Dad lit up, smiling at her.

"Why, here's the first teacher and coach that I can introduce you to who's on staff at the high school. Carson Andrews, meet my daughter, Mila. She coaches volleyball and teaches US history. Carson is going to replace not only Sam, but he'll also take on the AD duties from Jon Earl."

Surprise rippled through her. "Jon Earl is leaving?"

"No," Dad said. "He said he misses the classroom. He's going to be teaching government to seniors this coming year, as well as continuing as the Pirates' head football coach."

She turned to the new guy now and offered her hand. "It's nice to have you on board, Carson. I'd love to bend your ear since I was on my way to see Jon Earl. We need a new volleyball and track coach at the middle school. The current one has decided to stay home once she gives birth to her third kid in July."

"I'd be happy to talk it over with you, Mila."

"Why don't I give you a tour of the high school and athletic facilities while you're waiting for HR to finish up things on their end? We could also grab a bite to eat on the square if you're hungry."

"How can I pass up a guided tour and lunch with an insider?" Carson teased, his espresso eyes twinkling with mischief. "Dr. Perry said he grew up in Driftwood Bay and raised his family here. You'll know everything about everyone, I suppose, seeing this is a small town."

"Have you ever lived in a small town?" she asked.

"No. All I know about a small town is what I learned streaming that old TV show *Friday Night Lights*."

His answer caused her to laugh out loud.

"There are some similarities between it and Driftwood Bay. That town was centered around oil, though. A lot of the Bay's businesses deal with tourism and having the sea out our back door."

She glanced to her father. "Carson is in good hands, Dad. I'll have him back here to sign his life away in a couple of hours."

Mila left the building with the new coach, saying, "Let's do the tour first and get it out of the way. Then lunch won't be so crowded."

They crossed the street, and Mila showed him the front office, which also housed administrators and counselors. She walked him through the various hallways, pointing out the auditorium, teachers' lounge, gym, and copy room.

"There's a copier in the field house, so you'll use that one. Let's go out there now."

They cut through the cafeteria and went out the back

doors, crossing the teacher parking lot and entering the field house. Inside, she showed him the copy machine, break room, and conference room before stopping by Jon Earl's office. It was empty, as she'd suspected.

"Jon Earl is at lunch now. He likes to meet his wife at the diner on the square every weekday at noon. Hillary hates to cook, so they get a good meal in them mid-day and then have sandwiches or salad at dinner. Hillary's also a realtor. She can help you find somewhere to live. Do you have a family?"

Although Mila had not noticed a wedding ring on Carson's finger, there was always the possibility that he was married and chose not to wear one. Or he could be divorced. He looked to be in his early thirties and had that basketball, lean yet muscular build on what she guessed was his six-four frame.

"Thanks for the tip. I'll contact you after I finish up the paperwork with HR. I have a daughter who's four. Her name is Lily."

Carson didn't mention his wife, and she didn't want things to be awkward by bringing one up, especially if he were divorced.

Then he volunteered, "I'm a widower. I lost my wife two years ago. While I enjoyed the school where I coached and taught, everything everywhere reminded me of Angie. I decided Lily and I needed to get a fresh start. That's why we're coming to Driftwood Bay, along with Binky, our three-year-old beagle."

"I'm sorry to hear about your wife. Lily is such a beautiful name," she said. "I'm sure you'll both love it in the Bay. Will you be looking for an apartment or house?"

"I would prefer a house, especially having a dog. I'd like Lily to have a backyard to play in. She's a little shy."

"My brother has two kids. Bobby is four-and-a-half, and

Gina is three. Maybe Lily could come and play with them sometime."

"I'll have to figure out a lot of things," he said. "Thanks for that offer. I'll need to put her in preschool. Maybe you can suggest one. I also need to find someone who can sit with her nights and weekends when I've got games and tournaments."

"I can help you find someone," Mila volunteered, surprised that she was so willing to become this involved with someone she'd just met. But she felt some pull to Carson, not only a physical attraction, but something stronger. He seemed to be a decent guy who'd been dealt a difficult hand. After all, she was a Driftwood Bay native, and she could help him settle in with a few tips.

"That's kind of you. It's been hard, being a mom and dad to Lily. To be honest, I'm as scared as I ever have been, leaping into the abyss here. A new job. A new town. No back-up system. It's a lot to take on, along with the AD position, something I've never done before. While becoming the AD means more money, I know I've got a big learning curve ahead of me."

"You're going to do fine, Carson. One thing you'll learn about living in a small town is that people stick together. People are willing to offer a helping hand. The coaching staff at the high school is tight. It doesn't matter which sport you coach, everyone is friends and supports one another."

He looked at her, those warm, brown eyes causing her heart to speed up. "Thanks for being the first friend I've made in Driftwood Bay, Mila."

Chapter Two

Carson meant what he said about making a friend in Mila.

But he wanted much, much more.

He hadn't been attracted to any woman since Angie's death. He and his wife had been college sweethearts, and Carson couldn't remember the last time any woman stirred something within him. He'd been too guarded emotionally until Angie came and sat next to him in a required freshman political science course. The lecture hall had held close to two hundred, but she had plopped next to him and started up a conversation in her breezy, casual way. By the end of the professor's lecture, she had asked for his number and said they would be study buddies and ace the course.

That had been the start of their four years together in college. They both landed jobs in Houston before they even graduated, and after the morning graduation ceremony, they had gone to the courthouse and gotten married. Neither had family. They were everything to each other. Carson had numbed himself emotionally ever since her death. Not by using drugs or booze but simply turning off an imaginary switch that let him feel anything.

The only time he did experience any type of emotion was with Lily. He was one hundred percent involved and present with his daughter. He did his best to make up for the fact that she had lost her mom. Lily didn't really remember Angie, but Carson made certain to show her pictures of her mom every week and talk about Angie.

Coaching and teaching ate up a huge chunk of time, and the rest of any left over was spent in Lily's company. The idea of dating again, much less growing serious about someone and marrying her had not been on Carson's radar.

Until now.

Not that he wanted to marry Mila Perry. Talk about putting the cart before the horse. But she was the first woman who stirred anything inside him. It was as if while they talked and walked around his new professional home, he was a caterpillar emerging from his cocoon, long locked away from everything, and seeing the world for the first time. All Carson knew was he wanted to get to know Mila better.

She was the physical opposite of his wife. Angie had barely topped five-two and weighed just under a hundred pounds. She had delicate features and knew nothing about sports, even after going to plenty of his games over the years.

Mila, on the other hand, was built like an athlete. Dr. Perry said his daughter coached volleyball, and he could see where she had been a player, as well. She was probably an inch under six feet, slender but with great muscle tone. She wore a T-shirt and gym shorts which showed off shapely legs. Where Angie's hair had been ash blond and full of curls, Mila's honey- blond hair was board straight, pulled into a high ponytail. Angie had always worn makeup, being very particular about her appearance. He couldn't see a trace of it on Mila, but she still had flawless skin and blue eyes framed by thick, dark lashes.

Not only was Mila pretty, but she was friendly and outgoing. He was drawn to the warmth of her personality. Carson took a deep breath. He needed to keep things on an even keel.

And stop thinking about kissing Mila's lush mouth.

"I'm happy to be the first friend you've made in Driftwood Bay," she told him, her smile wide. She glanced inside the empty office they stood in front of. "I suppose Jon Earl will keep his office. It's the largest one in the field house. Since he's still the head football coach, he might want to stay here. On the other hand, you'll be serving as the new AD, so you'll need more room than Sam did. Let me take you to his office so you can see it."

They walked down the hallway, and she opened a closed door and turned on the light.

"This is the boys' basketball coach's office," she told him.

He could see it was only half the size of the previous one. While it would be adequate for basketball purposes, he might need more space for everything that went along with the AD portion of his new contract.

"It's nice." Carson stepped inside and looked around, seeing a desk, a few chairs, a round conference table with more chairs, and a huge whiteboard that would flip, allowing a person to write on both sides of it.

Mila went to the desk, where a stapler and phone sat, the rest of it blank. She opened the lap drawer. "Sam left a few pens and pencils. A box of staples."

She opened the rest of the drawers that moved along the left side of the desk. "Empty. Empty."

Then she froze when opening the last one. He watched her bend and retrieve a photograph. Her cheeks pinkened.

"Sam left a picture," she said brusquely, slipping it into her pocket. Then she brightened. "How about we go eat? I hope you like seafood, being so close to the coast. A lot of places scattered around town feature it on their menus."

"I'm coming from Houston, so I've had my share of seafood. I also would take Lily to the beach at Galveston. It was about forty-five minutes from our house. She's not much for getting in the water, but she does like to build sand castles."

"The ocean can be scary to little kids. My nephew is four and is just starting to walk out to where he's knee-deep. My niece, on the other hand, is like Lily. Give her a bucket and shovel, and she'll play in the sand all day if you let her." She paused. "I think we'll go to the Driftwood Diner if that's okay with you. They have a few fish items. Catfish. Tilapia. But the rest is pure diner fare. Any breakfast item you want all day. Burgers and chili dogs. And the most amazing French fries ever, plus homestyle favs. Chicken fried steak. Pot roast. You get the idea."

"Sounds good to me," he said. "If they do takeout, that might be dinner for Lily and me a few nights a week. I'm not much of a cook. I can make grilled cheese and scrambled eggs and bacon. That's about it."

"I like to cook. I just don't have a lot of time to do it," she told him. "And yes, Nellie and Neville definitely do takeout orders. I take advantage of that a couple of times a week myself." She grinned. "When I don't beg Mom to let me come to dinner. You'll have to come over and try her cooking. I think she's fabulous. She can do everything from paella to enchiladas to meatloaf and mashed potatoes."

Carson knew the invitation was just a casual, friendly one, but he would love to see how Mila interacted with her mom and dad. She seemed so normal, having two parents and being brought up in the same place. His idyllic childhood had ended with the car wreck which took his family's lives. Aunt Jayne hadn't been much of a parent at all, and he'd never felt wanted or loved by her. That was why family was so important to him, and he showered Lily with love and attention.

They returned across the street, and Mila offered to drive to the square.

"After we have lunch, I'll take you around town and show you a few highlights."

"I'll let your dad know what a great tour guide you are," he teased.

"I'm the Jeep over there," she said, and he got in, listening as she pointed out the police station, firehouse, and dry cleaners before they reached the town square.

"Here's where a lot of local businesses are," she said, pulling into a parking space that faced the gazebo, which was the focal point of the square. "Over there is Mom's shop, Coastal Charm Boutique. She carries things that focus on coastal life. Lightweight, breathable fabrics. Nautical-themed shirts. Mom has a great eye for fashion and stocks a good mix of trendy items, ones unique to the South Texas Coast, and even a few designer pieces. Do you want to go say hi since we're so close?"

"Sure," he said, getting out of the Jeep and moving past the gazebo to reach the opposite side of the square. Having already met Mila's dad, he was eager to see what Mrs. Perry was like.

He opened the door for Mila, who breezed in. "Hey, Mom. Here's the new basketball coach. Carson Andrews."

A tall blond with Mila's golden hair and blue eyes greeted him. "Why, hello, Carson. My husband told me you were coming to town this morning to sign your contract. We're so happy to have you in Driftwood Bay."

"Happy to be here, Mrs. Perry."

"No, I'm Laura. You can 'Dr. Perry' Bill all you want, but Mrs. Perry was my mother-in-law."

They chatted for a few minutes, Laura making him feel right at home. As they spoke, he looked around the shop, seeing mostly casual wear and coastal-inspired items bearing stripes, anchors, and seashells, along with swimsuits and activewear. One side of the store was devoted to accessories, including jewelry, handbags, and scarves.

"You'll have to bring your family over for dinner, Carson," Laura said.

"I told him you were an awesome cook," Mila said. "I think his eyes lit up when I mentioned enchiladas."

"Well, my chicken enchiladas are to die for, as are my shrimp ones," Laura said. "I'll make both and send some home with you. Just let me know when you get settled, and we'll have you over."

"Mila mentioned that Hillary Horton is a local realtor. I'm hoping to visit with her once I've dotted every *I* in my contract." He paused. "As for family, it's just my daughter Lily and me. She's four. My wife passed away a couple of years ago."

Sympathy filled Laura's eyes. "I'm so sorry to hear that, Carson. It must have been hard, trying to be strong for Lily and be both mother and father to her when your own heart was breaking."

"That about sums it up, but I'm hoping that Driftwood Bay will be a new start for us."

Laura handed him a card from a holder on the counter. "Just call whenever you're settled and want to eat a home-cooked meal." She glanced to her daughter. "Mila, you'll have to come, too."

"Hey, if you're serving enchiladas, you know I will be there. We need to grab some lunch now, Mom."

"All right, sweetie. Good meeting you, Carson," Laura told him.

They exited the boutique and went directly opposite it to the other side of the square, entering the Driftwood Diner. The smells that hit him as they walked in the door had his mouth watering. He hadn't eaten breakfast, being too nervous before his meeting with Dr. Perry, and Carson was now ravenous.

"Hey, Mila," a woman with white hair and a deep tan said. She looked to be in her early seventies.

Mila hugged her. "Nellie, this is Carson Andrews."

"The new basketball coach," the woman said. "Word is out all over town that you're replacing Sam." She glanced to Mila. "Sorry, honey."

"Nothing to be sorry about," Mila said, causing him to wonder what Nellie's remark—and Mila's reply—had been about.

"Nellie and Neville have run the Driftwood Diner for decades," Mila informed him.

"You came at the right time. An hour ago, I wouldn't have had a seat for you. Come on, let's grab you a booth."

Nellie lifted two menus from the stand and led them to a booth against the glass, giving them a nice view overlooking the town square.

"Any drinks?" Nellie asked.

"Water for me," Mila said.

"Same," he added. "I'm ready to dive into your menu."

After Nellie left, Mila said, "You can't go wrong with any of the burgers or grilled cheese. I'm actually going to get breakfast. It's my favorite meal, no matter what time of day."

Carson skimmed the menu, and when Nellie returned with their ice waters, he was ready to order.

Mila went first. "I'll do the Breakfast Bay Burger, with hash browns and fruit on the side."

Closing the menu, he said, "I'll take the Driftwood Diner

Number Two. Just curious, though. I didn't see a Number One. Am I missing something?"

Nellie laughed. "That's because there's never been one. How do you want your eggs cooked, Carson?"

"Over easy. I'll take the ham, hashed browns, and English muffin."

"No," Mila said, shaking her head. "Go with the biscuits and gravy. You won't be sorry."

"Okay. Biscuits and gravy," he told Nellie.

"Coming right up."

"I almost went with what you're getting."

"I love it. It's got the sausage patty instead of a beef patty. The sharp cheddar and the fried egg on top are perfection." She cocked her head. "Listen, I'm not opposed to splitting it if you want. You could have half my burger, and I could have some of your biscuits and gravy. That way, you could have more of a taste of things."

"You're on," he said enthusiastically, surprised she had suggested something so intimate. It had taken Angie and him six months to work up to sharing things from their plates with one another. "So, where have you coached? And how did you make your way back to your hometown?"

Mila laughed, a deep, throaty laugh that sent shivers running along his spine. "I played volleyball from third grade on. First at the Y and then at school. Driftwood Bay is too small for select teams, like more populated urban areas have, so I also worked as a photographer for the newspaper and yearbook staffs because I had more free time by not playing club volleyball. We won state my senior year, and my coach helped me earn a scholarship to play at Texas State."

Nellie arrived with a tray and distributed their food to them. Mila continued talking, slicing her burger in half and handing it over to him before picking up his plate with two biscuits and sliding one onto her own plate. She cut open the biscuit and spooned gravy on top of it.

"After college, I accepted a job in San Antonio as a volleyball assistant at a pretty large high school. Spent four years there and was getting itchy feet, ready to move on since the head coach was only in her mid-thirties and not going anywhere anytime soon. That's when my former high school coach called out of the blue and told me she was retiring—and she wanted me to take her place."

She paused, taking a few bites and sighing. Carson was right there with her, thinking the hash browns were the best he'd ever eaten and salivating after his first bite of biscuit and gravy.

"This biscuit is the lightest, fluffiest thing ever. And the gravy is outstanding," he said.

"It's sausage gravy. Neville does most of the cooking, and he won't share what goes in it."

"I hope he doesn't take his secret to the grave," Carson joked.

"It's common knowledge that the recipe is in his will and that when Neville is gone, it'll be published in the weekly newspaper, *The Drifter*. Until then, you have to come to the diner and pay to eat it."

"So, you returned home," he said, putting their conversation back on track.

"Yes. I interviewed with Jon Earl. As AD, he makes the final decisions on coaching personnel. You'll do the same now, I suppose. Anyway, he said I was the best candidate and offered me the job. I took it." Mila chuckled. "Breaking The Pact."

He frowned. "Pact?"

"My oldest, dearest friends and I—we met in kindergarten —always talked about getting out of Driftwood Bay. How we wanted to live in a place where no one knew everything about us. While it's great sometimes, living in a small town, people can get up in your business. We swore when we were thirteen that we would leave after graduation and never come back."

He sliced the last bite of ham and savored the smoky, sweet taste of it. "And are you the only one who broke it?"

"Yup. Layne is some hotshot computer tech person in Dallas. A CFO of her company. She's a former debater and can win an argument with the wall. Piper does regional theater and also travels in national productions. Layne is the last person who would come back to Driftwood Bay. She likes classy, Michelin star restaurants and high fashion. Piper is a nomad, living out of a suitcase. She doesn't even have a permanent address. She just goes from one production to the next. She did an off-Broadway play two years ago and rented a tiny place in Brooklyn during its run. That's the closest she's been to having a home since her college dorm room."

"Do you ever see them?"

"Some. Not often. We do FaceTime once or twice a month, though. We might not see each other in person, but we've stayed friends all these years. Piper and Layne are the people I depend upon the most."

Carson found himself a bit jealous. Because he lived with Aunt Jayne—and she'd been a hoarder from the time he'd arrived at her house—he'd never asked friends home. She would've flipped if he did. While he enjoyed playing with his basketball teammates, he kept to himself and had left high school without keeping up with a single soul.

When he got to college, he took a full load of classes and also worked about thirty hours a week, pulling shifts at a restaurant and refereeing basketball games. Summers, he kept the restaurant job and worked basketball camps and clinics. He'd had Angie—but she was really his only friend. He had made some during coaching, but he'd pulled away from those friendships after Angie's death, his responsibilities with Lily keeping him from staff happy hours and playing in a sports league.

The only exception was Rudy Cox, his assistant who'd been offered Carson's job when he resigned. Lily and Binky were staying with Rudy's family for a few days while Carson was in Driftwood Bay, but he was already missing his daughter and dog desperately.

Glancing at his watch, he said, "I guess you need to drop me back at admin." He waved to Nellie. "I'll get the check. Lunch is on me."

When the diner owner arrived and Carson asked for the check, she said, "It's on the house, honey."

"I can't let you do that, Nellie," he protested.

"Did you like the food? Will you be back?" she asked.

He grinned. "At least a few times a week."

"That's what I wanted to hear. Good to have you in town, Carson. Bring your little girl by soon. I'll have Neville make her some of his famous pancakes. He uses blueberries for eyes and strawberries for the mouth, and the hair is made up of choco-late chips."

Carson thanked Nellie for lunch, wondering how she already knew about Lily.

As they went to Mila's Jeep, she said, "You're thinking about how Nellie knew you had a daughter. I told you, Carson. You're in Driftwood Bay now. It's like the old show *Cheers*. A place where everybody knows your name."

They traveled the few blocks to the admin building, and Mila pulled up in front of its front door.

"Thank you for walking me around the high school," he said.

"I do need to talk to you about interviewing those volley-ball candidates."

"How many?"

"Three."

"Do we pay for them to come in for an interview?"

"No. Usually, we do those by Zoom. Did Jon Earl interview you that way?"

"He did, but he also wanted me to come in and meet your dad once he offered me the job."

"That's probably because Jon Earl was looking to hand off the AD position and knew Dad would need to visit with you in person."

He nodded. "That's the bulk of what your dad and I talked about. Okay, go ahead and set up Zooms with them. Do I need to be there for those?"

"No. Unless you don't trust me."

His gut told him that he could trust Mila.

"Do the interviews. Make the offer to the one you want. Just keep me in the loop."

"Will do. I should know by Thursday. Friday at the latest."

Going out on a limb, Carson said, "Would you like to have dinner and talk about it?"

Mila studied him for a long moment. "Sure. Why not?"

"Let's trade numbers so you can text me about the candidates," he suggested, hoping she wouldn't point out that once she'd hired someone, she could simply text him that info, as well.

They traded phones, inputting their information, and she said, "I'm also putting Hillary's number in here, as well." They handed their phones back to each other.

"Thanks again for everything, Mila," he said.

She gazed at him a long moment before speaking. "I hope you'll enjoy being here in Driftwood Bay, Carson."

He exited the Jeep and waved as she drove through the parking lot and turned onto the street. Carson entered the building to sign his contract and other papers, as well as receive his orientation packet. He had a lot to do. Set up a bank account. Contact the realtor. Find a place for Lily during the day and a responsible adult who could watch her when he was at practice or games, though that wasn't as pressing as everything else.

More importantly, Carson had some thinking to do.

And that revolved around whether or not he wanted to pursue Mila Perry.

Chapter Three

Carson entered the district's administration offices, and the receptionist greeted him brightly.

"Good afternoon, Coach Andrews. They're ready for you in HR. Go down the hall to your right and turn when it dead ends. Take it all the way until another dead end, and you're there."

"Thank you, Gretel," he said, reading the name tag she wore. He knew people enjoyed when a person used their name, and he certainly had a lot of new ones to learn in Driftwood Bay.

He followed her directions and found himself at Human Resources. He was shown in immediately, and the director introduced herself. Everything was set out on a round conference table, and they seated themselves. Mae Williams walked Carson through everything he was signing with brief but thorough explanations. The last time he'd been hired in his previous school district, it had been like herding cattle through, as several hundred new hires had been present, going to various schools throughout Houston.

This time, he was getting the personal touch. He supposed part of that was small-town charm, while the other was the fact that he was taking two important positions. Small towns in Texas were known for supporting their teams, and the district's athletic director would have his finger on the pulse of every sports team.

"That should do it, Coach Andrews," Mae said. "I'll have my assistant make copies of these for your records. Once you've established a bank account in the Bay, give me a call. I can set up direct deposit for you if you'd like to go that route."

"I would appreciate that."

"Thank you for taking on the additional title and responsibilities of being our athletic director," she continued. "While you may feel that this is a stretch for you, Dr. Perry and Jon Earl believe you have tremendous potential. Jon Earl has been the gold standard, so I'm not saying this lightly."

He found himself sitting up a bit taller. "Thank you for letting me know that." Setting down the pen, he asked, "Is there anything else?"

"If you have time now, Jon Earl is in his office at the field house and would like to speak with you," Mae said. "You won't officially be on the clock until June fifteenth, but he can pass over the keys you'll need, and you're welcome to come and go for the next two weeks. I know you also need to find a place to live."

"Yes, I want to find housing while I'm here for a few days. For my daughter and me."

"Talk to Jon Earl about that. His wife is a real estate agent and as sharp as they come. She'll want to make certain you're happy, so we can keep you in Driftwood Bay."

He stood and shook hands with Mae, and she asked if she could take his picture for his school ID. She handed him a lanyard that he could use with it, telling him she'd send the laminated card along with the copies of his contract.

"I'll text Jon Earl to let him know you're on your way over. I'll have everything from the contract to insurance copies sent to the high school in interoffice mail. I'll also set up your district email account now and forward it and instructions on how to activate it to the email you've used to correspond with us. I'll notify the webmaster that you'll need to be added to the district's website. He'll contact you directly about providing a picture and info for your page on the site." She smiled brightly. "Folks in the Bay are going to want to know all about you."

Carson got into his SUV and drove across the street, parking behind the high school and next to the field house Mila had showed him just a couple of hours ago. He still wondered at the connection he had felt with her, but that would take some deep thoughts. Right now, he needed to focus on the time with his predecessor. Jon Earl Horton held a wealth of knowledge about the district, and Carson was eager to soak up whatever the football coach passed along to him.

Knowing his way, he went straight to Jon Earl's office, where he was warmly greeted.

"Have a seat, Coach. Bill tells me you're all on board."

"I just finished up with the paperwork at HR, so it's official. I'm glad you're going to be around, though. I hope you won't mind if I have questions for you regarding the AD portion of the job."

"That's what I wanted to talk with you about." Jon Earl looked around. "You can see this office is a decent size, and it comes with the AD position. I'm going to move down the hall now that you're an official Driftwood Bay Pirate. I'll take the former basketball coach's office."

"You don't have to do that," he protested, although Carson was secretly happy he would have all the extra space.

"First of all, you'll need this office for storage. You'll accumulate a ton of things. Second, you'll be having meetings with everyone in the athletic department. That includes all the sports at the high school and the middle school. I'm happy to vacate the space and let you have at it."

For the next half hour, Jon Earl showed Carson where hard copies of various files were kept and gave him a rundown of a typical year for an athletic director, promising that once Carson had activated his school email account, he would inundate him with emails that contained attachments that Carson would need to refer to.

"When I decided to step down as AD, Hillary got on to me, gently nagging until I came up with a timeline of everything to pass along."

The older man picked up a notebook sitting on this desk and handed it to Carson.

"This is for you. It'll walk you through, month-by-month, in much greater detail than the overview I've given you, the kinds of decisions which need to be made by certain dates. Tasks which must be accomplished. Budgets are a huge part of that. It also has UIL info for all sports, not just basketball. You'll need to really study this, as well as everything I send to you so that you're familiar with the state's regulations for each sport and the Driftwood Bay's school trustees' plans for athletics over the next several years. I've worked with them on one-year, five-year, and ten-year plans. Of course, you'll want to put your own spin on things."

"Then I guess I need to thank you and Hillary. I've been told by two people that she's the realtor I need to speak with."

"We're done here," Jon Earl said. "I'll be out of your hair and moved from this office into my new one in the next twenty-four hours. I know you don't officially report until mid-June, but feel free to make this space your own starting tomorrow."

Jon Earl handed over a key ring stuffed with keys, each labeled meticulously, and they spent another quarter-hour going through all the places those keys opened.

"That's it for now," the older coach proclaimed. "And now that you're a part of Driftwood Bay, I'm going to give you a heads-up. This will be my last year of coaching and teaching. I'm going to retire at the end of this coming school year."

Carson guessed the coach was in his mid- to late-sixties and said, "We don't need to have this conversation today. You may change your mind."

"No. Giving up the AD's slot was the first step in cutting back and easing into retirement. I know it's hard to find personnel, especially in a smaller district, and I wanted to let you know what my plans were so that you'll have plenty of time to replace me. It's another reason I'm also going back to the classroom for a year. I haven't been there for a good many years, and I miss the teaching part. Yes, I do teach all the time when I'm coaching, but the classroom is a little bit different. I just wanted you to know about my plans, and I hope you'll keep that in a very small circle for now."

"Does Dr. Perry know about this?" questioned Carson.

Horton nodded. "He does. Bill's the one who suggested a transition year, so that I'd be around and able to answer questions for the new AD before I put in my retirement papers with the state. Would you like me to call Hillary and see if she has some time to visit with you now?"

"Sure, I'd appreciate an introduction."

The older man picked up his cell and tapped it. "Hey, honey. I'm with Carson now. Yes, everything is a done deal, and he is going to need a place to live. Sure."

Jon Earl passed his phone to Carson, who said, "Hi,

Hillary. You have been recommended to me by a few people today, and that doesn't even include your husband."

He heard her chuckle. "That's good to know, Carson. Why don't you come on over to my office? I'd like to hear what you're interested in, but I need to be very upfront. We don't have a lot of inventory open up in Driftwood Bay, so it may take time to hit on the right property for you and your family. People here like the area and seldom leave. Your best move would be to lease something for six months to a year. That way, I could keep my eye out for the kind of property you're looking for. If nothing right opens up over the next few months, I can suggest an architect for you to commission to come up with some plans and then build from scratch. Are you free now?"

"Free as a bird," he replied, a little disappointed that housing would be difficult to find.

"Good. Come on over, and we can visit a bit. Jon Earl will give you the address. I'm right on the edge of the square."

"Already familiar with that since I ate at the Driftwood Diner for lunch."

Carson ended the call and handed Jon Earl's cell to him. The other coach provided the address of his wife's real estate office, as well as directions. He found it amusing that Jon Earl didn't use street names. Instead, he gave directions which told him to turn at a gas station and then at the firehouse before reaching the square.

"Thank you, Coach," he said, standing and offering his hand. "I appreciate the time you gave me today, and I hope I won't drive you crazy with too many questions throughout the school year."

"That's what I'm here for, son. Anything you need, you just let me know. You're inheriting a solid staff, and your basketball assistant is a good one. I hope you'll make your home in the Bay for years to come."

Carson took the thick notebook with him, eager to read through its contents. While he felt very comfortable with the basketball piece of the job, being a district AD, even in a small school district, would be a tremendous responsibility. The fact that the residents of Driftwood Bay would be highly invested in their local sports teams meant a lot of eyes upon him and the decisions he made. That would be added pressure. He would not only need to be successful in basketball but also maintain a winning program in other sports, based upon his personnel decisions.

He arrived back at the square, the way already beginning to seem familiar to him, and entered the real estate office. He saw no reception desk. Instead, the small office held a large desk, covered with files and a desktop computer. It also held a conference table which would seat six. A woman who looked to be in her early sixties sat at it, along with a gentleman who appeared to be in his early fifties, graying at his temples.

Both stood, and he shook hands with each, as Hillary introduced herself and Dr. Pete Jacobs.

"Have a seat, Carson," the realtor said. "We may have a solution to your living arrangements, courtesy of Pete here."

Carson took a seat at the table, and Hillary said, "I'm familiar with every listing in Driftwood Bay and the surrounding area. Do you mind sharing in front of Pete what you're looking for in a house?"

Though Carson found it a bit odd to be talking in front of a stranger about something so personal, he said, "I'll be bringing my four-year-old daughter to Driftwood Bay with me, along with our beagle. I prefer a house over an apartment. I'd like a good-sized, fenced backyard. Probably three bedrooms and two baths. Although I am pretty handy, my new job is going to keep me really busy, so if a house is turnkey, that would appeal more to me than one which comes with projects."

Hillary nodded. "You'll probably want to be closer to town, as well, having a little one and working long hours. You don't want much of a commute." She chuckled. "Not that any place is very far away in the Bay."

"That's correct. The closer to work, the better."

She looked to Dr. Jacobs. "Have at it, Pete."

Carson turned his attention to the stranger, who said, "I'm a marine biology professor at a university in Corpus. I just learned that my yearlong sabbatical has been approved, and I'll be leaving shortly for Australia, where I'll be doing research with the Australian Institute of Marine Science, specializing in sea snakes. I hope to get at least two books out of my year abroad. Our daughter is in medical school. Our son just graduated from college and is headed for a job in San Antonio."

Carson wondered what all this had to do with him and waited patiently as the older man continued.

"We want to come back to our house this time next year. Hillary suggested we rent it. The Bay always has summer people coming and going, but I don't want to mess with hiring a cleaning service and someone to manage the property while we're away. I'd rather have one tenant—and it looks as if you might be it."

Carson now understood the connection. "Tell me about your house, Pete."

"It's a two-story. Four bedrooms. Two full and one half-bath. Close to town. If you'd be willing to put your furniture in storage and just use ours, I'd like to work out a caretaker deal with you. Hillary said she could draw up the paperwork for us. I wouldn't charge you any rent, Carson. I would ask that you pay for utilities and the internet. Keep the streaming services in place, too. Mow the grass. Trim the shrubs. That kind of thing. It would give you and your daughter plenty of room. We even have a swing set and slide in our backyard from when our kids were young. My wife didn't want to part with the play set, hoping we'd have grandkids who could come and enjoy it someday. What do you say?"

Carson couldn't believe his good fortune. He would save a ton of money by not paying any rent for a year, especially leasing something in a seaside community, where prices for rentals had to be through the roof.

"I don't mind covering the bills, and I do enjoy yard work," he shared. "Are you sure you don't want me to pay a monthly rent, Dr. Jacobs?"

"It's Pete. And no," the other man responded. "You'd be doing us a huge favor, especially if you let us leave some things in the drawers and closets. We can't take that much with us Down Under, but my wife would make certain to clear out plenty of room for you and your daughter. You could use our primary suite, and we'll empty those closets and put everything in one of the spare bedrooms. Your daughter could take the bedroom our daughter used. My son will be coming in a week to get the rest of his things to take to San Antonio with him. I would appreciate the favor, you taking care of the house for us."

Hillary spoke up, looking hopeful. "It would give us plenty of time to decide what you want to do about permanent living arrangements, Carson. There's rarely any properties for sale which open up in the summer months, but come fall, anyone who wants to sell will put their house on the market then. That way, we can see what inventory is available and if you need to build instead of buying an existing property." She smiled at them both. "To me, this looks like a win-win for you both."

"Before I commit, I'd like to see the property first," Carson said, his cautious nature rising. "If I think it'll suit our needs, then I'm happy to accept the deal."

"Great," Hillary said. "I'll begin drawing up the paperwork. I've never had an arrangement like this before, so give me about an hour to complete things. Pete can take you to the house and let you see what you think. If you're happy, head back my way, and we'll get the paperwork taken care of."

Pete offered to drive Carson, and they were only in the car about three minutes.

"The house is about six minutes from the high school," Pete told him. "Our neighborhood is friendly. My wife is close to Dotty Williams, a widow who lives next door to us. Dotty knows everyone and would be a great reference for you as you get to know the town."

They pulled into the driveway of a well-kept two-story, and Pete said, "It's about twenty-five hundred square feet. Should be plenty big enough for the two of you."

The house had great curb appeal, with a pristine lawn and flowerbeds blooming with color. He recognized Texas sage and black-eyed Susans among the blooms.

They went inside, and Pete walked Carson through the house.

"I can leave a list of people we use when things go wrong. The plumber. A/C guy. Handyman."

They finished their tour, and he turned to Pete. "This is going to be perfect. I was afraid Lily and I would have to stay in an apartment or a tiny rental while we were trying to find something permanent. This will work out well for both of us."

He offered his hand, and Pete shook it.

"Then let's go tell Hillary it's a done deal," Pete said.

They returned to Hillary's office on the square, and the realtor greeted them.

"Well, what did you think?"

"The house is in terrific shape. It's got a nice layout. Lily and I will be happy to serve as caretakers for it during the next year."

They sat at the table again, and Hillary walked them through the paperwork she had just created, combining a few templates which she'd found online.

"It does contain a clause stating that if Carson finds a house to purchase, he would be off the hook on his end," she shared. "At that point, I could rent it out for you, Pete."

"Even if that happens, I'd be happy to keep my eye on the place," he said. "Mow the yard. Handle any maintenance issue that came up. That kind of thing."

"Sounds good," Pete said cheerfully. "I just texted my wife to make our plane reservations. We're looking to leave in two days. We'll work on clearing space for you and Lily, Carson. I'll leave the keys with Hillary."

"What about your cars?" Carson asked.

"Glad you thought about that," Pete said. "I'd like to keep my car in the garage if that's okay with you. My wife has been needing a new car. I'll go ahead and sell hers so you can park your car in the garage. We can buy her a new vehicle when we get back. Anything else you can think of?"

"If you would just pull together a list of utilities and companies you use. Insurance. That kind of thing. I want to be able to continue making the payments on your accounts."

"I can help facilitate that," Hillary volunteered.

They signed the necessary paperwork, and Carson felt the stress of finding a place to live float from him.

Hillary offered her hand, and Carson took it. "It's good to have you in Driftwood Bay, Coach Andrews."

He left the realtor's office, feeling that he had accomplished so much today. He had a new job which would be challenging and rewarding. A house for Lily and him to live comfortably.

And he had made a friend—who might turn out to be more than a friend—in Mila Perry.

Chapter Four

Mila grabbed a can of sparkling water from the fridge and moved to the couch in her apartment. She decided to kill a few minutes before her FaceTime with Layne and Piper began and pulled up Instagram. Like everyone, she followed celebrities she liked. Local businesses in Driftwood Bay. Sports teams and figures she admired. And of course, friends.

She typed in Sam's name, something she had not done since he had abruptly resigned from the high school and left town for his new position. She went through a few of his more recent posts, seeing his apartment. A dinner out with fellow coaches. Surprisingly, she felt nothing.

And that felt really, really good.

She had been brokenhearted when she and Mark ended their romance. She had only been twenty-four, and it was her first serious relationship. She had tormented herself, following him on Instagram for a year, seeing how happy he was at his new school. When he had started dating someone and posting pictures of their outings, it had crushed her soul. She unfollowed him immediately, and had no idea where he was now or if he had married that girl from the pictures he posted.

Things felt different this time, with Sam, and Mila was glad to have made this breakthrough. Her phone rang, and she was excited to share this discovery with her two closest friends.

She clicked on the call, and Piper's friendly face filled the screen.

"Hey, girl," Piper greeted. "Let me patch in Layne."

Her other good friend appeared on the screen.

"Hi, everybody. I've got to tell you about a new app at work that I just finished working on. It's A-mazing, if I do say so myself."

For the next several minutes, Layne talked about the app she had created, saying it would make a huge difference in her company's productivity and efficiency, and that it might have long-reaching consequences for other companies who invested in it, as well.

When she finished describing it, Piper said, "I'm proud. I actually followed most of what you said just then. Thanks for learning how to explain tech-y things to us," she joked.

"I practiced on Jeremy before I called you two. You know he's as non-tech as they come."

"How are things with Jeremy?" Mila asked. "You haven't mentioned him for a while."

Layne frowned. "I hate to report that he's quit another job. He just can't seem to find work he enjoys. He's had a really bad run of luck finding a good boss to work under."

Mila had met Jeremy several times over the last few years on trips to Dallas. While he was very nice-looking and really smart, he wasn't a people person, the opposite of Layne. Mila also resented that Layne carried the financial burden in their relationship. Jeremy only contributed every now and then to their rent—and nothing else. She wished Layne would wake up and realize her longtime, live-in boyfriend was a user, but Mila wasn't going to go there. Layne would have to figure this out on her own. Jeremy would have to do something incredibly stupid to get Layne's attention. Then maybe she would give him the boot.

"Switching topics," she said, "how is *Les Miz* going?"

Piper brightened. "I've been getting some fantastic reviews. Fantine is a dream role for me. I get to sing my heart out and die dramatically almost every day of the week."

"Where are you, again?" Layne asked. "You travel so much, I lose track."

"Atlanta," Piper responded, laughing. "Sometimes, I can't even remember what city I'm in when I wake up. I check the weather on my phone to see where I am. We'll be in Atlanta for another two weeks and then swing through Florida before moving to New Orleans and then the Midwest."

"No stops in Texas?" Mila asked, disappointed because she enjoyed seeing Piper on stage.

"No. When I replaced the actress playing this role, they had already done a tour of Texas and the Southwest."

"I wasn't straight on why you replaced her," Layne said.

"She was having some vocal cord problems and had to stop singing for a while in order to rest her voice. I had just finished a touring production of *Rent*, so the timing couldn't have been better when the director contacted me. I was able to step in because I've played Fantine several times over the years. It was just a matter of a couple of rehearsals to help me gel with this cast. But enough about me. What's going on with you, Mila? How are your spirits? I know Sam leaving really had you down the last time we talked."

Mila sat up a little straighter. "Actually, I've come to the conclusion that I'm over Sam. Completely. We only dated six months. Yes, I had a lot of fun with him, but we never really went beyond surface level. I think when he left, I was more upset about the idea of not having someone to do things with, versus the idea of not having Sam in my life anymore."

"That's great, honey," Layne said. "All you need to do now is get back up on the dating horse."

She sighed. "You know what Driftwood Bay is like. There aren't a lot of single guys running around. Although I did see the architect for Tidewater at Pelican Point last weekend. He's pretty yummy. Too bad he'll be gone soon."

"How is Tidewater coming along?" Piper asked.

Her friend referred to the resort being built on the island a couple of miles off the coast of Driftwood Bay. It was supposed to open sometime next year and would cater to the wealthy looking for an escape.

"It's coming along. It should open by next summer, I think. Not that I could afford to stay there on my teacher's salary. Everyone's talking about how it'll be the ultimate in luxury, being a Wagner Enterprises Hotel and Resort."

"That should bring an influx of new guys to the area," Layne said. "They'll have to have people who manage the resort. Work the desk. Instructors for things like diving and golf. Even chefs and bartenders. Surely, some guy will come in and catch your attention."

Mila quietly said, "There's already a guy who has landed on my radar."

Her friends squealed in unison, and Piper said, "Spill it, Mila. Every detail, starting with how hot he is."

She laughed. "Actually, he is incredibly hot. Probably six-four or so. Rich, brown hair. Eyes the color of espresso." She paused. "Believe it or not, he's the guy who has taken Sam's place."

"Oh, no," Layne protested. "Not another coach. You said

you've sworn off dating coaches. That they only stay a few years and then leave for greener pastures."

"I'm not saying I want to date him," she said firmly. "Only that he's a very attractive man who's caught my eye."

"Where did you meet him?" Layne asked.

"I dropped by the ad building today to talk with Pamela about the curriculum I just finished revising. When I went to see if Dad wanted to have lunch with me, Carson was coming out of his office."

"Carson," Piper said. "Carson what?"

"Andrews," Mila supplied. "Wait, what are you doing?"

"I'm googling him, silly. I can't believe you haven't done that already. Or have you?"

"I'd prefer to learn things about Carson from him. I took him over to the high school and showed him around. Then we went to the diner and had lunch before I dropped him back at admin to sign everything at HR."

Piper got a funny look on her face, and Mila suspected what she was reading about.

"He's a widower," she told her friends. "Has a four-year-old daughter named Lily. He's coming from Houston."

"Do you want to get involved with someone who has a child?" Layne asked, concern on her face.

"First of all, I'm not involved with him. We just shared a friendly lunch while I told him about the high school and town. One coach talking with another coach. He really seems to care for his daughter. I'm sure all his free time is spent taking care of Lily."

Piper spoke up. "Do you know how his wife died, Mila?"

"No. He mentioned he lost her two years ago and that he was a single parent. Why?"

"I'm finding some articles about her death. It's really tragic.

His wife was *carjacked*. The little girl was in her car seat in the back, and Angie Andrews was hysterical, pleading for the carjacker to let her get her daughter out of the car when he shot her."

A sick feeling washed over Mila. "I didn't know any of that."

Piper's eyes were skimming the article as she said, "I think you owe it to yourself to look him up. Especially if you're interested in him."

She regretted sharing with her friends her attraction to the handsome new basketball coach.

Dismissively, she said, "Nothing is going to come of anything between Carson Andrews and me. I just wanted to share that I'm totally over Sam and I actually found another guy hot. End of story."

Layne quickly changed the subject, asking about a few things in Driftwood Bay. Mila knew what her friend was doing and answered all her questions as best she could.

Then Layne said, "I'm a little worried about Mom. We talk once a week, and she just seems... I don't know. Off."

"Have you asked your dad about it?" Piper asked.

"No. You know how Dad is. He would just dismiss my concerns. I just wondered if you might have run into her anywhere in town."

"No, but I can stop by the B&B and just chat with her."

"Don't do that," Layne said. "She'd know right away that I'd sent you, and that would piss her off. Maybe Mom is just in that menopause fog you read about older women experiencing."

"I'll ask my mom about her," Mila offered. "Since your mom usually comes into the boutique once or twice a month to shop."

"Would you?" Layne asked. "That would be great."

"Well, I need to go," Mila said. "I've set up three interviews over Zoom tomorrow."

"That's right," Piper said. "You've got to replace the coach at the middle school."

"Yes. She or he needs to coach volleyball in the fall and track come spring. Carson said I can pretty much hire whomever I want for the position."

"Wait a minute," Layne said. "Why would the new guy have anything to do with you hiring a coach?"

"Jon Earl Horton is stepping down as the district's athletic director," she informed her friends. "He wants to focus on football and return to the classroom, so he and Dad thought Carson might be a good choice to take over the open AD slot."

"That's a lot on Carson's plate," Piper observed. "Especially since I'm not seeing anything online about him having been in that role before."

"No, it's new to him, but he's a really sharp guy."

Layne grinned. "He's at least smart enough to know to let you hire the person you want for the job and just let him rubber-stamp it."

Mila laughed. "And on that note, I'll talk to you both in a couple of weeks."

Quickly, they all pulled up their phone calendars and agreed to a date for their next group call. While she texted almost daily with both women, it was nice to see her friends over these FaceTime calls and interact together.

"Thanks again for letting me share boring work stuff that neither of you cares about," Layne said, looking serious. "Jeremy never seems to be interested in work talk."

"We're always here for you," Mila said. "Especially when you dumb it down enough for us to have a clue what you're even talking about."

"Bye, everybody," Piper said, leaving the call.

Mila did the same and then clicked over to a set of questions she would be using in her interviews tomorrow. Some were standard ones provided by the district's HR office, while others were more in-depth ones which would allow her to see how well the candidates she interviewed knew about volleyball. Mila needed to find a coach who not only had decent knowledge of the sport but was willing to align the middle school program with hers at the high school. Too many times in a small town, staff was hired to coach a sport they'd never played, much less one they had personal knowledge of. She definitely wanted someone who had played volleyball and shared her philosophy regarding the sport and coaching athletes.

Taking time now to review their applications and résumés, she wondered which one would be the best fit. The first candidate was twenty-seven and had bounced around to three schools already since graduating from college. His résumé was solid, though, and she thought he was worth talking to. The second candidate was a recent college graduate, but she had played volleyball for almost fifteen years, from everything to the Y to club to her high school's team. She hadn't played on a university team, but she had run a coed intramural sports league for her college. That had included playing and reffing volleyball and other games, such as basketball and flag football. Mila liked that she was female and had organizational experience. She wasn't against hiring a male coach for a female sport, but she thought it was important for young ladies to have strong female role models.

The final woman she was interviewing was the wife of one of the new football coaches at one of Corpus Christi's high schools. Mila knew in a marriage where both the husband and wife coached, they would move to the job which was the most prestigious. The football job was with a 6-A school, several divisions higher than Driftwood Bay. Texas broke up competition based upon the population of a school, with new districts being drawn up every two years as student enrollments were updated.

While this third candidate had taught in a larger school than Driftwood Bay, it was obvious she was taking a step back in her career based upon the direction her husband's football career now headed. Because of the hours the husband would put in, most likely the couple would live in Corpus. Mila would have preferred a coach who chose to live locally, but she was still willing to interview this final candidate, seeking the best qualified coach for the position.

Satisfied with her list of questions and knowledge of each person seeking the job, Mila closed her tablet and got ready for bed. She had trouble falling asleep, though, playing bits and pieces of her conversation with Carson Andrews in her head. Frustrated, she sat up, turning on the light on her nightstand. Picking up her phone, she googled him just as Piper had suggested. Mila read several articles about the teams he had coached before turning her attention to his wife's murder.

Angie Andrews had been a nurse, well-beloved at the hospital where she worked, and had been married to Carson for eight years before her death. Lily had been their first child.

As Mila scrolled through several news stories, the witness accounts shocked her with just how brutal and senseless the murder had been. She couldn't imagine the hurt Carson carried in his heart, having lost his college sweetheart.

Setting her cell on the charger, Mila turned out the light again. Carson's life was going through huge changes right now. He was bringing his motherless daughter to a new town. He would have to find housing and childcare. Meet his new coaching staff and players. Learn an entire new job as the AD for the district. Like Mila, becoming involved with someone was the last thing either of them needed.

Or was it?

Chapter Five

Carson put his duffel bag into the back seat of his car and drove to the high school. He would leave today for Houston and claim Lily. Though they had only been apart a few days, he had FaceTimed with her each day he was gone.

He pulled up into the parking lot next to the field house and called Rudy, his friend and co-worker who had volunteered to watch Lily while Carson was out of town.

Rudy answered, his usual wide smile lighting his face.

"Hey, Coach. You ready to come home and claim your little princess?"

"That's the plan," he said. "I have a few things to handle at school. Hillary Horton texted me that she has the keys to the house. I'll pick those up before I leave town. That way, Lily and I will able to head straight to the new house when we return to Driftwood Bay in a few days."

After seeing the Jacobs' residence, both he and Pete had decided to move Pete's daughter's bedroom furniture into the spare bedroom, which had served as a guest room. While it would be a tight fit cramming the furniture into it, he thought

Lily would be more comfortable sleeping in her own bed and having her own dresser and shelves for her toys and books. That would be the only furniture they would move from Houston. The rest would go into a storage unit.

"Try to be here by dinnertime," Rudy advised. "Juanita is making tamales."

"You do know that's the only reason I hang around you," Carson teased. "Your wife's cooking is the best I've ever had."

"Is that Daddy?" he heard Lily ask.

Rudy said, "It sure is. Come here, kiddo."

Lily climbed into Rudy's lap and beamed at him. "Hi, Daddy. I miss you."

"I miss you, too, Peanut. I'll be coming home today, and then we'll drive to Driftwood Bay together."

She wrinkled her nose, still not quite understanding about the move to another city.

"Binky is coming?" she asked anxiously.

"Why, we can't move anywhere without Binky, can we? He's part of our family."

Lily visibly relaxed. "I love Binky. I love you, too, Daddy."

"I love you, sweetie. I'll see you by dinner tonight."

"Okay."

Lily scrambled off Rudy's lap, and his friend said, "We've really enjoyed having Lily with us. You know Juanita and I adore her. She's been great with the baby."

His friends had become first-time parents six months ago, on New Year's Day, and it made him feel good, hearing that Lily had done well around the newborn. Carson hadn't thought about remarrying in the two years Angie had been gone, but it would be nice to give Lily a brother or sister. He realized how lonely he had been and that he would enjoy the companionship of being in a marriage again someday. He didn't know if he had it in him to love again, though. Angie had been everything to him, and her death had hit him hard.

Still, thoughts of Mila Perry kept circulating through his head. He just might have to give love another chance. Or at least dating. Then again, he would technically be Mila's boss. With her dad serving as the district's superintendent, he didn't think getting into a relationship with one of his coaches would be the best move, especially being new to the job. Frustration filled him, and he shrugged it off.

"You think you're going to like this new place?" Rudy asked.

"I really do. I met a few of my basketball players at a pickup game in the park last night. I think I'm going to enjoy working with them. The AD piece of the puzzle is going to be a work in progress, but I'm excited about putting my stamp on this program across the board. We'll also be close to the beach. Lily will definitely enjoy that."

He raked a hand through his hair. "I'll let you go, Rudy. See you by dinner tonight."

Carson ended the call and went inside the field house. He had thought he would hear from Mila about the interviews she had conducted. Then again, maybe it was taking time for the candidate she wanted to make up his or her mind whether they wanted to come to Driftwood Bay.

Entering his office, he was thankful that Jon Earl had vacated it so quickly. Carson had spent all of yesterday afternoon reorganizing furniture and files and reading through bios of his coaches, as well as studying the budgets that had been submitted for the upcoming academic year. He had gone back and looked at won-loss records in every sport for the last three years and was eager to meet with the entire athletic staff and get to know them, both as coaches and people. Of course, they were all on their brief summer vacations now. Coaches usually reported back in July, attending coaching clinics and prepping for their upcoming year.

He had a basketball clinic to run at the tail end of June. It would be for elementary-aged kids to learn basic skills of the sport. Lisa Thornbach, the girls' basketball coach, would conduct a corresponding clinic for girls during the same time. Both would take place at the high school, and it would give him an opportunity to start implementing his philosophy regarding sports, as well as preview upcoming talent in the years to come. Both clinics had a little over one hundred attendees for each session, which he thought was a good number for a town this size.

Carson had reached out to Lisa via email, and she had responded that she was at a family reunion in Iowa. She promised to meet with him as soon as she returned to Texas, and they could talk more about the drills they would run and the skills they would teach at their individual camps.

Looking around, he decided everything in his office was arranged as well as it could be and was about to leave when he received a text from Mila.

> Have time to talk about the new hire?

He texted back that he was in his office and she could stop by if she wanted to see him in person. Mila responded she would drop by and fill him in, asking for his coffee order. He texted back:

> If you can grab any kind of latte, I'm all in.
> Hazelnut and vanilla are favorites. Sugar
> and a splash of cream, please.

She answered, saying she would see him in fifteen minutes. Giddiness filled him, a feeling he hadn't known in years.

Carson told himself to watch it. Play it cool. He and Mila weren't beginning a romance. She had expressed no interest in anything beyond friendship. He needed to let their friendship grow and play out before he approached her about moving beyond that.

If he said anything. His gut told him it would be foolish to become involved in a relationship with a subordinate whose dad was his boss and held Carson's future in his hands. He had to do what was best for Lily, not himself. She was his priority. Maybe Mila had a few friends outside of teaching and could introduce him around. He might even find someone to ask out on a date.

"Good morning, Coach."

Carson glanced up and recognized who stood in the doorway from his picture on the school's website.

"Jackson Rudd. Good to meet you."

Rudd was twenty-four and would serve as his assistant basketball coach. Already a week into June, Jackson sported a deep tan and sun-bleached blond hair. Carson imagined Jackson caused hearts to flutter wherever he went.

He moved to the doorway, offering a hand. His assistant shook it, and Carson invited him to sit.

"I went down to South Padre for a few days, but I got a ton of texts hearing the news about your hire. It's good to meet you, Carson."

"Same. I hope you're not disappointed that you didn't get the head coaching job."

The younger man shook his head. "I didn't even apply for it. I've only coached two years. Besides, I heard that the gig came with the AD position attached to it. They never would've considered me anyway. I want to learn everything I can from you, Coach. I'll know when the time is right to venture out and run a program of my own. Until then, I'm all yours."

Having googled his assistant, Carson knew Jackson had played college basketball at Tarleton State and was an outstanding three-point shooter.

"It's a two-way street," he said. "I expect I'll learn things from you, as well. A good coach always does. Give me your input on what you think about the varsity squad for the upcoming year."

For the next ten minutes, Jackson broke down the makeup of the team, commenting on both the strengths and weaknesses of the projected starters.

"The star of the team will definitely be Drake Duncan. He's been a starter on varsity since his sophomore year, and Sam named him team captain before he left. Drake's mom is the principal at the middle school. I would say that Marge is the loudest fan in the stands, hands down."

"Do you think Drake has any kind of chance at a scholarship?" Carson asked.

"Possibly." Jackson hesitated and then added, "Drake is pure talent, but his work ethic leaves a lot to be desired. He's breezed by on that talent, but he could be so much more if he applied himself. Same goes for academics. Drake's a smart kid, but he barely puts any effort into his classes."

Carson nodded. "Sounds as if Mr. Duncan and I will be having a come to Jesus meeting."

Jackson laughed and stood. "I'll let you get back to it, Coach. Just wanted to stop by and say hi."

As the two men shook hands, Carson saw Mila appear in the doorway. Jackson turned and grinned at her.

"Hey, Mila. Come bearing gifts to sweet talk your new boss?"

"Hi, Jackson. I hired a new coach for the middle school and came by to let Carson know a little bit about her."

"It'll be good to have someone new on board. Hey, guess what? I talked to Sam last night. He's settling in."

Carson saw a shadow cross Mila's face, and then she brightened. "That's good to hear. I hope he finds a lot of success with his new team."

"Well, I'll leave you two. Nice meeting you, Carson."

"You, too, Jackson," he responded, watching his assistant leave.

Mila entered the office and went to the table and set down a sack and the two coffees she had been balancing.

Taking a seat, she said, "Got you a hazelnut. Hope I doctored it the way you like."

He joined her, taking a seat and a sip of the coffee. "Perfect. Where did you get it? It's a lot better than what's in the break room here."

"It's a drive-through coffee hut which opened last summer. Coastal Roast. It did really well with all the tourists in town, but the coffee is so good that locals also patronize it."

She told him where it was located as she opened the sack. "This is a kolache from Seaside Sweets Bakery. I don't know if you like them or not, but in my opinion? I think they're a little bit of heaven on earth."

He'd heard of kolaches before but had never eaten one. Taking a bite, he savored the yeast in the roll as it blended with a bit of spicy sausage and melted cheese.

"Wow. This is incredible."

"They're even better if you heat them about twelve to fifteen seconds. You should get a microwave for your office. Jon Earl also had a coffeemaker in here." She laughed. "He never drinks the coffee in the break room."

"I guess I have some small appliance shopping to do. So, tell me about this new coach."

"It wasn't the candidate I thought I'd hire," she said. "The others both had teaching and coaching experience. Julie Shannon is a recent college graduate."

Mila explained how Julie had impressed her with her extensive volleyball knowledge, and she had also run track in middle school, which would be the spring sport Julie would coach.

"She's played volleyball most of her life. I liked her enthusiasm and her emphasis on teaching skills at the middle school level. She is especially interested in working on her players' serves. She ran a coed intramural sports league in college, scheduling everything from volleyball to pickleball to flag football. Besides preparing the schedules, she also had to provide referees for every game and even did some reffing of her own. She's not a green newbie out of college. She's invested a lot of her life into volleyball and is efficient and organized."

"Sounds like you two hit it off."

"We did. I also told Marge Duncan, the principal at the middle school, that Julie is our pick." Mila paused. "I used the word *our* because I really need your backing on this one, Carson. Marge can be set in her ways, and she doesn't like hiring teachers with no classroom experience."

"Jackson was telling me that Marge is a superfan with a kid on my basketball team."

She laughed. "Superfan is putting it politely. Marge can be really obnoxious. Sam had to speak to her several times about piping down because she was such a distraction. Anyway, I'm sure Marge is going to call you. Can you let her know Julie was the best fit for our program?"

"I've got your back, Mila," he said. "I mean it. I trust you made the right call. And if Julie needs help in the classroom, whether it's with discipline or teaching methods, we'll make certain she gets the tools she needs in order to be successful, on and off the court."

Mila smiled, and his stomach flipped over twice.

"Thanks so much. I won't forget this. I appreciate you allowing me to make this call, especially since we just met."

"Oh, I've been researching everyone in my new athletic department, from coaches to trainers. I've studied your pages on the district's website. Googled and got background on everyone. I like being prepared. You have great experience, both as a player and a coach. I even accessed your evaluations form Jon Earl. All were outstanding. You're a natural as a teacher and coach, Mila."

A blush tinged her cheeks. "I'll admit that I googled you, too." She grinned. "You took an inner-city program and really built it into something special, Carson. I hope you'll enjoy living in a small town after being in the big city for so long."

"Hey." He held up his cup. "I have a new coffee shop. A place to buy kolaches. I even have a house."

"Really?"

Briefly, he told her about Pete Jacobs' sabbatical halfway around the world and how he and Lily would function as caretakers for Pete's house over the next year.

"Hillary explained that inventory is pretty low in Driftwood Bay. While I might be able to find something outside the city itself, I prefer living in town and close to school. I want to become a part of this community."

"When will you move in?" she asked.

"I'm leaving town as soon as we finish up here. I'll stop and pick up the keys from Hillary before I go. I've got a few things to do in Houston concerning my house and wrapping up everything with my life there. I'm hoping Lily I and will be back in Driftwood Bay by next Tuesday. I still need to check out preschool for her. Pete says his neighborhood is very friendly and even has a few kids near her age on the block."

"It sounds as if you made a lot of progress in the last few

days." She glanced around. "I see this is your office and not Jon Earl's."

"He said the AD was located here. Jon Earl left me a lot of helpful information. I'm glad he'll be around this next year as a resource for me through each sports season for the first time."

Carson kept to himself about Jon Earl's plans to retire, knowing the football coach wanted the circle to be small regarding his decision.

Mila stood, draining the last of her coffee. "Then I guess I'll see you around. I'm looking forward to meeting Lily."

"She'll like you," he said. "She's shy when she first meets someone, but I think she'll warm up fast to you."

"Why don't you plan on bringing her to Mom and Dad's next Wednesday? Mom had offered to cook for you when you came to town."

He laughed. "You don't think she'll mind you planning a dinner without her knowledge?"

"Mom loves to entertain. She has never met a stranger and puts everyone at ease. She's the perfect superintendent's wife."

"I suppose her personality also helps her sell a lot at her shop."

Mila laughed. "That is very true. Summer tourists go in as strangers to pick up something, and they come out feeling as if they've made a new friend in Mom. I'll talk to her about it today and text you to let you know if next Wednesday is good for her and Dad."

"Thanks for everything you've done to welcome me, Mila." He hesitated a moment and then added, "Maybe once I return, you and I might have dinner together. Just the two of us."

There. It was out in the open. Despite believing he should hold back, he'd gone and blurted out that he wanted to see her. It was as if he'd lost all impulse control, along with any common sense he thought he had.

Her brows arched in surprise. "Are you asking me out, Coach?"

Rejection filled him. "Sorry. I know we talked about being friends. I didn't mean to push any boundaries. That would be crazy, going out with a coach who works under me."

A slow smile crossed her face. "It would be crazy," she agreed. "But I have been thinking about you nonstop ever since I met you, Carson."

Her words took him by surprise, but he found himself returning her smile.

"I think this calls for further discussion once I move to Driftwood Bay."

"Over pizza," she suggested. "My best talking and thinking always involves pizza."

"You're on."

Mila said goodbye and wished him a safe trip to Houston and back. Carson watched her go, already missing her as she vanished from sight. He hadn't been happy in a long time, but Mila Perry put a smile on his face—and made his heart just a little bit lighter.

Chapter Six

"Are we there yet, Daddy?" Lily asked for what had to be the tenth time since they had left Houston.

Calmly, Carson said, "Not yet, Peanut. But we should be there in the next ten minutes or so. As long as it takes to watch one Spidey cartoon," giving his words context that a four-year-old could understand.

"Can I watch *Frozen* when we get there?"

"Sure, sweetie," he promised. "Or *Frozen 2* or *3*," he teased.

The five hour trip from Houston to Driftwood Bay had taken almost six-and-a-half hours, thanks to having a small child and dog in tow. Where Carson would have driven straight through—maybe stopping mid-trip at a drive-through window for a drink—he had known that Lily needed to get out and stretch. They had stopped at McDonald's along the way for lunch and also stopped two other times to let her and Binky pee.

He had also told and retold a good many fairy tales. Lily would beg to hear stories such as Cinderella or Rumpelstiltskin, and he would oblige. Halfway into the stories, though, his

71

daughter would take over, telling them with a wide range of emotions and a good deal of drama. He wondered if she would be destined for the stage and supposed Driftwood Bay High School had a drama department.

If not, Lily Andrews would insist upon creating one.

"Let's talk some more about our new home," he said cheerfully. "We're going to be living in a new friend's house and taking care of it for him and his wife. They're going far away to live in Australia. He studies fish."

Carson substituted fish for sea snakes, not wanting his daughter to be afraid of stepping into the Gulf. Already, she was tentative about the water. He hoped living close to it now and playing in the surf on a frequent basis would alleviate her fears.

"I want a fish, Daddy."

He didn't think goldfish had extremely long lives, and he wasn't up to having ceremonial funerals and a flushing of a pet fish down the toilet, so he said, "You have Binky. He's way better than a fish. You can cuddle with Binky. Pet him. Play with him. A fish just swims around a bowl while you watch. That's pretty boring."

"Okay, Daddy," Lily said brightly, leaning over and patting Binky, who sat on a blanket next to her car seat.

"We're going to live in our friend's house," he continued, "while we're looking for one of our own. We may find a house that we like, or we could have someone draw a house on paper for us. Then other people could come and build it."

The more Carson thought about it, the more he liked the idea of commissioning an architect and building from scratch. It would be nice to see every nail hammered into a place which would be what he hoped would be a forever home for Lily and him. Though coaches bounced around from one job to the next, climbing the athletic ladder, Carson wanted stability for Lily, especially since she had lost her mother. He liked what he had seen of Driftwood Bay and thought this community would be an excellent place to raise his little girl.

"Daddy is going to be the basketball coach at the high school."

"You were a coach before."

"I was. I also get to be the boss of other coaches and help them do their jobs."

"Miss Gabby says you're not supposed to be bossy," Lily admonished, quoting her former preschool teacher.

"It's one thing to be bossy. It's okay to be a boss, though," he explained. "A boss is someone who is in charge. Miss Gabby is right. You don't want to boss people around, but if you are their boss, you need to be a good leader and help others."

Lily brightened. "I like being the leader of the line at school. The leader gets to take everyone to the restroom so we can go to the bathroom and get water for our water bottles. Then the leader walks the line back to our room." She paused. "Miss Gabby won't be here, will she, Daddy?"

"No, Miss Gabby has to stay in Houston, but we're going to find you another school in Driftwood Bay. You're going to make a lot of new friends and have a wonderful time. The best thing is that we live close to the beach now."

"I like the beach. I like making a sand castle. And a ..." Her brow furrowed. "What's the water thing called?"

"A moat," he supplied.

"A moat," Lily echoed, nodding her head. "Do I have to get in the water?"

"Only if you want to, baby."

She sighed dramatically, and Carson looked in his rearview mirror, seeing she was put out with him.

"I'm not a baby, Daddy. Don't say that. Babies can't walk

or talk. But I liked Baby Alex. I wish we had a baby like Rudy and Juanita. Do you remember when I was a baby?"

"You know I do. Don't we look at pictures all the time on Daddy's phone?"

He had hundreds of pictures on his cell of Lily from the time she was born until now. He regularly sat with her and went through those pictures, wanting his daughter to see her mother and what a big part Angie had played in Lily's life.

"Answer me, Daddy."

"What?" he asked, distracted.

"Can we get a baby?"

"Where do babies grow?" he prompted.

"In a mommy's belly. But we don't have mommy."

"No, we don't. So, I guess we won't be having any babies. At least not now. Maybe someday."

He made the turn which would lead them into Driftwood Bay as Lily asked, "Can we get a new mommy so I can have a baby brother or sister?"

"We'll have to think about that," he told his daughter. "First, Daddy would have to go out on dates. That's when you go and do something fun with another person, and you see if you like each other. If two people get along and enjoy spending time together, they might even fall in love."

"Like you and Mommy did," Lily said eagerly.

"Yes, just like Mommy and me. But I haven't been on any dates in a long time."

"Maybe you can go on a date here, Daddy." She frowned. "Where do we live again?"

"Driftwood Bay," he told her.

"Driftwood Bay," Lily repeated, saying it several times. "I'll remember. I promise."

"I hope we live in Driftwood Bay for a long, long time."

They had entered the town, and Carson now played tour

guide for his daughter. "There's the police station. Policemen help people."

"I see a fire truck!" Lily said excitedly. "Firemen also help people. Miss Gabby's husband is a fireman."

He pointed out the library and told her that they would get a library card for her soon. She loved being read to and was crazy about Dr. Seuss and *Pete the Cat*. Then he drove around the square slowly, pointing out some of the shops and the diner, promising her they would eat there soon.

Turning off the square, he said, "We live this way."

Carson turned on their street, and Lily asked, "Where is your school, Daddy? Where's my school?"

"I'll take you up to my school soon. We have to find a new one for you."

He turned on what would be their street for the next year and into the driveway. Glancing at the dashboard, he saw it was almost three o'clock.

"I'm tired. I don't like driving in the car that long."

"Well, we're here now," he said, undoing his seatbelt and climbing from the car.

He opened the back door and unbuckled Lily from her car seat before snapping Binky's leash onto the dog's collar. Lily climbed out of the car by herself, and he picked up Binky, easing the beagle to the ground.

Lily raised her arms high and stretched. "I can touch my toes," she said, leaning down and doing so.

A woman in the next yard was watering her flowers. She waved to him, and Carson returned the greeting. She set the hose aside and walked over to speak to them.

Wiping her hand on her shirt, she offered it to him, saying, "I'm Dotty Williams. You must be Carson and Lily."

Lily gazed at her with round eyes. "You know my name!"

"I sure do. Dr. and Mrs. Jacobs lived here and told me all about you coming."

"We're going to take care of their house. This is Binky."

"Well, hello, Binky," Dotty said, leaning down and scratching the beagle between his ears. "It's nice to have all of you come to Driftwood Bay." Glancing back to Carson, she asked, "Anything I can do to help?"

"Thanks for offering, Dotty. I just need to bring in some suitcases and boxes now. You wouldn't happen to know if there's a teenager on the street that might be willing to help me move in Lily's furniture? That's what's in the small trailer."

"I'll bet Keaton would help you."

Dotty waved, and Carson looked over his shoulder, seeing an SUV pull into the driveway across the street.

"Keaton just moved here last month from Colorado. He's a painter. Going to open an art gallery soon."

She motioned the newcomer over, and he crossed the street. He sported a tan which made his azure eyes stand out.

"Welcome to the neighborhood. I'm Keaton Maxwell."

Carson shook the artist's hand. "I'm Carson Andrews. This is my daughter Lily and Binky."

"I'm four," Lily said. "How old are you?"

Keaton laughed. "I'm thirty-three. Way older than you. I'm also new to Driftwood Bay, same as you. It's a friendly place."

"Carson needs some help moving in Lily's bedroom furniture," Dotty said. "Pete told me you were bringing Lily's things."

"I thought it would be easier for her to settle into a new environment if she were in a familiar bed."

"You're a thoughtful father," Dotty praised. "If you'd like, I can take Lily with me and feed her a snack while you and Keaton move things in. Binky, too."

"That would be terrific. Lily is all over the place, and it

would be hard to keep an eye on her and get everything moved in."

"Whenever you're done, just come on over and get them," Dotty said. She took Binky's leash from him and held out a hand. Lily took it, and Dotty said, "I have all kinds of things for snacks. Strawberries. Trail mix. Peanut butter crackers."

"I love peanut butter," Lily declared as the pair walked off, hand-in-hand.

He turned back to Keaton. "Sorry Dotty roped you into this."

"I don't mind at all. It's great that you were able to step in and look after the place. Let's do the heavy stuff first, and then we can follow up with boxes."

Carson went to the small trailer attached to the back of his car and unlocked the doors. With the two of them, it only took a short time to bring Lily's furniture to her bedroom.

"We need to make the bed for her," Keaton suggested. "That would be more inviting." He chuckled. "As an artist, I'm all about the setting."

They returned to the trailer and made several trips, bringing in suitcases and clothes, as well as boxes of Lily's bedding, books, and toys.

The two men quickly made the bed. While Carson hung clothes in the closet and filled the dresser drawers, Keaton arranged books and toys on the shelves.

He glanced around the room. "She's going to be happy to see everything from our old house in place here. Thanks so much, Keaton. At the very least, I owe you a few beers. Even dinner."

"There's a great craft beer place which opened last month. Bayside Brewery. Take me there, and I'll collect on the debt you owe me," Keaton said, smiling. "Dotty would be happy to watch Lily."

"You have kids?" Carson asked.

"No. I'm not sure I even want any. I didn't have the best childhood. I grew up in foster care, and it was pretty rough."

"So did my wife," he said quietly. "I'm a widower."

"I'm sorry to hear that. Does Lily resemble your late wife?" Keaton asked.

He nodded. "I see a lot of Angie in Lily. Sometimes, it's a great thing. Other times, it hurts like hell." Then he sighed. "Sorry. Didn't mean to dump on you, especially since we've just met."

Keaton placed a hand on Carson's shoulder and squeezed. "It's good to have you as a neighbor, Carson. And hopefully, as a friend. I'll let you get to the rest of your unpacking."

The men traded cell numbers, and he thanked Keaton and saw him out before going next door. He didn't want to take advantage of Dotty's hospitality by leaving Lily too long with the older woman. A long driveway ran between his house and Dotty's, and he had seen her and Lily enter a door off it. He went there now and knocked, and Dotty answered.

"Done already?"

"Lily's room is all set up. I just need to put my clothes away, and I can do that after she goes to bed tonight. Thanks for watching her, Dotty."

"I suppose you'll be wanting to put her in home daycare or preschool," his neighbor said.

"She was in preschool in Houston. She's at an age where I think the socialization is important."

"I can think of a couple in Driftwood Bay. A little girl down the street goes to Happy Hearts, and her parents are pleased with it. It's only about five minutes from here. You might want to see if it has any openings."

"Happy Hearts," he repeated. "Thanks for the tip."

Lily appeared. "Binky made friends with Ginger. Miss Dotty said I can go with her when she walks Ginger."

"I hope you don't mind," Dotty said. "I never had kids but always wanted them. I've been a widow for over ten years now and am the unofficial grandma of the street. If you ever need me to watch Lily, just let me know, Carson."

"Actually, I am going to need to find someone beyond preschool hours to watch her. I'm the new basketball coach at the high school. Once the season begins, we have night games and a few tournaments on the weekends. I need a reliable, permanent sitter for those times."

"Look no further than next door," his neighbor said cheerfully. "I'd be happy to watch Lily. She can come to my house, or I'd be happy to watch her at yours. That might be easier. That way, she could have her bath, brush her teeth, and go to bed at her usual time in familiar surroundings."

Dotty patted Carson's forearm. "We can talk about it later. Basketball season is several months away, but just know if you have other things going on, I'm always happy to sit with Lily."

"Thank you, Dotty." They exchanged cell numbers and then he looked to his daughter. "Let's go get Binky."

They went to the backyard, and Carson saw the two dogs curled up together on a patio lounger, fast asleep.

"Don't wake up Binky, Daddy," Lily said. "Can he stay here for his nap, Miss Dotty?"

"He sure can. I'll bring Binky back after he and Ginger are up and about again."

Carson smiled gratefully at the older woman and ushered Lily out the backyard gate.

He took her inside the house, walking her through the rooms downstairs.

"They have a TV, Daddy. Do they have *Frozen*?"

He had asked Pete if they got the Disney+ streaming channel. Pete had told him no but said he would see that it was added.

"They do. You can watch your movie in a few minutes. Let's go look at your new room first. It's upstairs."

"Ooh, I like a house with stairs," Lily said, scampering up them to the top.

She found her room. "This is so big, Daddy. Bigger than Houston. We can have a picnic here with my dolls."

She raced to her drawers and opened them, seeing that each one held the same things as before. Lily ran to him, and he scooped her up, giving her a tight hug.

"I like Driftwood Bay," she told him.

"I do, too," he agreed, taking her downstairs and finding the remote.

Once he turned on the TV and queued up the movie, he said, "I'm going to let you watch this while I go unpack my clothes. Okay, Peanut?"

"Okay," she said, her eyes fixed upon the screen.

Carson went to his bedroom, finding that all the drawers in the dresser had been emptied. The closet had two-thirds of it freed up, which turned out to be plenty of room to hang his clothing. He was happy to have met Dotty Williams, thinking the older woman would not only be a good neighbor but a terrific sitter for Lily. He also had enjoyed meeting Keaton Maxwell and hoped that he might make a friend in the artist.

His cell chimed, and he pulled it from his pocket, seeing he had a text from Mila.

I hear you've already arrived. That's the small-town network for you! Hope you and Lily had a good trip from Houston and she's happy to be in DB. Mom is looking forward to having you two for dinner tomorrow night. My brother and SIL are also coming with their 2 kids, so Lily will have playmates. Holler if you need anything before then.

Just reading her text caused a warmth to rush through Carson. While he would never forget Angie, he was ready to leave his old life behind in Houston and start a new one in Driftwood Bay.

He texted back, asking for the address and time and if he could bring anything. She replied, telling him they would eat at five-thirty and to be there around five so the kids could play a little before dinner. Mila said an appetite was the only thing he should bring.

Carson sent a thumbs up emoji and slipped his phone back into his pocket. He had always been a careful, cautious man, weighing options and deliberating before he made important decisions. For the first time in years, however, his heart was overruling his head.

He looked forward to seeing Mila tomorrow night—and hoped it might be the start of something good for both of them.

Chapter Seven

Nerves flitted through Mila as she finished mixing up the guacamole, a specialty of hers. She covered it with foil and placed it in the fridge.

"Anything else, Mom?" she asked.

"No, honey. You're done with kitchen duty. Go visit with Cecily and rescue her from the kids."

She walked out the kitchen door and onto the covered patio, where Dad was grilling fajita steak and chicken strips on a large tray. Michael was standing next to him, sipping on a beer as they talked. Bobby and Gina were running around the backyard, begging Cecily to chase them.

"You watch your kids," she told her brother. "I'm stealing your wife for girl talk."

"Ooh, sounds serious," he teased.

She motioned to Cecily, who headed her way, a grateful expression on her face.

"I told Michael he's on dad duty. Come inside and take a break from mom-ing."

They cut back through the kitchen and went to the den,

where Cecily said, "Are you still up for babysitting while we take a getaway? It would be soon."

"You know I am," she assured her sister-in-law. "Just tell me when and for how long. And sooner is better since I'll be tied up with my volleyball camp in a couple of weeks."

"Michael actually has four days in a row off. This Friday through Monday. Could you handle any or all of those days?"

Knowing how badly the couple needed adult time together, she said, "I'll cover the entire four days. What time do you want me at your house on Friday?"

"Early. Michael wants to leave no later than six. Will that be a problem?"

"I'm always up early, even if it is summer. My body clock was set a long time ago to rise before the sun. Where are you two going?"

Cecily took out her phone and started typing rapidly. "Now that I have you booked, I need to grab the places we're going to stay. Don't worry. As a nurse and a mom? I can multi-task with the best of them. Talk away."

"I hope you'll get away from the coast. Most people think going to the beach is a vacation, but living here, you guys need to do a totally different getaway. Adult beverages. Adult conversation." She smiled impishly. "Adult...activities."

Cecily laughed. "Oh, I've got a great plan. We're going to head up on Friday morning to Fredericksburg. It's a little over three hours from here to there, and we're going to start by treating ourselves to brunch at a place where I ate at a bachelorette party several years ago. They had the most divine Eggs Benedict I've ever eaten." Cecily grinned. "And they taste even better washed down with a mimosa."

Mila laughed. "I hope you'll hit up a winery or two while you're in Fredericksburg."

"We will that afternoon. At least one, and then go back

into town for a little antique shopping. It's time Gina transitioned into a big girl bed, not just the twin one the crib converted into. I would love to buy a sleigh bed for her."

"Brunch. Wine. Antiquing. That all sounds terrific. What else?"

"We'll get up early Saturday and head to New Braunfels. Go tubing along the river all day. Just fun in the sun, floating down the river. Then we'll drive into San Antonio around four. After that, Mexican food and margaritas on the Riverwalk."

"I love that. What about Sunday?"

"Sunday is a lazy day," Cecily said. "Go buy a newspaper and sit in chairs along the river. Drink coffee and do the *New York Times* puzzle with no interruptions. Just whatever the spirit moves us to do. While Friday and Saturday are planned, Sunday is wide open."

Cecily tapped her phone. "Okay. I have a B&B booked in Fredericksburg. Reservations at a winery for a tour and tasting. And tubes reserved for Saturday. I just need to find a place to stay in San Antonio Saturday and Sunday night, and we're ready to rock and roll."

"There's a really cute boutique hotel near La Villita Market," Mila said. "I've stayed there twice before when I've gone to coaching conventions. It's small. Private. Quiet."

She pulled up the website on her phone and texted it to Cecily, who grinned.

"This looks heavenly. And it's a great price. I'll see if we can get a room. Thanks for covering for us, Mila. We're going to owe you big."

"So, you'll come back sometime on Monday?"

"Yes. Since I'm trading a shift to be able to do this getaway, I need to cover someone's three to eleven shift on Monday. We'll get up early on Monday and drive back. We should be here no later than ten or eleven. Michael always needs time to decompress after a trip, and I'll get him to do the laundry while I go into work. Yes! They have a room. Got it booked. Oh, I can't wait to have a few days to ourselves. We seem to pass each other, coming and going, these days."

"Having two little ones is tough," Mila said sympathetically. "It won't always be this hard."

"It can be a lot, but we love them like crazy. They will go to preschool on Friday and Monday. You'll need to do drop-off and pick-up on Friday, then have them the weekend. Once you take them Monday morning, you're free and clear. Michael will collect them that afternoon."

Cecily put aside her phone. "Trip is done. Enough about me. Give me some good gossip, starting with this new basketball coach coming to dinner tonight."

Mila hadn't shared a single text with Layne or Piper about her last conversation with Carson before he left for Houston, and she was bursting at the seams to tell someone.

"I like him," she blurted out.

Cecily cocked her head, frowning. "You like him?" Then understanding dawned in her eyes, and her hands flew to her face, making her resemble Macaulay Culkin in *Home Alone*.

"You *like* like him?" her sister-in-law whispered.

"I do. That's not good, is it?" she asked, doubt filling her.

Cecily took Mila's hand and squeezed it. "First, I think it's great that you're looking at guys again. I was worried when Sam left that you would go into a funk like you did when you and Mark broke up."

"I was way more serious with Mark. That about destroyed me when he left. Sam was a lot of fun to hang out with, but things never grew serious between us. I'm happy for him. Yes, I may have pouted a little bit because he left so abruptly, but it's a good opportunity that he couldn't pass up."

She smiled. "Besides, Carson wouldn't have come to Drift-wood Bay if Sam would've stayed.

"Tell me everything," Cecily encouraged.

"On a one to ten scale, he's a good twelve or thirteen," she said, causing Cecily to roar with laughter.

"He's thirty-two. Tall. Six-four or six-five. The most gorgeous brown hair that I want to run my fingers through. Eyes the color of an espresso. He's built like the basketball player he was. Lean but muscular. You know the type."

Her sister-in-law nodded. "Go on."

"He seems to have a real heart for kids and turned around a Houston inner-city program he headed up. He's smart. Kind."

Cecily frowned. "I don't get why he would leave a big school to come somewhere as small as Driftwood Bay. Unless the athletic director job drew him here. I could see that."

"He didn't even know about that," Mila confided. "That was something they sprang on him after they offered him the head basketball job. While he's never held that position anywhere before, he'll be able to figure it out. You can tell not much gets past him. He's also got Jon Earl around to help answer any questions."

Mila bit her bottom lip. "What I'm worried about are two things."

"Which are?" Cecily prompted when Mila didn't speak.

"First, his wife died two years ago—and he's got a little girl. Lily. She'll be with him tonight, and I'm hoping that Bobby and Gina will get along with her."

"You're reluctant to become involved with him because he's got a child?"

"No, that doesn't bother me. He's already talked a lot about Lily, and it's easy to see he has genuine affection for her. That he's a good, caring dad." She hesitated. "What I'm worried about is competing with a ghost."

Cecily nodded. "I get that. You think he's put his wife on a pedestal. That she's the perfect woman, and no one can ever live up to her."

"That about sums it up. They were college sweethearts. She was murdered, Cec. A violent carjacking. She was trying to keep the carjacker from driving off with Lily in the car when she was shot."

Tears sprang to Cecily's eyes. "Oh, that's terrible. As a mom, I can't imagine being confronted with such an awful situation."

"She died trying to defend her daughter. So, I'll also be compared to someone who spent her last breath being totally heroic."

"That is a lot to worry about," her sister-in-law agreed. "Do you know if Carson has gone out with anyone since her death?"

"I didn't ask him. I get the feeling he hasn't, though. And I did let him know that I am interested in him. We have a tentative date to eat pizza tomorrow night."

Cecily beamed at her. "That's a good thing, Mila," she encouraged. "Maybe with a move to a new town, Carson is ready to put the past behind him and start fresh."

"Remember I said there were two things I was worried about?"

"That first one was huge. I hope the next one is small potatoes compared to it."

"I'm afraid it's even bigger. Think about it, Cec. Carson is the new basketball coach—*and* the new athletic director." She let that sink in.

"Oh. I get it. As the AD, Carson will be your boss. He would be responsible for the sports part of your yearly evaluation."

She nodded. "Exactly. While I'll have an assistant principal come in and observe me in the classroom for the academic eval, my athletic future is in Carson's hands. Now, I've always received terrific numbers from Jon Earl. He's been a fair evaluator. Given me some great tips on the coaching side of things. He's also effusive when it comes to praise."

Mila shrugged. "But how can I be dating the guy who's supposed to judge my performance on the court?"

"Have you consulted the district's handbook? Surely, something like this has come up before."

"That's a great idea. I need to look it up on the website since they don't provide hard copies anymore. I know when two people are dating in the district, they have to report it to HR. Sam and I did when we first started going out. And last year when two teachers in the science department got married, the department chair stayed at the high school, while the new wife moved down to teach life science at the middle school. That's because department chairs have input into evaluations and can recommend whether or not an employee should be offered a new contract," she explained.

"Well, don't put the cart before the horse," Cecily advised. "You might go out with Carson and find he's not what you're looking for. If you click, though, you are going to be in a pickle." She hesitated. "You'd have to tell your dad."

"I know," Mila said worriedly. "That would totally suck. You're right. I need to take baby steps. See if we actually do go on a date. If it goes well enough that we go out again. Then if we go out several times and decide we'd like to be in a relationship, then we'll have to notify HR—and Dad."

The doorbell rang, and Mila jumped to her feet."

It's him," she said, butterflies exploding in her belly. "I'll get it." She took a few steps and turned. "Do I look okay?"

"You look perfect, Mila," Cecily assured her.

She went to the front door and opened it. Immediately, her

gaze connected with Carson's, and her stomach felt as if she were riding a roller coaster.

"Hey," she said casually and then glanced down, seeing he held Lily's hand in his.

Kneeling, Mila looked Lily in the eye and smiled. "Hi, Lily. I'm a friend of your daddy's. My name is Mila. I'm so glad you've moved to Driftwood Bay." She looked around. "Did you bring Binky with you tonight?"

The little girl had stared at her cautiously, but with the mention of her dog, she seemed to relax.

"You know Binky?"

"Well, I haven't met Binky, but your daddy told me all about him and you. I also work at the same school where your daddy will be coaching basketball."

"Are you a coach?"

"I am. I coach volleyball. Have you ever been to a volleyball match?"

Lily shook her head solemnly, and Mila said, "You'll have to come and see one of my games. If it's okay with your daddy, you can sit on the bench next to me. We can watch the game together. Would you like that?"

The girl nodded and then turned her face into Carson's leg.

"That would be a lot of fun, Lily," father told daughter. "Why, you've never even sat on the bench with me and my basketball players."

"You might play basketball one day, Lily. Or you might play volleyball. We have lots of sports in Driftwood Bay for you to try. There are other things to do, too. You could take dance lessons or learn how to play the piano. I was in Brownies and Girl Scouts, and I had a lot of fun doing that."

Lily turned her face back to Mila. "I dance with my dolls," she said softly.

"You have dance parties with your dolls? That must be so

much fun. I have dance parties with my niece and nephew. They're in the backyard now. Their names are Gina and Bobby. Would you like to go meet them?"

Lily nodded and Mila rose, holding out her hand. When Lily took it, warmth rushed through Mila.

"Let's go find them," she said. "Your daddy can come, too. My brother is here. He's Bobby and Gina's daddy, and their mommy is also here. They'll be eating dinner with us. My mommy and daddy live here, and they're making the food we're going to eat."

"That's a lot of people," Lily said worriedly as they reached the kitchen.

She saw Cecily had joined Mom and was stirring taco meat on the stove.

"Hello, Carson," Mom greeted.

"Thank you for inviting us over for dinner this evening, Laura. Lily, this is Miss Laura. She's cooking dinner for us tonight."

"My daddy can't cook," Lily shared. "He can make cereal and grilled cheese. That's it."

Carson ruffled her hair. "Thanks for ratting me out, Peanut."

Mom told the young child, "Any time you'd like to learn how to cook, Lily, you come and see me. We could start by learning how to bake cookies. Do you like cookies?"

The little girl nodded eagerly.

"Sugar cookies are always the best cookie to start with," Mom continued. "That way, we can put sprinkles on them. We can also spoon icing onto them. I'll work it out with your daddy, and you can come bake with me soon."

"Thank you," Lily said, shyness turning to eagerness.

Mila indicated Cecily. "This is my sister-in-law, Cecily Perry. Cec, this is Carson Andrews and Lily."

Cecily shook hands with Carson and did the same with Lily. "My two kids are playing outside, Lily. You want to go outside with them?"

Mila felt Lily grip her hand more tightly, and she looked down at her. "I'll go with you if you want me to. Daddy can come, too."

"Okay," Lily agreed.

They went into the backyard, and Mila took Lily over to the swings where her niece and nephew were. She introduced her to Bobby and Gina and told them, "This is Lily. She's new in Driftwood Bay." Glancing over to Carson, she asked, "Have you found a preschool for her yet?"

"My next-door neighbor recommended Happy Hearts. She said a little girl down the street goes there. I have an appointment with them tomorrow morning."

Michael joined them. "That's where our rug rats go. Michael Perry." He offered his hand, and Carson introduced himself.

"Good to have you in town. Dad says you'll be coaching basketball."

"Yes, I will be."

"I played basketball through the end of middle school and then gave it up to concentrate on track. I ran cross country in the fall and then ran hurdles and did high jump in the spring. We go to some of the Pirates' basketball games, though. Football and volleyball, too. Bobby is showing a real interest in sports."

By now, Lily had released Mila's hand and gone over to Gina. Bobby ran and brought back a ball and asked if Lily wanted to kick it with him. She said she did, and the three kids began running around the yard, kicking the lightweight ball.

Carson's eyes followed Lily. "She's really warmed up fast. That's unusual. She doesn't always take to people so quickly."

Glancing back to Michael, he asked, "So, you like this preschool?"

"We do," her brother said. "There are a few in town, but our kids have been at Happy Hearts ever since Cec went back to work. She's a nurse in Corpus. I'm a fireman here in the Bay," he added.

"Then I hope they'll have an opening for Lily when we talk with them tomorrow," Carson said.

Mila's dad began removing the chicken and beef from the grill, saying, "Time to eat. Head inside. Good having you here, Carson. Lily, too."

"Thank you, Dr. Perry."

"That's pretty darn formal. Sure you can't call me Bill?"

"How about we compromise and I go with Dr. P?" Carson countered. "At least for now."

"Sounds good to me," Dad said, leading the parade inside.

Her mom had everything to be served spread out on the kitchen's island.

"I changed the menu on you, Carson," Mom said. "I thought tacos would be easier for the kids to eat than enchiladas. I decided to add fajitas to that. I have all the fixings here. Guac. Grilled onions and mushrooms. Cheese and tomatoes. Chips and queso. There's also some Spanish rice."

"Looks like a feast, Laura. This is a great welcome to Driftwood Bay."

Carson fixed plates for both Lily and himself, and Mom pointed them outside, where they would eat. Mila retrieved pitchers of iced tea and lemonade and asked Carson if he would prefer a beer.

"Iced tea is good for me. I never drink when I'm out with Lily."

They enjoyed a pleasant hour, talking and eating. The kids finished their meal quickly and went back to kicking the ball and then playing in the sandbox. Mila noticed Carson always kept a watchful eye on his daughter. She couldn't imagine being married and losing her spouse and knew Carson watched over Lily with extra care, playing the roles of both mother and father to his daughter.

Cecily said, "I hate to break up such a fun time, but we need to get the kids home for baths and bed." She looked to Mila. "I'll type up a list of everything you need to know."

"I'll be there by five-thirty Friday morning," she promised.

Carson also rose. "I should get Lily home, too. This was a terrific meal, Laura, Dr. P. Thanks for your hospitality."

Everyone brought their plates inside, and Mom nudged Mila. "Go ahead. You can leave. Dad and I will clean up everything."

"If you're sure."

"Yes, sweetie."

She retrieved her purse and walked out with Michael's family and Carson and Lily. As her brother led his crew to their Suburban, Carson lingered, turning to her.

"Are we still on for pizza tomorrow night?" he asked hopefully.

"I'd like that. What time does Lily go to bed?"

"Usually by seven-thirty. She's in PJs by seven, and we read a couple of stories before I put her down."

"I could swing by Pizza Perfecto and pick up a pizza and bring it by once she's asleep."

Lily looked up. "Are you coming to our house, Miss Mila?"

She liked how Carson had instructed his daughter to call all the women by the polite title, and she nodded. "Yes. Since your daddy doesn't cook and we need to talk about school stuff, I thought I could bring by a pizza."

"School stuff is boring," Lily declared, causing Mila to laugh.

"Yes, school stuff can be boring, but it's our job."

"Would you come read me a story?"

The small sprite's request touched her heart. "Yes, I'd like that."

Carson said, "Then come at seven. I can put the pizza in the oven on warm. I know enough to do that."

She laughed. "Seven tomorrow. I'll see you both then."

Lily suddenly stepped toward her and threw her arms around Mila. She hugged the little girl. Lily released her and ran to their car. As Carson helped buckle his daughter into her car seat, Mila headed to her own car, a glow filling her. She looked forward to tomorrow night, more than she had anything in a long time.

She reached her car and turned, seeing Carson close the door. Their gazes met, and they both smiled.

Mila knew that one smile of his would have her floating through the rest of tonight.

Chapter Eight

Carson awoke, already feeling at home in the house he and Lily would live in for the next year. He didn't jump out of bed, as he usually did. Instead, he reflected on last night's dinner at the Perrys' house.

And Mila.

It was hard to put his finger on why he was drawn to her. Yes, she was a fellow coach, so they had that in common. She also was very pretty, with her heart-shaped face and those incredibly blue eyes which drew a person in. She was also kind, offering him a helping hand as he settled into life in Driftwood Bay.

More importantly, he had now seen her interact with Lily. Though Mila had no children of her own, she had gotten down on Lily's level when they first met, focusing on Lily exclusively. His daughter had also taken to Mila, and that was no small feat. Usually she was clingy and didn't want to leave Carson's side. The fact that Lily had been the one to ask Mila to come and read to her this evening spoke volumes.

He jumped in the shower and got ready for the day, shaving

and dressing in slacks and a sports shirt for his meeting at Happy Hearts this morning. Then he went and got Lily up. She always slept deeply, but once awake, she was bright-eyed and full of questions, jabbering away.

As they shared a breakfast of Cheerios, blueberries sprinkled on top of the cereal, Lily asked about her new preschool.

"We're going to go see one today. I hope it'll be one we both like. It's called Happy Hearts. Bobby and Gina go to school there."

Lily smiled at the mention of the two kids. "I like them. They're nice. So is Mila. And she's pretty and has a ponytail like me."

"She is," he agreed, taking another sip of his coffee.

It was nice to be in a fully-stocked kitchen, with everything from a coffeemaker to toaster to microwave. He had put all their furniture and appliances in a storage unit in Houston. It had been easier to keep everything in Houston since he wasn't familiar with the Driftwood Bay area yet and hadn't known what they had available. Once the time came and he and Lily had a house of their own, he would return to the storage unit and have everything moved to Driftwood Bay.

Or the Bay. He had noticed several of the locals referring to the small town that way. He and Lily were now locals, and he would try to do the same.

Carson got Lily ready for the day. Rather, she mostly got herself ready. His daughter already had strong opinions on what she would wear every morning. Today, she picked out a pink and white striped T-shirt dress. She pulled on a pair of pink shorts to wear underneath it, and they went into the bathroom so she could brush her teeth. In the next week before he started his new AD position, he still needed to find a pediatrician and dentist for Lily. It would be smart for him to find the same for himself, as well as somewhere to get his hair cut. He hoped Happy Hearts would the right fit for Lily so he could complete all the tasks on his to-do list as they acquainted themselves with life in their new hometown.

"I want a ponytail today, Daddy," Lily instructed, picking up her brush and running it through her curly locks.

Angie had always been the one who had done Lily's hair. When that task fell to him, he had worked hard, watching YouTube videos of how to do a toddler's hair.

"One ponytail coming up," he said cheerfully, taking the brush and using it to gather up her mass of hair.

"And a bow. A pink one. Not white."

He did as requested, tightening the hair tie and then removing a bow from the bow tree sitting on the bathroom counter. After he slid the bow into place, Lily studied herself in the mirror, smiling at her image.

"Good job, Daddy," his daughter praised.

Pride swelled in his chest, knowing Angie would approve of how Lily was turning out. She was a thoughtful child and always thanked others promptly. She was smart, too, and he hoped whatever preschool she wound up at would challenge her.

"Time to go," he said, filling her neon pink water bottle, something she never left home without.

Lily went and picked up her backpack, which he always kept filled with snacks and a change of clothes. Preschoolers could be messy—and also have an accident every now and then —so he always wanted to be prepared for the unexpected whenever they left the house.

"I don't think you'll need that, Peanut," he said, thinking they'd only be gone for an hour or so.

"But if I *like* my new school, I want to stay," she said firmly.

In that moment, a lump formed in his throat, seeing how

much his daughter reminded him of Angie. Strong. Opinionated. Pretty.

Swallowing it down, he said, "Duly noted. Let's go."

He'd googled where the preschool was last night and didn't need to pull up directions to reach it. It was across the street from the town library, which was on his way to the high school. The convenient location was already a plus in Carson's book.

They went to the front door, which was locked. It had a keypad on it, but he had no code to get in.

A woman appeared at the door and opened it.

"Good morning. I'm Miss Debra. I bet you're Lily and her daddy."

Lily smiled up shyly at the woman, who looked to be in her mid-forties and had auburn hair and a sprinkling of freckles across her nose and cheeks.

"I'm Lily," his daughter confirmed.

"And I'm Carson Andrews," he said, offering his hand to the owner and director of Happy Hearts.

"We are so excited to have you come and visit with us today, Lily," Miss Debra continued. "Let's go inside so you can see our school."

They entered the large foyer, which had a glassed-in reception area, and another door which also had a keypad. Miss Debra typed in the code and opened it for them to go through.

"How old are you, Lily?" the older woman asked.

"I'm four," Lily said proudly, holding up four fingers on her left hand.

"Then let's go look at the Orange Room. That's where the four-year-olds are."

They moved down a corridor lined with artwork done by children, passing rooms that were labeled Green and Red. When they reached the Orange Room, Miss Debra paused.

"I see they're having story time now. Miss Andi is the teacher for the Orange Room. Could you go join the learning circle and listen to the story she's reading?"

His daughter nodded solemnly and moved quietly into the room, setting down her backpack and water bottle before going to the circle of children. Carson saw her take a seat next to Bobby. The boy grinned, patting Lily on the shoulder, and then returned his attention to the teacher.

"We can talk quietly here for a few minutes, Mr. Andrews. That way, you can keep an eye on Lily."

"I appreciate that. We lost Lily's mother two years ago, and I can be a little overprotective sometimes. And please, call me Carson."

"I almost called you Coach," she admitted. "I've heard you're taking over the boys' basketball program at the high school. My son will be a sophomore this coming year. He played on the JV, but he has aspirations of moving up to varsity this fall."

"Then you must be Caleb Connors' mom," he said, recalling her last name from the website.

"My, you already know players' names. That's a good sign. You'll find Caleb is a hard worker. He's not like most teenagers who dig in their heels when you talk to them. He'll be easy to coach. I promise. Now, let me tell you about Happy Hearts."

Debra Connors explained to Carson the philosophy of the preschool, saying that learning was key—and that laughter was a part of that learning experience.

"We want our children at Happy Hearts to truly be happy to come to school each day. We aim for a balanced education. Children learn everything from numbers and colors to farm and zoo animals. We work on fine motor skills and even expose them to conversational Spanish. Music and art are a huge part of their day, as is physical activity. A strong body helps with a strong mind."

Carson liked the fact that it was a balanced curriculum. He had thought Lily's last school leaned a little too heavily into academics, but he hadn't wanted her to change schools when it was the only place she had ever known. He had a good feeling about Happy Hearts.

"Michael Perry recommended Happy Hearts to me."

Miss Debra smiled. "Michael and Cecily have both their children with us. Gina is in the Green Room now. I noticed Lily went and sat next to Bobby."

"We met them last night at dinner. Dr. Perry had us over to welcome us to the community."

"Bill and Laura Perry are lovely people. Bill has done wonders for the school district, and I can't go into Laura's shop without coming out with something new. Would you like to see the rest of our facility, Carson?"

By now, story time had ended, and Lily had joined other children sitting at a table. Bobby was sharing crayons with her.

"I should let Lily know where I'm going."

"Let me do that," Miss Debra said gently. "We prefer to keep parents in the hallway so the classroom isn't interrupted."

The owner went into the room and spoke briefly to the teacher, who smiled and waved at Carson. Then she went to the table where Lily sat and knelt, talking to her for a minute. Lily nodded and looked up, smiling at him. He waved and she grinned before going back to her coloring.

Miss Debra joined him again. "Lily feels comfortable with us leaving."

He saw the rest of the school, and they returned to the director's office.

"We do have a spot open for Lily. If you would like to put

down a small deposit to hold that spot while you think things over, I'd advise you to do so."

"That won't be necessary. I believe that Lily has found a new home at Happy Hearts."

"That's terrific. Let me pull out paperwork for you to fill out, Carson."

He did so, explaining that he would need to leave a few things blank. "We've just arrived in town. Before I start work, my goal is to get us completely settled. That means finding a doctor for Lily, among other things."

"If you'd like, I can recommend a pediatrician."

She opened one of the desk's drawers and pulled out a card. Handing it to him, she said, "Dr. Dickey is wonderful. My own children go to her. She's smart as they come and gentle with her patients."

"Thank you for the recommendation," he said, sliding the card into his pocket. "When can Lily start at Happy Hearts?"

Smiling, Miss Debra said, "I think she already has. Would you feel comfortable leaving her with us today?"

"I really would," he said, surprising himself. "Her backpack has extra clothes and a snack. I didn't pack a lunch, though."

"That's never necessary. We provide a morning and afternoon snack, along with a healthy, nutritious lunch. Did you note any allergies on Lily's paperwork?"

"She doesn't have any."

"Then I think it would be good to allow her to remain with us today."

The woman gave Carson an orientation packet, which detailed procedures at Happy Hearts.

"Can I go and tell her goodbye?" he asked anxiously.

"Of course. Follow me."

When they reached the Orange Room, he saw Lily was in a circle and the children were playing some kind of game. Again, he stood in the hall while the director entered the classroom and spoke briefly to Lily. His daughter nodded enthusiastically and then looked up at him, waving. He waved back, and Lily turned her attention to the game again. It was good to see joy on his daughter's face. His anxiety melted away.

"I'll be sending you an introductory email, along with some frequently asked questions by parents," Miss Debra told him. "I'll also add you to our parent text chain. We change the code to the outside door once a week. When you arrive to pick up Lily, you may use it to gain entrance into the foyer."

She led him to a notebook sitting on the ledge in front of the receptionist's window.

"You'll sign Lily in and out each day when you arrive and leave. We usually find it better if once you sign your child in, we buzz open the door and let Lily go to the Orange Room on her own. At the end of the day when you arrive, you'll sign her out, and the receptionist will notify Miss Andi to send Lily to the front. It's less disruptive that way. Her teacher will always put a brief note into Lily's backpack about what she did today. We also have a place on our website for parents to create an account and log in. There are cameras in each of the rooms so that you may observe your child. We also post, within that private page, pictures of your child each day. I promise those will never appear on the general website. We do everything we can to ensure your child's privacy."

"I like how secure Happy Hearts is," Carson said. "In a way, it surprises me because this is a small town. My daughter's last preschool in Houston wasn't nearly this security conscious."

Miss Debra smiled sadly. "The world has changed in many ways, and we want to keep the children at Happy Hearts as joyful and innocent as we can during their time with us."

"Then I guess I'm off," he said, turning to the log book and officially signing Lily in for the day. "You have my cell number if anything arises."

"We will take good care of Lily, Carson," Miss Debra assured him.

"Thank you. This was the biggest piece of the puzzle I needed to solve in moving to Driftwood Bay. I think Lily will be very happy here."

Carson went by the pediatrician's office which Debra Connors had recommended. He waited twenty minutes and then had a brief sit-down with her. He found Dr. Dickey to be warm and nurturing, and she agreed to take on Lily as a patient, especially after he mentioned Debra Connors had recommend Lily come to this practice.

"Has Lily seen a dentist yet?" Dr. Dickey asked.

"No. I didn't know we needed to this early. I'm Lily's sole parent. Her mother died two years ago."

"That must have been difficult for both of you," Dr. Dickey said sympathetically. "Yes, it is time for Lily to see a dentist. By five, I also suggest that she see an eye doctor."

She pulled two cards from her lap drawer and handed them to Carson. "This is who I would recommend. Full disclosure, the dentist is my husband. He's the only pediatric-certified dentist in the Bay. The eye doctor sees patients of all ages, however."

"Thanks for the recs, Dr. Dickey. Do you have any for me?"

She laughed. "Keeping it in the family, I could recommend my brother as your PCP." She took one of her cards and jotted his name and address on the back of it. "There are a few dentists

in the area, but we see Dr. Melvin." She added that name and address and then passed the card to Carson.

"I should have come to you first," he joked. "You're like a

one-person Chamber of Commerce. Do you have a suggestion for a barber?" he asked, only half-kiddingly.

Dr. Dickey chuckled. "My cousin has a barber shop on the square. His name is Hank. He does walk-ins and appointments. That's what you get in a small town, Carson. Everyone knows everyone and seems to be related somehow to most of the town."

"I appreciate you taking on Lily as your patient."

"If you would, have her previous doctor's office forward her medical records to me. I want to see her history and make sure she's up-to-date on her vaccinations. I'd also like to see her in a week once I receive this info, so I can establish a relationship with her. You can make an appointment with my receptionist on your way out."

Carson rose. "Thank you again, Dr. Dickey."

"It's good to have you in Driftwood Bay, Carson. And by the way, my sister is Lisa Thornbach, the girls' basketball coach at the high school."

"She just texted me last night and said she was home from her family reunion. We set up a time to meet tomorrow. I guess you didn't make the reunion?"

"It was her husband's family who held the reunion out of state. You'll like Lisa. She's easy-going—until it comes to sports. Then she's a killer on the court, as are her players."

"I've checked her teams' records for the last few years. She's built a solid program. Good meeting you, Doc."

He left the pediatrician's office after making an appointment for Lily the next week and then called her pediatrician in Houston to have the records forwarded. He then made stops around town, scheduling dental appointments for both of them, as well as an eye appointment and physical for himself. Dr. Hopewell had a cancelation occur while he was filling out paperwork, so Carson stepped into the empty appointment, meeting his new PCP and finding he liked him quite a bit.

By day's end, he felt he had accomplished a good deal and had enjoyed getting to know more residents of Driftwood Bay. He returned to Happy Hearts and claimed Lily, who was a chatterbox the entire way home, talking about Miss Andi and the Orange Room and all the new friends she had made.

"I love Happy Hearts, Daddy," Lily said, finally winding down as they reached home. "And I get to go back tomorrow."

"Right you are, Peanut," he said, helping her from the car seat and going into the house.

Carson fed her grilled cheese, yogurt, and fruit for dinner, and then got his daughter into the bathtub. She played with her plastic figures from *Toy Story*, lining them up on the edge of the tub and then knocking them into the water, laughing as she did so.

In that moment, he knew the move to Driftwood Bay had been the right one.

For Lily—and him.

He got her into her pajamas and unpinned her hair since this hadn't been a hair wash night.

"Let's go wait for Miss Mila," she told him, scurrying down the stairs.

Carson heard the doorbell ring, and his heart skipped a beat, knowing he was about to spend the next few hours with Mila Perry.

Chapter Nine

Mila stood on the porch, her finger poised above the doorbell. Once she pushed it, there would be no going back. Either she walked away now, her heart intact, or she rang it.

And hoped she was making the right decision.

Taking a deep breath, she braced herself and touched the doorbell, pushing hard, hearing it chime. She heard a faint squeal and determined it was coming from inside. From Lily.

While she was guarding her heart when it came to Carson Andrews, she had already fallen headfirst for Lily. The sprite was a cute, clever child, and she had gotten along beautifully with Gina and Bobby. In fact, no matter how tonight went between Carson and her, Mila had decided to ask if Lily could come for a playdate this weekend while she kept the kids.

She heard the lock turning and swallowed her nerves. The door opened, and both Carson and Lily stood there. She ignored the thumping of her heart and smiled brightly.

"Hello, you two."

"Hi, Miss Mila." Lily smiled up at her. "You brought

Daddy pizza. He likes sausage and pepperoni, but I like cheese."

"Well, it's a good thing I brought sausage and pepperoni." She had taken a chance since she had forgotten to touch base with Carson and ask him his preferences, going with standard toppings, and was glad now of her selection.

"Come on in," Carson said, taking the pizza box from her. "I'll go put this in the oven. I have it on low now."

She leaned down and retrieved the sack she had placed by her feet as Lily took her hand.

"Come see my room."

As they went up the stairs, Lily said, "I saw Bobby today but not Gina. Bobby and I colored, and I played a tambourine and had bananas and peanut butter for a snack."

"Sounds like you visited Happy Hearts."

"That's my new school," Lily said matter-of-factly. "I like orange, and I'm in the Orange Room. I wish they had a Pink Room. Pink is my favorite color."

They arrived at Lily's bedroom as Mila said, "I certainly like those pink pajamas you have on. Is that Sleeping Beauty?"

"Well, her name is Aurora, but she went to sleep for a long time. This is my room."

"I see Binky."

The dog was curled up by the pillows on the bed, in the middle of a dozen stuffed animals. He raised his head hearing his name and looked at her in curiosity.

Lily scrambled onto the bed and kissed the beagle's head. "This is Miss Mila, Binky. She's Daddy's friend. She's a coach like him." Lily frowned. "What do you coach?"

"Volleyball," she reminded the child. "It's where a net is put up in the middle of a court, and each team stands on one side of it. One person serves the ball, which means it goes over the net to the other side. Then players hit it back and forth, over the net, until someone misses."

"Can Binky come sit with me when I go to your game?" Lily pleaded.

"I'm afraid animals aren't allowed in the school gym. Binky will have to stay home and keep your stuffed animals company."

The little girl sighed dramatically. "All right." Then she looked at the sack Mila had placed on the bed. "What's that?"

"Your daddy said you like to read, so I brought you a book."

"Yay!" Lily stood and began jumping on the bed.

Mila wanted to correct her but didn't think she should get on to a child who didn't belong to her.

"Lily Angeline! Stop that right now," Carson barked from the door.

Lily got in a final bounce, landing on her bottom. "Sorry, Daddy. I forgot."

He came and sat on the bed. "Did you really forget? Or did you try to do something you knew you weren't supposed to do?"

"I was excited. Miss Mila brought me a book!"

"You can find a better way to show that you're excited. I hope you thanked her."

Lily thrust out her bottom lip. "No. I'm sorry." She looked to Mila. "Thank you for my book. Can I see it?"

She pulled the book from the sack and handed it to Lily. "These are two characters that Bobby and Gina like to read about. Their names are Gerald and Piggie."

"Gerald is the elephant," Lily said. "He's gray. I like Piggie because she's pink. What's the name of this book?"

Mila climbed onto the bed, pushing aside a few stuffed animals, and Lily snuggled next to her.

"Mo Willems is the author of all the Elephant and Piggie books. That means he wrote the book."

She read the title page, and Lily insisted on turning the pages for her. Mila's voice moved into the rhythm of the book, and soon Lily was laughing aloud at the adventures of the two friends.

"Again!" she cried once they had reached the end.

Knowing how Bobby and Gina liked the repetition of reading a book several times, Mila turned back to the beginning and read it from start to finish. Lily began joining in on the repetitive parts. So did Carson.

After she had read it a third time, Carson said, "Okay. That's enough Gerald and Piggie for tonight. Time to say your prayers and hit the sack, Peanut."

Lily scrambled from the bed and knelt beside it. Carson did the same. Both closed their eyes and bowed their heads. She sat quietly, watching and listening.

"God bless Mommy. God bless Daddy. God bless Binky," Lily said. She paused and then added, "God bless Bobby and Gina and Miss Andi. And Miss Mila."

She was touched hearing her name, and a warmth spread through her limbs.

"Amen," Lily said, and Carson echoed the word.

They both rose, and he began moving stuffed animals so that he could turn back the covers. Mila set the book on the nightstand beside the bed and helped remove more of the stuffed friends. Lily climbed into bed and pulled the covers up as Carson replaced the plethora of stuffed animals. Binky, who had gotten up during the process, now settled himself against Lily's leg.

Carson went and kissed his daughter's brow. "Goodnight, Peanut. Sleep tight."

"Goodnight, Daddy. Goodnight, Miss Mila."

"Sweet dreams, Lily," she replied, going to the door and stepping through it as Carson turned on a sound machine and clicked off the light. A nightlight was visible now, glowing faintly.

Carson blew Lily a kiss and closed the door. He raked his fingers through his hair.

"Another day in the books." Then he grinned. "Thanks for bringing Lily a book. I think."

"Why do you say that?"

He chuckled and parroting a line from the book, said, "We need a map. Map! Map! Mappy-map-map!"

She couldn't help but laugh as they went down the stairs. "It's a real earworm, I know. When I first read that book to my niece and nephew, it seems I turned every one-syllable word into the same sing-song for a week. Walk. Walk. Walky-walk-walk. Wash. Wash. Washy-wash-wash. Sorry. I know it'll probably drive you crazy."

"I don't mind. Lily learns with repetition. I can tell she's crazy about the book. Thanks again for bringing it to her."

They entered the kitchen, and he went to the oven, donning mitts to remove the pizza.

"I think it's important to encourage reading," she said. "Naturally, with my dad's line of work, education was big in our household. How about yours?"

She saw a slight frown cross his face before he said, "Yes. Education was emphasized."

Mila decided not to push the issue now, but she believed there was a story to be told about Carson's childhood.

Opening a cabinet, he removed two plates and set them next to the pizza. "Fork?" he asked.

"Please. I start out using one, and then as I eat closer to the crust, I abandon it."

He plated two slices for each of them and then asked, "Would you like a glass of wine to go along with it?"

"Yes. That sounds good. And some water, too."

"Bottled water is in the fridge. I'll open the wine. Let's eat in the den."

She grabbed two waters, napkins, and forks and took them to the den, returning for the plates of pizza. Carson joined her, balancing the wineglasses in one hand and the bottle of wine in the other. He poured each of them a glass and took a seat on the sofa beside her.

"Lily was a bundle of energy," she remarked, taking a bite of her pizza.

"She always is. She crashes pretty fast, though."

"Does she sleep through the night?"

"She does now. Right after Angie died, she would get up a couple of times during the night. Needing a drink of water or to go to the potty. She was restless as she slept. Finally, that all calmed down as she adapted to our new normal."

"It had to be hard for her, losing her mommy and not really understanding why. How much does she know about what really happened to Angie?"

"Not much. Back then, I just told her Mommy had gone to heaven and would watch over us. She was too young to remember the carjacking itself. We look at pictures from back then on my phone, and I also display a few of Angie."

"I saw one on her dresser."

He smiled wistfully. "That was from Halloween. Angie always wanted us to dress up to take Lily trick or treating. I don't want her to ever forget Angie, but I think it's good we've come to a new place. It'll help me distance myself from what happened. Houston held nothing but bad memories, and I always suffered through the whispers of being the guy whose wife was murdered."

She placed a hand on his thigh. "It's okay to feel sad. It's also okay to live your life, Carson. From everything I've seen, Angie did a great job raising Lily, and you've stepped up and kept things rolling. You won't ever forget Angie and what she meant to you, but you have to keep moving forward."

Mila removed her hand, self-conscious about having touched him. She took another bite of pizza and chewed thoughtfully.

"Tell me the Mila story," he urged, changing the subject. "What was it like growing up in Driftwood Bay?"

"The Bay was a terrific place to be a kid. The beach being so close makes it a magical place. Michael is four years older than I am, and he was always a protective big brother. We would get on our bikes and just roam. I mentioned my two best friends to you—Layne and Piper—and I was just as at home in their houses as I was my own. The three of us did everything together in elementary and middle school. We pursued our own interests in high school, though. Layne played soccer and was a debater. Piper danced on the drill team and was editor of the *Pirate Press*, our school newspaper. She also was big into choir and theater. We went to each other's events and supported one another. Even though we're far apart now, we have that shared history."

"That's great. I don't really have any childhood friends." Carson paused and then said, "My younger brother was my best friend. We were sixteen months apart and did everything together. Then he and my parents were killed in a car wreck when I was twelve. I had to leave behind my home and everything I knew to move in with my aunt Jayne, Dad's sister."

Mila couldn't believe how tragedy had struck Carson not once, but twice. "I'm so sorry to hear that."

He shrugged, biting off a piece of his crust and chewing a moment. "She wasn't a warm, fuzzy person, if you know what

I mean. Never came to a single game I played in. Didn't attend either my high school or college graduations. I studied hard for my grades in college and also worked a part-time job. There wasn't a lot of time left over after that for friends. Angie became my best friend and then my girlfriend. We had each other."

"What about after college? Were you close to anyone at work?" she asked.

"To my assistant coach. Rudy was offered my coaching position when I left. His wife Juanita and Angie were good friends. They had a baby six months ago. They're the ones who kept Lily when I came here to interview. Other than that, I'm a bit of a loner."

Trying to lighten the mood, she said, "Loners still have interests. What do you like to do, Carson? Apart from playing dad to Lil?"

He chuckled. "Lily takes up a lot of time. I am fascinated by anything related to World War II. I've read a lot of books on the subject and see every war movie ever made about that era. I also enjoy running and Pilates. How about you, Coach Perry?"

She took a sip of her wine. "I'm also a runner. I'm into photography, especially black and white. I think shooting in black and white adds so much more depth to a photo. I teach US history, so I'm interested in that, too, especially the Old West after the Civil War. Give me a Western to watch, and I'm happy."

They finished off the pizza, talking about different movies and historical documentaries they had enjoyed. Mila told him about the 5K run held on Labor Day each year.

"The city hosts that one, and the local Y sponsors another 5K on Thanksgiving Day. You should enter."

"I don't run as much as I used to," he admitted. "Before, I would strap Lily into her stroller and run for an hour or more.

She's not big into that now, so the running is more if I have time at school. With the AD position, I doubt I'll have much free time to work out. It'll probably be at-home Pilates on my app for the foreseeable future. Tell me some more about my new town."

They talked for another half hour, with Mila talking about traditions at Christmas and what the summer tourist season looked like versus when school started and the tourists abandoned Driftwood Bay.

"We do have a small group of snowbirds who come down from the north each year. Minnesota. North Dakota. Montana. Most of them reside at the trailer park in motorhomes they drive down, but a few have cottages near the shore."

"We made a big move today," Carson said. "Lily and I chose Happy Hearts for her. She's in Bobby's class. I'm glad they met last night because he really made her feel welcomed."

"I'm glad you've found a preschool for her."

"Also, our next-door neighbor, Dotty Williams, will probably watch Lily when I'm gone for basketball. She's great with kids, and Binky and her dog Ginger really get along."

Mila nodded. "I'm happy for you, Carson. All the pieces seem to be falling into place for you."

He set his empty plate on the coffee table in front of them. "Most of the pieces. The biggest piece is one I'm struggling with, Mila. And that's you."

"Me?"

Carson nodded. "I haven't even thought about going on a date since my wife died. Then I came to Driftwood Bay and met you. Suddenly, you're all I can think about. Then you told me the same thing. I'm not sure if I'm ready for a relationship. Part of me is holding back, wanting one, but scared shitless to try again."

He had taken her hand as he spoke, his thumb stroking her palm, sending shivers dancing along her spine.

"What about you? You're an attractive woman. Have you ever been married? Or had your heart hurt?"

"No, to marriage. Yes, to the heart," she said quietly. "I dated a guy who coached at a rival high school when I first got out of college. We were together two years. I saw a future for us, but Mark wasn't ready to make that kind of commitment. Then he got a job offer and left me behind, brokenhearted. It took a long time to get over him. I finally left San Antonio when I got the call to come and coach here. Then last November, I started dating our basketball coach. The one you're replacing."

"Ouch."

"I know, right? It wasn't serious, but I had fun with Sam. When he left the Bay, I swore off dating coaches."

"Double ouch," Carson said, his hand wrapping around hers now. "Yet here we are."

"Exactly. I'll be honest, Carson. I don't know if I have it in me to invest in another relationship with a coach who's going to leave when greener pastures call."

He took her other hand. "I'm not going anywhere, Mila."

"You say that now."

"I mean it. I like the slower pace in Driftwood Bay. The opportunity to remain a head coach while also serving as a district athletic director means I'm not interested in looking elsewhere. Professionally, this is a great situation for me. Personally, I want to give Lily consistency. That means staying in one place. I don't want her to have to make new friends every few years when I change jobs. I want to raise her here in the Bay. Give her a real home, with a community that is like extended family."

Carson gazed deeply into Mila's eyes. "I plan to be here a

long, long time. I've realized that while I put my life on hold these past two years in order to focus on Lily, I'm ready to do something for myself now." He paused. "And that something is getting to know you, Mila."

"Would we be making a mistake, though, starting something between us?" she asked.

"You're my boss. You oversee all aspects of athletics in the district. You'll be responsible for evaluating my performance and deciding whether or not to keep me on contract. The optics of dating your subordinate don't look good, Carson."

"Is that the only thing holding you back?"

She was afraid to voice how she worried about living up to his memories of Angie, and so Mila said, "That's a pretty big concern."

"If I can get that straightened out, are you willing to take a chance on me? On us?"

"More than anything. That's exactly what I want," she replied truthfully.

"We seem compatible. My gut tells me that we have the same values. I know innately that you're a good person and wonderful coach. But I think before we decide to pursue this any further, there's something we need to do."

"What's that?" she asked, her heart hammering against her ribs.

"Kiss. If we're going to fight for this relationship, we should see if we have chemistry. I already feel the pull between us, but I think we need to see if that spark is real."

Carson gazed at her. "May I kiss you, Mila?"

"I thought you'd never ask."

Chapter Ten

Despite her reservations about beginning a relationship with Carson, Mila was ready for his kiss. He was right. They could talk all night about whether or not they should start up something between them, but the physical attraction had to be there.

She was certain it was.

His hands framed her face, the simple touch stirring something deep within her. As he lowered his mouth to hers, anticipation filled her.

The kiss began tenderly, full of unspoken promises. It was gentle and moved her, tears filling her eyes. She inhaled his clean, masculine scent, reveling in his nearness. Then his lips, firm and yet pillowy soft, increased the pressure, sparking a thrill within her, causing desire to ripple through her. One hand slipped to her nape, cradling it as his kiss grew more insistent.

Mila had never been one for romance novels. That was something Piper enjoyed, but she felt as if she were now starring in her own romance story as Carson continued to kiss her, heating her blood. This kiss was different from any she'd experienced before, and she wanted more of it. More of him. She leaned into him, needing to be closer, and heard a low growl in his throat. He broke the kiss, and they gazed at one another a long moment, the air crackling between them. She felt on the precipice of something unknown to her, yet she was ready to dive in.

His mouth came down on hers hard now, one arm snaking around her waist, holding her close. He teased her mouth open, and she invited him in, his tongue sweeping against hers sensually, beginning a playful warring of their tongues.

New sensations poured through her, foreign to her. Her arms went about him, not wanting to let this man go.

They kissed for a long time, the variety of kisses changing from minute to minute. At times, he explored her leisurely, as if he wanted to memorize everything about her. Other times, his kiss grew demanding. Bold. Taking and taking—yet giving himself in return.

Finally, he ended the kiss, resting his brow against hers, both out of breath, their breathing erratic, coming in short spurts. In this moment, she knew she had never kissed—or been kissed—in such a poignant, passionate way. Carson had set the new standard for what a kiss could be.

He lifted his head from hers and gazed deeply into her eyes. Things had definitely shifted between them, and Mila no longer had any doubts about pursuing more than friendship with this man. She wanted to see where this relationship might lead them.

Carson leaned back against the couch, his arm going about her, drawing her to him. Her cheek rested against his heart, and she felt its beat. She flattened her palm against his chest, feeling the hard wall of muscle resting beneath her fingertips. A possessive wave swept over her, wanting to shout to the world that this man was hers.

"I think I could stay curled up next to you forever," she told him.

"I hear you." The back of his fingers caressed her cheek, and he kissed the top of her head. "That was something."

"If I were a coach rating your kissing skills, you would receive an A+ and be named team captain," she said flirtatiously.

"I haven't kissed anyone in a long time," he admitted. "Angie was everything to me. We met on the first day of college and literally matured into our adult selves together."

He cupped her cheek, the pad of his thumb sensually stroking it. "But I don't ever want to compare you to Angie, Mila. You are your own person—and one terrific kisser yourself."

She smiled at his compliment. "I haven't done a lot of kissing myself for quite a while. I was so busy in college, playing on a volleyball scholarship, that I didn't date much. I've only had one serious relationship I told you about, and those kisses were a long time ago."

"What about Sam?" he asked. "He was pretty recent."

"Sam wasn't much into kissing. Or foreplay. He was more of a 'let's get to the main event' kind of guy. We enjoyed doing things together, but even I knew nothing serious would ever come from us seeing one another. I hate to say it, but I was marking time with Sam." Mila paused. "Maybe because I was waiting for you to come along."

She brushed her palm back and forth against his chest. "I liked kissing you, Carson. You made me feel cherished. At the same time, I definitely felt the passion between us. I've never kissed anyone as long as we just did. It was pretty incredible."

"Do you believe it's worth it to invest ourselves in a relationship?" he asked softly.

"Before we kissed, I was walking a tightrope regarding that question. Now? I'm all in," she assured him. "That doesn't mean it'll be smooth sailing for us, though. I expect a lot of rough bumps along the way. People throwing obstacles in our path."

She lifted her head, their gazes connecting. "You have far more at stake than I do. Not only do you have to prove yourself on the court with your team, but you also have the eyes of Driftwood Bay on you, watching as you supervise all sports in the schools. Fans here can be pretty harsh in their assessment of coaches, and that includes the athletic director responsible for all sports programs."

"What do you suggest as our first move?"

"Something which may be the hardest thing I've ever done. We need to tell my dad." She hesitated. "Just because we feel something between us doesn't mean we'll receive the green light to pursue it. Your job—and providing for Lily—has to be your priority. This isn't like when Sam and I went to HR and notified them we were dating. We were coaches on equal footing in different sports." Mila shook her head. "This is way different. I report to you."

"I think I want to run this by Jon Earl before we approach Dr. P and HR," Carson said. "He might have greater insight into this situation than either of us. Do you want to be with me when I speak to him?"

"No, I think it should be between you two guys. It's the smart move to loop him in, but Jon Earl is a bit old-fashioned. I think he'll be more frank if I'm not present during your discussion when you let him know what's brewing between us."

"I guess this is the right time to bring up something else." Carson took a deep breath and let it out slowly. "I hope you don't mind, but I'd like to take things slowly. This is the first time for me to be with a woman since Angie's death. I don't want to mess things up by moving too fast. I also have Lily to consider. I've already introduced you to her, and she knows you're my friend and that we work together. I don't want to confuse her and let her jump to the conclusion she's going to have an instant mommy."

"I get that. Slow is definitely the way to go. And no PDA in front of her."

"I'm already aching for your taste again," Carson admitted. "Are you up for round two?"

She broke out in a huge grin. "Where your kisses are concerned, I'm ready to roll."

He began kissing her again, pulling her into his lap. Mila entwined her arms about his neck and leaned into him, kissing him back with everything she had. Their kisses ran the gamut, from sweet to scorching. By the time they stopped again, she was hot all over, burning need pulsing within her. She had to agree with Carson, though. They were both fragile and didn't need to leap into anything too quickly.

Mila slid from his lap and said, "I'm keeping the kids for Michael and Cecily the next four days. They haven't had alone time together in forever and are taking a short trip up to the Hill Country."

"Will the kids be at Happy Hearts tomorrow? Lily will be disappointed if Bobby is among the missing."

"I'll drop them off at Happy Hearts in the morning and then pick them up that afternoon. Maybe we could all have dinner together tomorrow night," she suggested.

"Lily would like that." He leaned in and kissed her softly. "*I* would like that."

"Does Lily have any favorite foods?"

"She could live on mac and cheese. She's also a fan of hamburgers and hot dogs."

"Then we should meet at Burger Barn. It's a kid-friendly place. I've decided to take the kids to the beach on Saturday morning before it gets too hot. You and Lily are welcome to join us if you'd like."

"That's a great idea. I'm going to try and reserve weekends this summer to be a work-free zone. A trip to the beach would be a good start to our first summer in the Bay."

He took her hand, lacing his fingers through hers. The simple gesture meant a great deal to Mila.

"What do you have on your agenda this summer?" he asked.

"I run a volleyball clinic the last week of June. Mornings are for elementary-aged kids, and the afternoon sessions are for middle schoolers. I also have made a big commitment regarding my future."

He looked at her quizzically. "About what?"

"Not that I would do anything about it anytime soon, but I've decided to pursue my master's degree in administration. I love coaching—but I love having options more. The day may come when I'm ready to leave the classroom and court and challenge myself in new ways. I want to be prepared."

"I've never looked into that," he admitted. "What does it involve?"

Briefly, she outlined the online program she had registered for two days ago and how many courses she would take for the degree, as well as the tests she would need to pass for certification.

"Fortunately, I can take all my classes online, so I'm going to get started with that this coming Monday, the first day of the summer session. Once my coursework is completed, I'll need to do an internship. Hopefully, George Crumby, our principal, will help facilitate that. I've seen others do it, and it usually involves pawning off grunt work assistant principals don't like bothering with. Issuing textbooks to teachers. Assigning lockers to kids. That kind of thing."

"How long will it take you to earn your degree and certification?"

"The university suggests two years, but once volleyball season ends, I have more free time and can devote myself to my studies. I'm hoping to finish a year from this coming Christmas."

"That's ambitious." He grinned. "I find ambition very sexy."

Carson kissed her again, a long, slow, delicious kiss that caused her toes to curl.

Breaking it, he cradled her face in his large hands. "If I don't stop kissing you now, I'll keep doing it all night long."

She understood he was trying to cool the heat between them so things didn't progress any further tonight.

Mila came to her feet, and he did the same.

"I plan to pick up the kids at five. We'll head straight to Burger Barn from Happy Hearts."

"I'll do the same. Let me walk you to your car."

Hand-in-hand, they went outside to where her Jeep stood at the curb. She knew he was as reluctant as she was to part.

"Talk to Jon Earl tomorrow," she urged. "I don't want this to go any further until we've been given permission to proceed. We have to be realistic, Carson. HR might shut this down."

He squeezed her fingers. "While Lily is my top priority, she's 1A and you're 1B, Mila. I'm going to fight for us and make certain this works for us and our district."

She climbed into the driver's seat, and he leaned in, giving her a soft, parting kiss.

"I'm meeting with Lisa Thornbach tomorrow morning

about the clinics we're putting on, but I'll see Jon Earl after that."

"Thank you," she said, starting the Jeep. "I'll see you and Lily for dinner tomorrow night."

Carson placed a hand on her shoulder squeezing it. "I have complete faith this'll work out for us."

His hand fell away, and Mila put the Jeep into gear. She waved as she pulled away from the curb and drove down the street, watching him in her rearview mirror.

Tonight, a seismic shift had occurred inside her. She was still dealing with feelings so new and unfamiliar that it would take time to wrap her head around them. All she knew for certain was that she needed Carson Andrews in her life and was willing to do whatever it took to give their relationship a chance to blossom.

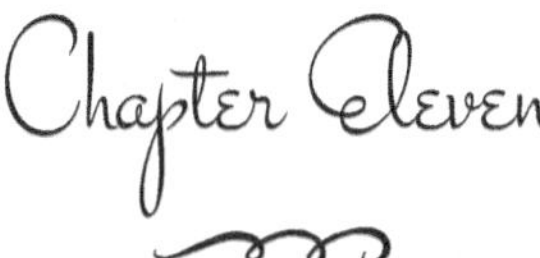

Chapter Eleven

Carson punched in the code to the front door at Happy Hearts and ushered Lily inside. He signed her in, and the receptionist buzzed the door leading to the classrooms. Lily was still too small to open it on her own, so he did so for her, handing her water bottle to her.

"Have a good day, Peanut!" he called as she raced down the hall, eager to get to the Orange Room.

Returning to his car, he drove to the field house for his meeting with Lisa. As he pulled up, he saw a woman getting out of her car. She noticed him and waited.

"Coach Andrews?" she asked. "Lisa Thornbach. Thanks for making time to meet with me."

"You resemble your sister," he said, shaking her offered hand as he balanced the box containing the coffeemaker he had bought.

"You must have kids," she said, laughing.

"A four-year-old. Lily. Dr. Dickey is her new pediatrician."

They entered the building and went straight to his office. Carson looked around and set the box down.

"Mind if I set this up while we talk?"

"I need to go to my office to grab a few things regarding the clinic. Be back in a few."

By the time she returned, he had the coffeemaker plugged in but realized he still needed to buy pods for it. He'd brought in a mini fridge yesterday so he'd have access to a place for creamer and drinks, as well as a place to keep his lunch. He rarely left school grounds once he arrived, preferring to eat at his desk or with other coaches.

Lisa spread out a few folders on the table, and he retrieved ones which Sam had left behind regarding summer camps. He also brought over his laptop, seeing Lisa had hers. They spent the next hour discussing the general overview of what their two camps, running simultaneously, would accomplish, as well as smaller, organizational details. He had managed basketball clinics at his previous assignment, and he brought a few ideas to the table that he wanted to implement for the boys' sessions. She liked everything he had to offer and promised to incorporate his suggestions into her own camp. It was good that Lisa was so willing to be on the same page, and he felt they'd gotten off to a good start.

They talked their personal basketball philosophy next. Both prioritized player development and skills, with an emphasis on creating a positive, supportive team environment. Each shared specific examples, and by the end of their conversation, Carson knew they would get along well.

"I like that you promote sportsmanship," Lisa said. "Too many kids pout when they lose."

"It's important to learn how to be a good winner, as well as being a good loser," he said. "I try to make a lot of my basketball lessons life lessons. I want my players to be good people on and off the court. Winning at all costs is not in my playbook."

"Can I ask one thing?" Lisa hesitated. "How do you interact with your athletes?"

"I'm not sure where you're headed," he replied, knowing she must have had a previous conflict.

She sighed. "Are you a yeller?"

"No way," he said immediately. "I want my players to respect their opponents, as well as their coaching staff. I believe respect is a two-way street, and I would never yell at them. I may get a little over enthused at times, but belittling and berating a player isn't in my nature. Yes, I will get on to someone if they're slacking. If they make a wrong move in a game, we'll watch film of that together and go over what they should've done and what their reaction should be the next time. But I'm pretty even-keeled, both in practice and during games."

"I like hearing that," Lisa said, her relief obvious. "I have that same outlook, though I can get a little heated during a close game. I think a positive attitude is important, both as a coach and player, and I try to model good character, as well."

"Agreed. I want players to have the opportunity to grow. To become part of a team. To develop as players and into leaders. I also give positive feedback anytime I have something negative to say, trying to balance things out." He paused. "But I do believe in discipline. I have clear rules and consequences for breaking any of those rules. I hold players accountable, both on and off the court."

She smiled. "We're going to get along great, Coach. Our counterparts at the middle school definitely buy into what you're saying. They'll also be here for the basketball camps. Have you met Jackson Rudd yet? He's your assistant."

"I have briefly. He told me he's also a part of the clinics. I've included him on the schedule. I've got campers rotating between various coaches for working on specific skills. Dribbling. Shooting. Footwork. Then we'll come together in small groups to put those skills into play."

Lisa stood. "Okay. I'm glad we're in sync. I'll be in the girls' gym, while your camp takes over the boys' gym. We used to have to share, but two years ago when the bond issue kicked in, we got a new basketball arena out of it."

"I've seen it. It's a beauty. I haven't studied the schedule too closely yet," he admitted. "I'm trying to familiarize myself with the fall sports and their schedules before turning my attention to basketball."

She looked puzzled, and he told her, "I'm the new AD. Jon Earl is stepping back."

"Didn't know that."

He realized she had been out of town and that the district administration hadn't sent out any formal announcement to its coaches. He would follow up on that today and see if they would do so or if they thought that announcement would be more appropriate coming from him.

Lisa left, and he wandered down to Jon Earl's office, not certain if the football coach would be there since most football personnel wouldn't report back until right after the Fourth of July. Jon Earl was at his desk, though, and he motioned Carson in.

"Finding everything you need?" the older man asked.

"I am. I've got things arranged as best I can for now. I know once the school year kicks in, things will get a little chaotic. I'll probably have to live through an entire school cycle and all its sports before I'm truly comfortable with the job. Thanks again for the files you left and the instructions regarding what I need to do on a month-to-month and sport-to-sport basis. Those have been extremely helpful."

"I want this transition to be as smooth as possible, Carson. Sometimes, people hog all the knowledge they've garnered over the years. Don't help out their replacements. Even want those taking their spot to look bad. That's not me. I'm a team player and Team Pirates all the way. You look good? We all look good."

"I appreciate hearing that. And just having you here during this coming year to bounce ideas off is going to be really helpful." He paused. "I have something important I'd like to discuss with you now if you've got a few minutes."

Jon Earl's brow furrowed. "Close-the-door important?"

"Yes."

"I've got time."

Carson stood and shut the door, returning to his seat. After Mila left last night, he'd consulted the district's website pages for employees, searching through HR for any mentions of employees dating. Only a brief paragraph occurred, stating that while Driftwood Bay ISD did not specifically prohibit a romantic relationship between employees, it strongly discouraged ones between supervisors and subordinates.

"I want to begin dating Mila Perry."

Jon Earl let out a low whistle. "That's probably the last thing I thought would come out of you." He sat a moment, nodding to himself. "Have you and Mila talked about this? Because that's serious stuff, Carson."

"We have. I know she dated Sam before I arrived, and she said they informed HR about their relationship early on. I know this is different, though. Have you experienced this situation during your years in the district? Or somewhere else?"

"In my last position, which was two decades ago. The assistant principal started dating a teacher. He was divorced for years. She was a widow. Then he was promoted to principal.

She was a department head and had to transfer schools. She went from being a big deal at the high school to teaching Texas history to seventh graders."

"This is different," he said. "Even if things grow serious between us and Mila moved down to the middle school, she'd still be a member of the athletic department. One I supervise."

Jon Earl shook his head. "It's a sticky situation, son. That's for sure. Have you really thought this through? You're new to the Bay. You have a lot to prove. Your little girl to think of."

Stubbornness filled him. "You aren't saying anything I haven't thought of, Jon Earl. If I didn't feel so strongly, I would've let it go. But there's something there. Something I can't even explain. Mila's...special."

The coach smiled broadly. "That she is. I'm glad you've taken a shine to each other, but this is above my pay grade. My advice? Go to HR now. Get out in front of this before some busybody sees you with her and starts calling school board members. This is a small town. Everyone is up in everyone's business. Gossip is the biggest pastime. If you want to try and make this work—both your new job and a relationship with Mila—you need to be proactive."

Carson stood. "Thanks for your advice. I'll call her now. See if we can go to admin together and give them a heads up."

Jon Earl leaned back in his chair, pillowing his hands behind his head. "You're going to have a helluva fight on your hands."

"Mila is worth it."

He left the football coach's office and texted Mila, asking her to call him ASAP. His cell rang less than ten seconds later.

"Hey. Did you talk with Jon Earl?"

"I did. He said we need to get our asses over to HR right away and tell them. Dr. P, too. He warned me in friendly terms that with this being a small town, someone might stir up trouble with the school board if we don't take the bull by the horns."

Mila sighed. "I was afraid of that."

"Are you having second thoughts?" he asked, praying she wasn't.

"Not at all. This is a good thing. Let's meet at admin now. What are you wearing?"

"A T-shirt and shorts."

"We want them to know we'll be going by the book, so we need to look professional when we drop in. Go home and change," she advised.

"Do you think I need to wear a suit?"

"No, just a nice shirt and slacks. Maybe a tie."

"Will do. Meet there in half an hour?"

"See you then."

Carson returned home and changed into dark blue pants and a pale blue shirt. He retrieved a tie and decided Mila was right. They needed to present a united front and let the powers that be know they would be professionals regarding their relationship.

He arrived in the parking lot, seeing her Jeep was already there. Hurrying inside, he found her in the lobby, wearing a sleeveless, blue and white seersucker dress and dressy sandals. Her usual ponytail was absent. Instead, her honey-blond hair fell in waves past her shoulders.

Approaching her, he said, "You look beautiful. Wear that on our first official date."

"Last night wasn't a date?"

"It was an in-house date. Once we get the go-ahead, I'm going to take you somewhere for a nice steak. An impress-you first date."

"You're on, Coach." She wet her lips nervously, causing desire to rocket through him. "Let's do this."

She led them to her dad's office, greeting his secretary.

"Hey, Sandy. Does Dad have any openings in his calendar today?"

The secretary eyed them with interest. "He's got a two o'clock meeting in Corpus at the Region 2 Service Center with other superintendents. He'll leave here at one for that."

"Then we need to see him now," Mila said firmly. "In an employee capacity."

"I see. Anyone else need to sit in on this meeting?"

Carson could tell Sandy had an inkling of what was going on, and he said, "Mae Williams from HR."

Sandy nodded. "That's what I thought." She picked up the phone and dialed. "Mae, could you come down to Bill's office for an impromptu meeting? Great." Sandy looked up. "She's on her way. Good luck, you two."

The secretary stood and went to her boss' open door, rapping on the frame. "Mila Perry and Carson Andrews are here to see you. And Mae Williams will be here to sit in on your meeting."

Carson sensed Mila tensing and took her hand, squeezing it briefly before releasing it. She reached for it again, though.

"We're going to do this," she said, her voice firm as she led him to the door. Then she said, "Dr. Perry, we need a few minutes of your time."

Carson supposed with her addressing him in that manner, her dad would know there was a serious issue to discuss. Then he saw Dr. P's gaze fall to their linked hands and back up.

"I see. Come in. Let's sit at the table, shall we?"

They seated themselves as Mae arrived.

"Come on in, Mae. Mila and Carson want to notify the district about something."

The HR director walked briskly across the room, setting

her tablet on the table and taking a seat. She looked at Carson expectantly.

"Mila and I have decided to embark upon a romantic relationship," he began. "We've read what the district policy in the employee handbook is and wanted to inform you."

Mae frowned. "While it's commonplace for two teachers to date, this situation is different, Coach Andrews, because of your position. There are considerable risks involved, despite there being no specific state law against a superior dating a subordinate."

"We understand," he said, taking Mila's hand openly. Just touching her let his confidence soar.

The gesture didn't get past Mae, who crisply said, "You are in a supervisory position as our athletic director, while Mila is an employee who would be evaluated by you. There are certain issues to consider."

"I know favoritism would be one," he said. "Whether it's actual or perceived. Mila is already a head coach, however. The only promotion I could award her would be to my position as AD. So that argument doesn't hold water."

"We need to be concerned about other employees being resentful," Mae continued. "Your relationship could have a negative impact on the workplace."

Mila spoke up. "I don't see that becoming a problem, Mae," she said evenly. "We both have solid work ethics. I'll stay in my volleyball wheelhouse and wouldn't think to give Carson advice regarding other coaches in the district."

Carson took up the banner. "And I assure you that we will keep professional boundaries so that our relationship doesn't affect our work environment. Or the educational environment for students. I will attend a couple of practices to see Mila in action and get a feel for her coaching style, but we would never act in anything but a professional manner in public."

"There is the matter of evaluations," Dr. Perry pointed out. "While Mila has an evaluator to observe her academic performance in the classroom, you are the supervisor regarding her athletic performance. If you're seeing one another, there is a loss of objectivity in your evaluation as you review and rate her."

"I would suggest that for this academic year, we task Jon Earl Horton to step in and do Mila's evaluations," he pitched. "He is familiar with her coaching, and that would take me out of the equation altogether."

Dr. Perry nodded, looking at Mae. "That would be an acceptable compromise if Jon Earl would be willing to take on that responsibility."

"I would be more comfortable with that," Mae said. "It would eliminate any conflict of interest." She paused, glancing from Mila to him and back to Mila. "My biggest concern is a sexual harassment claim."

"What?" Carson and Mila both cried in unison.

"If your relationship ends badly, Mila could claim it wasn't consensual or that she was pressured into it."

"That's ridiculous," Mila said. "We are informing you before we ever start dating, and I will sign anything necessary to indicate that I am entering into this relationship with Carson of my own free will. We plan to conduct ourselves in a professional manner. If things don't work out between us, we will still behave in a responsible manner."

She looked to her dad. "You know me better than anyone. You know I'm not going into this lightly. Carson and I have discussed the ramifications, but we believe there is definitely something present, and we wish to pursue it. I think having Jon Earl in charge of my evaluations is sufficient, but if you request that I resign, I will do so."

"No," he said quickly. "I can't ask you to do that."

She looked at him, her clear blue eyes assuring him. "I feel strongly enough to do so. If the district isn't comfortable with the solution we've approached them with, I would rather resign my position and coach somewhere else."

"That won't be necessary," Mae said quickly, obviously not wanting to lose Mila, much less dealing with the fallout from her father if Mila resigned. "You've done the right thing by informing HR and the superintendent of your intentions to pursue a romantic relationship. I'm comfortable with this. Are you, Dr. Perry?"

The superintendent chuckled. "You mean as the head of the district—or as Mila's dad?"

Dr. Perry turned to Carson. "I thought enough of your character to hire you as both our basketball coach and athletic director. That hasn't changed. I know you will conduct yourself as a gentleman and a professional with my daughter, Carson."

"I promise that I will perform my job to the best of my ability and treat Mila with the respect she deserves."

"That's all I can ask for."

He squeezed Mila's hand, and she squeezed it back. They looked at one another, and both grinned.

"Thank you, Mae," Dr. Perry said, and the HR director excused herself. Once she was gone, he said, "I don't think this will be as big a deal as Mae made it out to be. As you said, Carson, Mila's already a head coach. You wouldn't be promoting her over other people. Having Jon Earl complete the evaluation is a smart idea."

He smiled. "As long as you don't make out in the stands at the first football game, I think the community will be behind you. And you have my support. Laura's, too." Looking at Mila, he said, "You better call your mom and let her know. If she hears about this from anyone else, you'll be toast."

They laughed, and Mila said, "I'll stop by the shop on my way home and let her know."

Carson rose. "Thank you, sir. I know this is an unusual situation. One more thing to ask."

He explained how Lisa Thornbach hadn't known he was the new AD and if he should send something out.

"You're welcome to do a group email to your coaches if you'd like, Carson. The announcement regarding your hiring goes out in today's town newspaper, and it's also going up on the website as we speak. I usually send out a Monday morning email to the entire district, and your hiring will be one of the items I mention in it."

"Thank you. I just didn't want to overstep."

They left his office, still holding hands. Sandy smiled at them as they passed her desk and left the building.

Mila blew out a long breath. "Wow. That was hard. Not as hard as I'd thought, but still pretty intense." She gazed up at him. "I hope you think I'm worth all this trouble."

"If we weren't standing almost directly outside your dad's window, I'd kiss you and let you know you're exactly worth any hoops I have to jump through."

He walked her to her Jeep. "Still on for Burger Barn?"

"Yes. I told the kids about it when I dropped them off this morning." She smiled shyly. "I also told Michael and Cec about us. They were thrilled. Cec is already planning a double date for when they get back from their trip."

Carson laughed easily, his spirits considerably lighter than when he had entered the building. "I'm looking forward to that. Go see your mom."

"I have a sneaky suspicion that Dad's already called her to give her a heads up."

He kissed her lightly. "See you soon."

Opening the door for her, he helped Mila into her vehicle. She beamed at him.

"I feel we're off to a great start."

"I couldn't agree more," he replied, heading to his own car.

Announcing their involvement to HR had been a big step. Carson knew word of their relationship would spread quickly.

And that was fine with him.

Chapter Twelve

Mila fixed scrambled eggs and bacon for the kids' breakfast. She sipped on a cup of coffee and nibbled on a piece of toast. She thought back to how well last night's dinner at Burger Barn had gone with Carson and Lily.

Carson was unlike any other guy she had ever gone out with. She liked how he had not played any games, instead letting her know he was interested in a relationship with her, despite the formidable obstacle standing in their way. The fact that he immediately went to bat for them with both her dad and HR let her know just how invested he was in seeing if they might have a future together.

Her cell rang, and she saw it was her mom calling. After she left admin yesterday, she had gone straight to Coastal Charm Boutique to let her mom know about the new man in her life. As she suspected, Dad had already phoned Mom and shared the good news.

She answered. "Hey, Mom. What's up?"

"Just checking in to see how you and the kids are. And how last night went."

"Bobby and Gina are having breakfast now, and we'll head to the beach once they're done."

"You didn't answer everything. What about your dinner with Carson and Lily?" Mom asked.

"Carson and Lily enjoyed Burger Barn, if that's what you're asking. After dinner, we went our separate ways, but we're meeting them at the beach."

"That sounds like fun," Mom said brightly. "You'll need some alone time with your new fellow, Mila."

She laughed. "That'll have to wait until Michael and Cec get home."

"Why don't you let us babysit the kids tonight? That way, you and Carson can have some adult conversation."

"I appreciate the offer, but Carson would still need to find someone to watch Lily. I'm not sure how comfortable she'd be being left with someone new so soon after arriving here."

"Well, she met us and seemed just fine. Your dad and I can come over to Michael's and keep all three kids. Why, Lily could even spend the night. Then Carson wouldn't have to wake her up to take her home."

The idea appealed to Mila, so she said, "Let me talk to him and see if he would let Lily stay over. I'll get back with you. Thanks for the offer, Mom."

"Talk to you soon, honey."

She thought a moment, not knowing where Lily might sleep, since Gina's twin bed would only fit her. She supposed the girl could sleep with her, but that might make Gina or Bobby jealous. Mila decided to run things by Carson before she dealt with logistics.

She took the last sip of her coffee as the kids were finishing up breakfast and then loaded the dishes into the dishwasher and started it. Last night, she had taken time to gather snacks for the beach and had put drinks for everyone in a cooler this morning. Carson had said he would contribute peanut butter sandwiches for them all.

"Time to put on your swimsuits," she told her niece and nephew. "And potty first."

Mila placed things into Cecily's car since it contained car seats for the kids. She already wore her swimsuit underneath a T-shirt and pair of gym shorts. She placed a bag with towels and sunscreen into the car, as well as one with beach toys. She pulled on a ball cap and sunglasses and waited for the kids to appear. They came downstairs and raced outside, and Mila buckled them into their car seats.

The trip to the beach took less than five minutes. She had taken for granted growing up so close to the water and had missed it during college and her years in San Antonio. Piper and Layne said the same thing, neither ever having time to get to the coast because of their busy jobs. Thinking of Layne reminded her that she had forgotten to talk to Mom about Mrs. Larson and Layne's concern that her mom was slightly off-kilter these days. She typed a quick note into her phone to remember to do so. She wanted to check in with Mrs. Larson before they had their next FaceTime chat. That would certainly be an interesting call, with everything that had happened with her and Carson, as well as embarking on earning her master's degree coursework.

They reached the parking lot by eight-thirty, and Carson pulled in right after she did, parking next to her. The kids all squealed when they saw one another, and she told them to stay close while she unloaded the car. Carson helped since he didn't have as much as she did, taking the cooler and the duffel with the towels and sunscreen.

"Looks like it's going to be a pretty day," he said as they left the parking lot and hit the sand.

"Cec is very careful with the kids not getting too much sun

at their age. That's why I wanted to bring them early. The rays are just too intense from noon on." She grinned. "Plus, it never hurts to tire them out early so they'll sleep well tonight."

They found a prime spot in the sand and set out a few of the towels. Mila took the bottle of sunscreen and shook it, spraying Gina and then Bobby's legs before squirting some into her hand and smearing it on their faces. Their swimsuits covered their trunks and arms and continued a high SPF factor, something very different than what she had worn at their age. She put Gina's sun hat on her head and tied the strings under her chin.

"I think I like that spray a lot better than the lotion I brought. It takes forever to coat Lily in it."

"I'll spray her. Come over here, Lily."

The little girl scampered over, and Mila sprayed the sunscreen along her exposed skin.

Lily giggled. "That's cold."

"It is a little cold, but it helps protect you from the sun's strong rays. We don't want you to burn and peel."

Lily then looked at her apprehensively. "Do I have to get in the water?"

"Only if you want to," Mila assured her. "Gina likes to build sand castles on the shore."

"So do I," Lily said eagerly.

They took the bag of toys and walked through the soft sand to where it was firmly packed from the waves washing onto the shore. Mila had peeled off her T-shirt and shorts and saw that Carson had removed the T-shirt he wore. She couldn't help but snatch quick glances at his muscular chest and flat belly. She longed to run her fingers over the ridges of his six-pack.

The five of them embarked upon building their castle. Bobby and Gina were experts at this, having come to the beach many times. Lily was more tentative, but she soon joined in. Bobby ran to the water with a plastic cup, making numerous trips to bring back water for the moat surrounding the castle.

"Can I swim now, Mila?" he asked once their masterpiece was completed.

She hesitated, and Carson said, "I'll take you, Bobby. We'll leave the girls here."

Mila mouthed *thank you* and watched him take Bobby's hand in his, walking to the water's edge. Now she had a nice view of his broad shoulders and narrow waist. Damn, the man even had gorgeous calves. She supposed that was from the running he did. She had the urge to run her tongue over them, shocking herself. She had never been adventurous when it came to

sex, but suddenly, all kinds of wicked ideas floated through her head concerning Carson Andrews.

As the girls played with plastic figures, making up a story about the king and queen who lived in the castle and a wicked witch who'd put a spell on them, Mila kept her eyes on Carson and Bobby. Carson didn't let them go out too far in the surf, just enough for Bobby to splash. His laughter carried through the air as he squealed and soaked Carson.

"Bobby is having a lot of fun in the water," she said casually, causing both girls to glance up and watch for a minute. "Would you like to go and put your feet in the water? Maybe we could even get Bobby wet."

Gina looked to Lily, and both girls nodded.

Standing, she held out her hands, and the girls took them.

"I only get my feet wet," Gina told her new friend.

"I'm scared of the water," Lily admitted quietly.

Mila squeezed the young girl's hand. "I'm right here, Lily. I won't let go of you. I promise."

She stopped and let the next wave glide into shore, coming to them. It splashed up to the girls' ankles.

"Hold on to me," she warned. "You'll feel some of the sand under your feet pull away and head back with the water."

"I feel that!" Lily exclaimed.

"Here comes another wave!" Gina cried.

Again, they stood as the water lapped about them before it retreated.

After several more waves came in, Gina said, "Can we go a few more steps, Mila?"

"Only if Lily wants to." She looked down at the girl. "What do you think?"

Grinning, Lily said, "I'll go with Gina."

They moved farther into the water, and the next wave came in, striking the girls at the knees this time.

Gina leaned down, her hand dancing through the water. "Splash me!"

Lily echoed, "Splash me!"

Soon, everyone was wet from head to toe, especially Mila, since the girls teamed up to soak her. She took a few steps back to more shallow water and sat in the sand, both girls laughing, and they joined her.

"I like the water," Gina said.

"Me, too," Lily agreed, and Mila was happy progress had been made regarding Lily's fear of the water. She was old enough to take swim lessons now, and Mila decided to suggest it to Carson. Maybe he could enroll her at the same place where Cecily took the kids.

Carson must have heard his daughter's words as he and Bobby approached. "You like the water now, Peanut?"

"It's fun, Daddy." She grinned mischievously. "Gina and I splashed Mila. A lot."

Bobby grinned. "We saw a fish. He swam by us. He touched my leg!"

"Was it a clownfish like Nemo?" she asked.

"No," Bobby said. "Nemo is orange. This fish was gray."

"I think it's time for a snack," she said, and they returned to the towels.

They dried off the kids, and Mila coated them with another layer of sunscreen. She got out juice boxes, grapes, and string cheese. The kids talked animatedly as they ate.

Pulling a bottled water from the cooler, she offered it to Carson.

"Thanks." His eyes swept over her, and he quietly said, "You look amazing in that swimsuit."

She had accumulated several swimsuits since her return to the Bay. This one was a form-fitting tugless tank in midnight blue. It had a scooped neck and was cut high on her legs.

He leaned closer. "Your legs seem a mile long. I had trouble keeping my eyes on Bobby because they wanted to stay on you," he said huskily.

"I noticed you have a decent set of legs on you," she teased. "Runner's calves."

"I want to get back to running," he said. "I think when I drop off Lily at Happy Hearts each day, I'll try to get in a workout at school before showering and starting my day. Working out always energizes me."

The kids wanted to build shapes with shells, so they took time to walk along the shore and collect shells of various sizes in their sand pails. By the time they had made a rectangle, circle, square, and octagon, a good hour had passed. Carson broke out the PBJ sandwiches, and Mila added blueberries and chips for their feast.

Once they finished eating, Lily begged to go back to the water, causing Carson's brows to arch.

"Wait a minute. Is this the same girl who didn't like to get her big toe wet?" he teased.

"Gina and I like the water," Lily said matter-of-factly.

"Switch with me," he said to Mila. "I'll keep up with the girls, and you can take Bobby."

"Let's race, squirt," she told Bobby, and they ran to the water.

After playing for half an hour, she could see her nephew was quickly losing steam. She took his hand and motioned to Carson, who led the girls back to where their towels were.

As they wrapped the kids in the beach towels, she said, "Mom and Dad have offered to babysit tonight so that we could maybe go to dinner or something. Mom said it might be easier if Lily spent the night. That way, you wouldn't have to wake her up and take her home."

He frowned. "She's never spent a single night away from me. I don't know how she would handle that."

"She would have to sleep with me. Gina only has a twin bed."

"I hope you don't think this is too forward, but I'd like to sleep on the couch," he said, pulling his T-shirt over his head.

"That wouldn't be a problem," she assured him, sliding into her shorts and slipping into her shirt.

They gathered up all they'd brought and she quietly said, "Why don't you ask Lily about it and see what she says? One way or another, I need to let Mom know."

"Hey, Peanut," he called. "Would you like to sleep over at Gina's house tonight?"

Lily's eyes widened. "Can I?"

"Mila and I are going to go out to dinner. Bobby and Gina's grandparents would come stay with you while we were gone. They'd play with you and help you get ready for bed. If you'd like, I'll spend the night, too. I'll sleep on the couch downstairs in case you need me."

"Okay, Daddy," the little girl said brightly.

Bobby said, "We can play camping. When Brian came for a sleepover, we got in sleeping bags and slept in the loft."

"Actually, that's a great idea, Bobby," Mila praised. "That way, all three of you can camp together."

"If you'd like, I'll get up early and bring back donuts for breakfast," Carson volunteered.

"Donuts, donuts, donuts," Gina began chanting, and the other two joined in. Gina added, "Sprinkles, sprinkles, sprinkles," and the new chant began.

He looked at her, and Mila felt herself going warm all over. "I guess it's a date then. Wear that dress. And tell me somewhere fancy I can take you."

Without hesitating, she said, "Steak on a Plate. We'll need to make a reservation, though. It's tourist season and a Saturday night, so places get crowded."

"I'll make one and text you the time," he told her.

"Bring Lily over for dinner," she suggested. "Five-thirty. That way, we can get the kids situated before we leave. If our reservation is later, we can stop for a drink somewhere."

"I like how you think." Carson gave her a smile Mila wasn't likely to forget anytime soon.

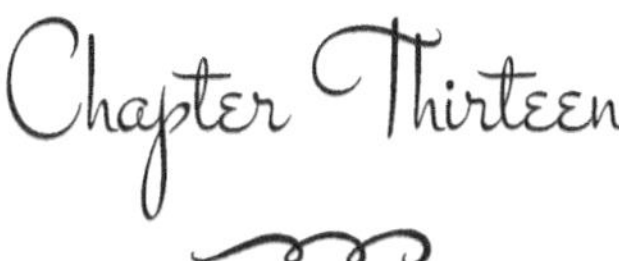

Chapter Thirteen

"Are you sure you're ready to spend the night away from home?" Carson asked Lily.

His daughter opened a drawer, pulling out her PJs. "Daddy, *you're* spending the night, too."

Well, she was right about that. Not that sleeping on the couch was where he wanted to be.

He would rather be in Mila's bed.

As Lily put her nightgown into her backpack, Carson told himself to put on the brakes. After all, he had been the one who had told Mila that he wanted to take things slowly. Yet here he was, chomping at the bit, like a thoroughbred in the gate at the Kentucky Derby, ready to race when the bell sounded. He needed to take his time getting to know Mila.

Yet his heart told him he already knew everything he needed to know.

Carson had never believed in falling in love at first sight. Even with Angie, they had started as friends and study partners. It had taken months before he'd gotten the notion to kiss her. When he did, his gut told him she was the right person for him. He had never looked at another woman after that.

Meeting Mila seemed to awaken him after some deep slumber. The only thing he could liken it to was Sleeping Beauty, who had been cursed by an evil fairy and slept one hundred years. He had been ravaged by Angie's murder, but he had pulled himself together for Lily's sake. Carson had numbed himself to all feelings, burying himself in work and caring for his daughter. When he was introduced to Mila, however, it was as if a heavy curtain had been drawn back, and he could see the world clearly for the first time in a long while.

He was torn, though. His loyalties should lie with Angie— but the deep loneliness which had filled him ever since his wife's death had become too heavy a burden to bear. Mila was all light and sunshine and exuded positive energy. That's what he had been drawn to. Her goodness. Her outlook. It was why he had been willing to risk a job he had just accepted. Because he saw a future with her.

And that scared him shitless.

That's why he needed to rein in all the crazy feelings running through him, the giddiness of a schoolboy who'd asked his crush to the school dance and went to the moon and back when she said yes. He felt he would be doing Angie a disservice if he got too involved too fast with Mila. Still, he eagerly looked forward to their date tonight. He also couldn't help but recall how Mila had said Angie would want him to move forward with his life and not be stuck in the past.

"Daddy, these don't fit," Lily complained, trying to shove her tennis shoes into her backpack.

"Hold on, Peanut." He moved to her. "Let's take out what you've already put in."

Carson emptied the backpack, pulling out clothes for

tomorrow, clean underwear, and her nightgown. He also removed Ralph Rabbit.

"Ralph is taking up too much space," he told his daughter.

"But I can't leave him!" Lily said, her voice rising in hysteria.

He had learned touch calmed her, and so he gently put his hands on her shoulders, saying, "Let's pack your clothes and shoes. You can carry Ralph. I know you don't want to leave him behind because he wouldn't be able to sleep without you."

She sniffed. "Okay."

Folding what he had just removed, he replaced everything in her backpack, including her tennis shoes.

"I need Crocs," she announced. "Gina has them. So does Bobby. And some of the kids at Happy Hearts."

"Then we'll get you a pair soon," he promised. "I'll have to find out where to buy them." He zipped the backpack closed. "Ready?"

They went downstairs, and Carson slipped into the sport coat he had hung on the back of a kitchen chair.

"You look nice," Lily told him.

"Why, thank you."

Carson had wanted to dress up since they were going to a fancy steakhouse. He wore slacks and a crisp, white dress shirt. No tie. He thought that would be too over the top, but the navy jacket gave him a more polished appearance. As they went to the car, he found his heart beating faster in anticipation of spending tonight with Mila.

When they reached her brother's house, he saw another car sitting in the driveway and assumed the Perrys had already arrived. Mrs. Perry opened the door and greeted them.

"Hello, Lily. I'm glad we're going to hang out tonight. We're going to play Chutes and Ladders and Disney Yahtzee."

"I love Disney Yahtzee," his daughter said enthusiastically as they entered the foyer. "I have Elsa on my pajamas."

"That's wonderful. Hi, Carson."

"Hello, Laura. Thanks for giving Mila and me a break and watching the kids tonight."

"Oh, it's a pleasure. Michael and Cecily don't go out of town often. When they do, we usually watch Gina and Bobby. Since it was summer, though, and I'm busy at the boutique, Mila was available to do so. We're happy to help out."

"Lily!" Gina cried. "Come to my room."

Both girls ran up the stairs, giggling. He placed the backpack at the foot of the stairs.

"She's got her nightgown, toothbrush, and clothes for tomorrow inside it. Shoes, too. You wouldn't happen to know where to buy Crocs, would you?"

"There's a children's store on the square," Laura said. "They have a variety of colors." She told him the name, and he decided he'd take Lily by there tomorrow. He recalled feelings of being left out, when kids at school wore something he didn't own. Aunt Jayne had never been interested in helping him fit in, and that meant never buying what she had termed "trendy items." He never wanted his daughter to experience the teasing and loneliness he had.

Laura led him into the kitchen, where Mila and Dr. P were sitting at the kitchen table.

"Carson," the superintendent greeted.

"Hello, Bill," he said, grinning at the older man.

"Oh, so *now* I'm Bill?"

"I'm trying. Doesn't mean I won't slip and forget."

Laura went to the stove and stirred something boiling in a pot. "I hope Lily likes spaghetti."

"She does. But she's not big on the sauce. She prefers butter on it."

"Until she sees Gina eating it with sauce," Mila said. "Kids that age imitate one another all the time."

"You, Layne, and Piper certainly did," Bill said. "If one of you said you didn't like green beans, the other two would pipe up, stomp your feet, and declare you also hated green beans."

Mila laughed. "One time, Chief Roberts paid me a dollar to say I liked carrots."

"Elmo did what?" her dad asked, amusement in his eyes.

"Piper barely ate vegetables, so her dad pulled me aside and told me he'd give me a dollar if I said I liked them. I didn't have to eat any. I just had to say I liked them." She shook her head. "I told him I would say it *and* eat some if he gave me five dollars."

"Mila Marie Perry," Laura chided. Then she paused. "So, did Elmo give you five?"

She smiled smugly. "He sure did. Told me I could stay for dinner. Mrs. Roberts served carrots and English peas."

Bill laughed. "Even I know you don't like peas."

"I ate them," Mila revealed. "I was afraid not to. I thought Chief Roberts might ask for his money back. It's so funny because Piper loves vegetables now. She could eat her weight in zucchini or broccoli or corn. I like to think I put her on the road to good eating habits."

"So, what's Steak on a Plate like, besides serving steaks?" Carson asked.

"Their salads are cold and crisp," Mila said. "Their best sides are sautéed mushrooms and mac and cheese, but the mac and cheese is delicious ."

"I get enough mac and cheese with Lily," he joked.

"Then try their roasted carrots with honey herb butter or the mashed potato casserole."

"Their steak fries are good," Bill added. "Laura likes their sautéed green beans with pomegranates."

"Hmm. That sounds different," Carson said. "To be honest, I haven't had steak in forever. This is a real treat, getting to dress up and go out with a beautiful woman and eat a fancy dinner."

"Save room for dessert," Laura cautioned. "Their coconut chiffon cake is to die for."

"Nope, it's chocolate bread pudding for me," Mila said. Looking to Carson, she added, "And that's not something I plan to share. Sides? Yes. Chocolate? Never."

Everyone laughed, and he said, "We better get going. It's a six o'clock reservation. Sorry it's so early, but all the later times were booked up."

"I don't mind," Mila said. "I never like to eat late."

Laura removed the pot from the stove and dumped the spaghetti into a colander. "Why don't you go and say goodbye to the kids? And have them come downstairs since dinner's almost ready."

Carson went upstairs with Mila. She stopped at the loft.

"Here's where the kids will be sleeping. Since Lily didn't have a sleeping bag, I got Cecily's for her."

"Thanks again for letting me sleep downstairs."

"I know it's probably rougher on you than it is Lily to be away from her. Now you're in the Bay, though, she'll be making all kinds of friends. Going to birthday parties and sleepovers. Tonight will help ease you into that."

"I don't know if I'm ready for her to be big enough to spend the night away from me."

"Get used to it, big guy. You're going to blink—and she'll be dating."

He groaned. "Don't go there. I hope I have at least a decade before all that starts. Hopefully, longer."

They gathered the kids and brought them downstairs, where Laura had ladled spaghetti into melamine bowls. Cups of milk sat next to the bowls, and the kids climbed into chairs.

"We're going to go now, Peanut," he said, kissing his daughter's head. "Be good for Miss Laura and Dr. P."

"I will, Daddy."

Mila picked up her purse from the counter and slid into a pair of heels which sat by the door.

"I usually don't torture my feet this way," she told him as they went out the door and to his car. "But they do look good with this dress."

"This dress was made for you. You look beautiful tonight." He leaned over and sniffed her as they reached the car. "And you smell divine."

Grinning, she said, "I got into Cecily's perfume. She's probably got half a dozen different bottles." She lifted her wrist to her nose and sniffed. "This was something with vanilla in it."

He took her wrist and inhaled deeply, feeling her shudder. "It was meant for your skin," he said, his voice low and rough.

This was not the way to slow down. If anything, Carson was accelerating.

Once in the car, she gave him directions. It only took ten minutes to get to the posh restaurant.

"I see the appeal of a small town," he said. "Everything is so close. Do you eat here often?"

"Not on my coaching salary. Of course, you're making the big AD money, so I thought you could afford it," she teased.

He cut the ignition and gazed at her. "You're worth it."

She gave him a dazzling smile. "You're pretty smooth, Coach."

"I've got a good audience to play to."

Carson opened her door and placed his palm on the small of her back, guiding her inside the restaurant. It was inviting, with candles flickering on every table. He had booked the last available time and table and as the hostess led them to it, he was pleased to see it was on the glass, overlooking the water. He held out Mila's chair for her and then seated himself.

Their server arrived promptly with glasses of water and a basket of hot, sliced bread. The butter had a hint of garlic to it. As they each buttered a piece, the server ran through the specials and left them with menus.

Glancing over it, he said, "I think I'm going with the New York strip."

"The filet mignon is calling my name," Mila said.

The server returned, asking if they wanted to order drinks. Mila asked for a glass of the house red, and he said, "Make it two."

When their wine arrived, they ordered, then she said, "This is a perfect spot. It's got a wonderful view of the bay."

"Your cheeks are slightly pink. You definitely got some sun today." He sighed. "It was a good day. Thanks for inviting Lily and me to the beach with you and the kids. Your brother and sister-in-law have done a great job with them."

"They are good kids," she agreed. "I'd say the same about Lily, though. You're a really thoughtful father, Carson." She paused. "That's very attractive."

"Really? I thought being a dad would make me not as attractive to other women."

"I'm not other women. I'm me. And I'm complimenting you on being a terrific parent. Lily is well-adjusted. You're comfortable with one another. It's easy to see you spend a lot of time together."

He reached and took her hand. "I want to spend time with you, Mila. I want us to be comfortable with one another. I already feel as if I've known you forever."

She smiled. "I feel the same way. It's as if we've cut through all the trappings and have gotten down to just you and me."

She paused. "You're different, Carson. In a very good, very appealing way."

"That is a compliment I will accept with grace," he said.

Their salads arrived on plates which must have been stored in a freezer. The greens were just as cold and crisp as Mila had promised. His steak was boldly seasoned and seared to perfection, while the sides were excellent.

While they ate, she talked about the coursework she would be completing this summer.

"I'm actually one of those nerds who enjoyed my education classes, so I'm looking forward to what's ahead. While I'm disappointed I won't have any interaction with my fellow educators, being able to take all the classes online is a gift. It takes a good half hour or more to drive into Corpus to the university and then back again, plus sitting through the class itself. I'll save tons of time being able to log in from home—or even school—and working on assignments."

"What classes will you take first?" he asked.

"I've got two courses which run concurrently. Introduction to the Principalship is one. Public School Law is the other. I should be through with both those right after the Fourth of July holiday. I've signed up for a class on supervision of instruction and another on the teacher appraisal system after that, but volleyball starts the first of August. I'd like to plow through those additional two classes in July and then take a break when my season and then school begins."

"Refresh me on when your team plays. That's something I need to get familiar with regarding all the sports we offer."

"I issue equipment and start workouts the first week in August, then scrimmages start the second week. After that, preseason games and tourneys begin. District wraps up by the end of October." Mila paused. "I have a decent team this year, Carson. I'm hoping to make it through at least two rounds of the playoffs. The state title game is right before Thanksgiving. Not that I think we'll go that far, but that's the official end of the Texas volleyball season. I think I can handle taking one class during that time. And right when I wind down, you'll gear up."

He laughed. "I already have October twenty-third circled on my calendar. That's the first day of practice. First scrimmage is a week later, then the season is in full swing through mid-February. That's when the playoffs start."

Taking her hand, he said, "I plan on coming to your games."

"Not all of them, I hope," she said, laughing.

"My fair share. I'd like to bring Lily to a few. I think she would get a kick out of it. She's never been to any of the ones I've coached. It was hard enough arranging childcare beyond the school day for her, much less having someone bring her to sit in the stands. And she was too young anyway. My games went well past her bedtime."

Carson told her more about his neighbor becoming his go-to sitter during the season.

"Dotty is friendly. Lily likes her and likes her dog even more."

"Maybe she can come to a game or two. Just to see you in action. I think it's important for kids to see what their parents do."

"Did you?"

Mila chuckled. "Michael and I were put to work both places at a young age. When Dad was still teaching when we were young, he had us putting up bulletin boards and placing posters on his classroom's walls. Mom had us come to the store and help do inventory a few times a year. We also worked at the boutique one day a week during the summers, free of charge.

They wanted to instill a healthy work ethic in us, as well as letting us see how hard earning a living is."

Their server appeared. "Dessert tonight? I've already sampled the key lime pie and can highly recommend it."

"How about getting it to go?" Mila suggested. "And as hard as it is for me to say this, I'll split with you."

"One chocolate bread pudding to go," he told the server. "And the check, please."

"I like that you not only listen to what I say. You remember everything," she said, and he heard admiration in her voice. "After six months of dating, Sam couldn't have told you what my favorite food was, much less the kind of movies I like to watch."

"What's your favorite kind of movie? Besides Westerns."

She smiled. "Action/adventure. I like the *John Wick* and *Mission: Impossible* franchises. How about you?"

Carson shook his head. "I haven't been to the movies in years. The only thing I watch at home, besides sneaking in a little *Sports Center*, is Disney+ and all those Disney princesses. And Spiderman. Lily is wild about a cartoon series where Spidey is a kid. His sidekicks are Spin and Ghost Spider, a real kickass girl. They fight crime."

"Ooh, I may have to watch that with Lily and Gina," she teased.

He paid for their meal and escorted Mila to the car. When they arrived back at the house, Laura and Bill were watching a movie. Actually, Laura was watching and Bill was napping in a chair.

"How were they?" he asked, pulling off his sports coat.

"Tired," Laura said. "I could tell their trip to the beach wore them out. After dinner, we played one game of Yahtzee and two Chutes and Ladders. By then, all three were yawning, so we got them ready for bed. Teeth brushed. Prayers said. They were out like lights."

"Thank you again for babysitting," Carson said. "It was nice to have a date with your daughter."

Laura smiled at Mila. "I'm glad to see she has such a good guy to take her out." She leaned over and shook her husband's foot. "Rise and shine, honey. The pre-bed nap is over."

Bill Perry stood up, a sheepish smile on his face. "Hope you two had fun."

"We did. Thanks, Dad." Mila brushed a kiss on his cheek.

The Perrys left, and Mila kicked off her heels. "Ah. That is so much better."

He set the Styrofoam box with dessert on the coffee table. "How about a foot rub?"

"Seriously? I've never had one."

"Then you're in for a treat. Come sit on the couch."

She got situated, stretching out her legs. Carson put them in his lap and began kneading, bending her foot and using long strokes. Mila made some very appreciative noises.

"I'm sorry," she apologized. "I sound like I'm enjoying an orgasm. This is actually better than an orgasm, I think."

He paused, meeting her gaze. "Then you haven't been with the right man. When the time is right, I guarantee I'll knock your socks off."

"Ooh, I like bold Carson," she purred. "And I will look forward to that earth-shattering orgasm. When the time is right for both of us," she added softly. "Until then? I suggest five more minutes of footwork. Then dessert. Then lots of kissing."

"You're on."

He massaged her feet, enjoying her sighs, sad that none of her previous partners had spoiled her in such a way. While she plated dessert for them, he went upstairs to the loft to check on the kids, seeing they were fast asleep.

After one bite of the bread pudding, he said, "This dessert is pretty orgasmic itself."

"I'm a chocolate fiend," Mila admitted. "You're the first person I've ever shared anything chocolate with."

He took the plate from her hands and placed it on the coffee table in front of them.

"I hope I'm also the last."

Carson took her in his arms then, kissing her for a good hour, relishing the feel of her body and the taste and scent which was all Mila. He finally ended the make-out session, feeling like a high school kid.

Mila fanned herself. "My goodness, you get my blood singing, Coach Andrews."

They finished their dessert, and she said, "Let me get you a pillow and blanket."

"Yes to a pillow. No blanket is necessary."

She retreated down the hall and returned with a pillow. "Powder room is to the right. Do you need a glass of water or anything before bed?"

He pulled her to him, encircling her in his arms. "No. Just one very passionate goodnight kiss from my girlfriend."

Her face lit up. "I guess I am your girlfriend."

He took her mouth with his for a long, searing kiss. If his daughter hadn't been upstairs, Carson might have done much more than kiss Mila.

Breaking the kiss, he told her, "Goodnight."

She left the den. He retreated to the bathroom, pulling his toothbrush from his pocket. He brushed his teeth and returned to the couch, stretching out his long frame, and snuggling against the pillow.

Today had been a perfect day. Beach time with the kids. A dinner date with Mila.

And what Carson knew was the starting point for the rest of his life.

Chapter Fourteen

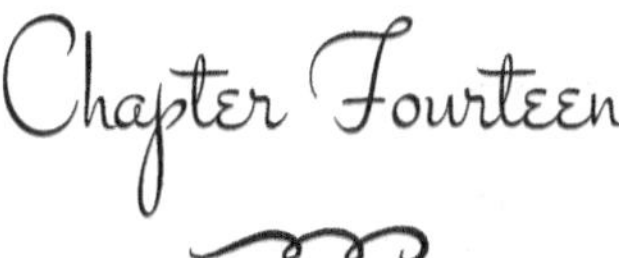

Carson escorted his daughter and Binky next door to Dotty's house. The older woman had babysat Lily several times over the summer. Tonight, they were going to make sand art, and Lily would spend the night.

"Don't forget Binky's treats," he reminded.

"That's okay, Daddy. Ginger has treats. She'll share."

He scooped some kibble into a Ziplock bag and walked Lily and the beagle next door, where Dotty greeted them.

"Thanks for taking Lily this evening."

"Do you and Mila have plans?" she asked.

"Actually, we don't. The lady coaches in the district have a tradition of going out the last Friday before school starts on Monday. I'm going over to Keaton's to watch a baseball game and have dinner."

"Just let me know if you need me tomorrow night then, Carson. You know I'm always happy to watch Lily, and you and Mila need a last hurrah before school starts and you both hit the ground running."

"You've been a real gem, Dotty. I couldn't have gotten through this summer without you."

He kissed Lily goodbye and returned home. The summer had flown by as he had settled into the rhythm of Driftwood Bay. His basketball camps had gone well. He was getting a good handle on his new position as AD. By now, the entire coaching staff knew he was seeing Mila, and several had ribbed him that he'd come in and swept up the prettiest coach. It had all been in good nature, though, and he didn't think he was abusing his authority by dating a subordinate. While he did talk over aspects of his job with her, he would always refrain from discussing sensitive information, such as personnel. She understood that line, and he knew she would never cross it.

They seemed to be in sync as a couple. They had spent time together these past couple of months, building a firm foundation of friendship. The underlying passion was ever-present, and he planned to do something about it.

Tomorrow night...

If Mila agreed, he wanted to introduce sex into their relationship. They had refrained from making love until now, but he was ready to take the next step. He wouldn't be doing this if he didn't envision a future with her, especially because Lily was involved and always a piece of the puzzle he kept uppermost in his mind. Already, Mila had been woven into the fabric of his and Lily's lives. In turn, he and his daughter had also become as extended family to the Perry clan. They had gone on a few double dates with Michael and Cecily, which proved to be a lot of fun, as well as had Sunday family dinners with Bill and Laura. In time, Carson knew he would want to make things permanent between Mila and him.

He had even FaceTimed with her two closest friends. Layne was smart and sarcastic, never mincing words, while

Piper was funny and charming. He liked both a great deal, and Mila had passed along that her friends approved of him, too.

Going to the kitchen, he pulled out a six-pack from the fridge, his contribution to tonight. He was happy to have found a friend in Keaton, who had a bit of a reputation around town as a loner. It was nice to talk with someone not in the school business. The artist had opened his gallery to booming business, tourists flocking to it. Once Carson had a house of his own, he planned to buy a piece or two from the painter.

It was slim pickings as far as house inventory in Driftwood Bay went, though. Hillary touched base with him weekly to let him know if any new properties had become available. The few that had simply didn't appeal to him, so he'd told Hillary to begin looking for land for him to purchase and build on. He didn't care if it were in a neighborhood or off to itself. It was simply time to move ahead in the process.

He walked across the street, six-pack in hand, and rang Keaton's doorbell. His friend opened the door and ushered him into the foyer.

"I hope you don't mind, but I invited someone to join us tonight."

"As long as you ordered another pizza, we should be good," he joked. "Let me run back. I can grab some more beer."

"Not necessary. I have plenty. Sullivan also brought wine."

They went into the kitchen, where Carson saw the newcomer opening a bottle of wine. He looked to be about six-two, with dark brown hair and hazel eyes.

"Carson Andrews, meet Sullivan Shepherd."

The two men shook hands, and Sullivan said, "I hear you're the new basketball coach."

"And district athletic director," Keaton added. "The fate of Driftwood Bay's sports is in this guy's hands."

"What do you do, Sullivan?" he asked, not having seen Sullivan around town.

"That is up in the air right now. My degree is in architecture design. Tidewater is my latest project for Wagner Enterprises."

Carson knew of the ultra-exclusive resort being built offshore from Driftwood Bay. It was to cater to a wealthy clientele. He hadn't really paid much attention to it since he never anticipated visiting the resort.

"So, you drew up the plans and have stuck around to watch it being built?"

Sullivan shrugged. "More or less. I'm not the project manager, overseeing every detail, but I am stepping in and advising on a few things. The thing is, I've taken a shine to the Bay. I like the slower pace of life. I also have a job where it's easy for me to work remotely while I'm designing various projects. Usually, I go from one job site to the next to oversee various stages of the build, but I'm getting tired of the constant travel. For now, my boss said I can work from Driftwood Bay—with a few trips to properties I'm designing for Wagner Enterprises."

The doorbell rang, and Keaton said, "Pizza's here. I'll go get it."

Sullivan said, "Keaton told me that you're renting the house across the street and looking for one to buy."

"I haven't had much luck with that. People who come to the Bay seem to enjoy staying here. Not much has been on the market."

"Would you ever consider drawing up original plans and building?"

"You read my mind. I'm at a point where I told my realtor yesterday to start looking for land I can purchase and build on. I know you said you just designed a fancy resort, but would you ever consider taking on a smaller job?"

"I'd be happy to give it a whirl. You see, I'm ready to step away from my job with Wagner altogether. I can't decide if I want to open my own architecture design firm—or a furniture store."

"What? Those are two very different pursuits."

Keaton entered with three pizza boxes, and Sullivan said, "Let's get settled, and I'll explain."

Their host retrieved plates, and they each piled several slices onto them. Carson got beers for him and Keaton, while Sullivan poured himself a glass of the wine he had brought. They sat at the kitchen table.

"My grandfather worked with wood," Sullivan shared. "Growing up, I spent a lot of time with him. He designed and carved furniture. Taught me everything he knew. Not to brag, but I come from a pretty wealthy family. Dad married into Mom's money and went to work for Wagner Enterprises, which he founded with a friend. Even though I wanted to craft in wood as PawPaw did, that wasn't good enough for my parents. I went ahead and earned my degree in architecture from a prestigious university and went to work for Wagner Enterprises. Zane, my college roommate, is a Wagner and my closest friend, so that makes stepping away even harder."

Sullivan paused, taking a bite of pizza and chewing thoughtfully.

"The thing is, although I'm great at big projects, my heart is telling me to go back to my roots. To do what PawPaw taught me to do. Craft furniture. I was thinking I might open an architecture firm of one and design projects on the side to bring in income, but most of my time would be spent working with wood."

"As an artist, I'm naturally nudging Sullivan to follow his heart and go the artistic route," Keaton said. "The Texas Gulf

Coast is a haven for many artists and artisans. I think he could do really well here."

"Is that what drew you to this area?" Carson asked. "I never asked how you turned up in the Bay."

"That—and the water," Keaton replied. "There's just something soothing about being near the water. I'm renting this house and hoping that eventually I can buy something directly on the water. I wanted to get my gallery up and running before I took time to think about my living arrangements." He grinned. "Maybe I can talk Sullivan into designing a home for me, too."

Keaton had a boat, and Carson had gone fishing with him twice, taking Mila one of the times. Keaton said he did his best thinking on the boat and had mentioned how much he enjoyed living close to the Gulf.

"When do you have to make a decision about your future?" he asked Sullivan. "Staying with your present firm or breaking out on your own?"

"Soon. My parents will be livid if I decide to stay in some backwater small town, but I figured out that I can't live my life for them." He smiled. "Enough with shop talk. I'm a basketball fan. Football, too. How does Driftwood Bay stack up in district this year?"

They talked sports during the rest of dinner, with Carson sharing what he knew of the two high school teams. Keaton thought that he and Sullivan should invest in season tickets for the football games, and Carson said he would email them a link with that information.

"I think we're also going to field strong soccer teams, both guys and girls," he added.

"I haven't been here long, but I gather the town is a strong supporter of high school sports," Keaton said. "You must be feeling a lot of pressure, Carson. Not only from a basketball perspective, but overall."

"Yes. This is the first time I've been in the spotlight so much. Everywhere I go in town, people know who I am and are eager to talk sports. Residents in the Bay are serious about their teams. In a way, it's a real rallying point, having an entire community support the one high school and all its athletic teams. Mila tells me there's always a great turnout for other activities beyond sports, such as plays put on at the high school."

"Who's Mila?" asked Sullivan.

With pride, he said, "She's our head volleyball coach. We've been seeing each other all summer."

"From the look on your face, I think it must be serious," Sullivan said.

"It is," he confirmed. "I've been admittedly cautious. I was married before. My wife was killed a few years ago."

"I'm sorry to hear that," Sullivan said. "Any kids?"

He nodded. "One. My girl Lily is four."

"And where is Miss Lily this evening?" Sullivan inquired.

"She's staying with my next-door neighbor, Dotty Williams. Dotty is great with her and will be watching Lily the nights I have basketball games or other athletic events I need to attend. It all seemed like fate, me stumbling into renting the house from the owner who was leaving for a year's sabbatical to Australia. I've found Dotty and Keaton and am friendly with a few other neighbors on the block. We'll maintain the house until the end of next May."

"If you're really serious about building a place of your own, you'll want to have some plans drawn up soon," Sullivan advised. "So that you can break ground and have your house completed by the time your lease runs out. My offer stands, Carson. If you would like me to design a home for you, I'd be happy to do so. You could be my first client at Sullivan Design Studio."

Sullivan looked surprised that he had thrown out a name for his firm, but he said, "That would work, two-fold, both for architecture plans and woodworking designs." He grinned and repeated the name. "Sullivan Design Studio. I like it."

"I guess if you've already named your new firm, it must be official," Keaton proclaimed.

He raised his bottle of beer, and Carson and Sullivan tapped their drinks against his bottleneck,

"To Sullivan Design Studio," they said in unison.

Keaton cleared the kitchen table and told them to stay and talk house plans. He returned with some blank paper and a pen, giving both to Sullivan.

Sullivan looked at Carson. "What do you want in your house?"

"I want it to feel like a home. I grew up at my aunt's house, which was full of antiques that I wasn't supposed to touch. On top of that, she was a hoarder, and it was hard to maneuver a path through the house without feeling claustrophobic. I want openness. Space. Rooms to flow one into another and be invit-ing." He paused. "And I want room for a family. I want to have more children. That's important to me."

Sullivan was taking notes as Carson spoke. "One or two stories? Ranch? Beach vibes?"

They batted around several ideas.

"Need a home office?"

"No to that," he said firmly. "I work long hours as it is. I don't want to bring work home. I want to enjoy time with Lily. And Mila."

They talked the number of bedrooms. Size of the kitchen. Whether or not to go totally open concept or have a few tradi-tional, divided rooms.

"You've given me plenty of food for thought. I'll start working on something, but it would be good before we get too deeply into the process for you to have the size of lot you're building on. Knowing those dimensions will influence my design."

"I'll give Hillary a call tomorrow and tell her to kick the hunt into high gear then," Carson said.

"Enough business," Keaton said. "The Astros are up over the White Sox two to one."

They retreated to the den, where the game was in the third inning. Keaton brought new beers for them, and Carson relaxed, enjoying the game and time with his new friends.

He couldn't wait to tell Mila that he had commissioned an architect, and he definitely wanted her input into the design.

Because he planned for this to be *their* home.

Chapter Fifteen

Mila was eager to see what her varsity squad would do in today's match. They had played two scrimmages already this week, winning both times, but today's opponent would be a bit of a challenge. She knew the turnout would be big in the gym because it was the first Saturday match to be played of the season. Although football was the revenue sport, its profits paying for all the other sports at the high school, there was a loyal fan base which was wild for volleyball. Since volleyball was the only game in town right now, she expected a heavy crowd. The fans would include her parents, Michael and his family, and Carson and Lily.

Mila had sat with Lily several times this summer, calling up YouTube videos of volleyball games, telling the four-year-old all about how to score points. She seemed fascinated and had told Mila that when she got big, she was going to be the best volleyball player ever.

Summer couldn't have gone any better. She had been busy with her new university courses, but she was a disciplined person and set aside a good amount of time to complete them.

The first two classes had gone so well that she had felt confident enough that she could complete two more before the start of school. Even with volleyball starting at the beginning of August, she was able to carve out time in her schedule. Tomorrow, she would submit her final paper for her supervising instruction course. She had already turned in her last assignment in the appraisal system class three days ago.

She had only registered for one course this fall, knowing that not only would she have volleyball practices and games to deal with, but she would also add teaching her US history classes into the mix. She was a student who had been antsy when teachers didn't return papers or tests in a timely fashion, and Mila made certain she had a decent turnaround time.

Now, she stepped into the locker room, hearing the girls teasing one another. This squad was very loosey-goosey, at least at this point, and she wasn't going to step in and play dragon master by messing with their chemistry and squelching their fun. As long as they took the game seriously when they were on the court, she didn't mind them having fun in the locker room. It helped keep tension down and built camaraderie amongst the athletes.

She had known she would depend upon the two seniors on the squad, but she had been surprised at how much growth she had seen in two other players. Annie Morgan was a sophomore, six-one, and an intuitive athlete. She had moved to the Bay two years ago and played volleyball for the first time at the middle school. Mila had been salivating, biding her time for Annie to join the ranks at the high school. As she had thought, Annie was an excellent player for the JV last year as a freshman, but she had come on even stronger than she had in middle school with a sweet serve, as well as dominating at the net.

The player who had really surprised her since practice had begun a few weeks ago was Belinda Carter. Belinda was only five-six, but she also played basketball and softball, a natural athlete. She had been a member of the JV volleyball squad last year and had been good but not great. Mila didn't know what had happened over the summer, but Belinda was making plays left and right during this first week of play, taking a strong leadership role as the team's setter. If Mila had to name only one player whom she thought would land on the all-district team at season's end, it would be Belinda.

Belinda spotted Mila and gave a loud, shrill whistle. "Coach in the room. Listen up!"

"There's not much I have to say to you today," she began. "You've looked crisp in your first two outings this week. The Blue Devils will be a much tougher opponent than the teams we've already faced, however. They were their district's champions last year and only graduated one starting player. They have a talented team and a deep bench."

Deirdre Echols, a senior, said, "We're more talented and deeper, Coach."

She smiled as the girls all nodded in agreement and clapped at the remark.

"I think we have what it takes to be winners this year," Mila continued. "Now that you've gotten your feet wet, we'll be setting goals next week when school begins. You've seen where you are, based upon your play and those around you, so you'll have a better handle on the goals you wish to attain. We'll set individual goals, as well as team goals. We'll also set one academic and one personal goal."

"Is praying I pass geometry a good goal, Coach?" Annie asked, causing everyone to laugh.

"You just think you're math challenged, Annie. Don't worry. We'll get you the tutoring you need." She looked around, zeroing in on Fiona Garrison, the other senior on the team. "Fiona, you're our resident math whizz. You need to make certain Annie makes it through geometry."

"Will do, Coach," the senior responded, giving the sophomore a grin.

"Let's bring it in. Pirates on three."

Mila stepped to the center of the locker room, thrusting out her hand, and each player stacked a hand on top.

"One, two, three," she called out.

"Pirates!" reverberated through the locker room.

They went out to the larger gym, with its bigger seating capacity. She had told Carson that she wanted it reserved for this afternoon's match. As they came out onto the court, she saw the place was about ninety percent full and figured by game time that the few remaining seats would be filled. It pleased her that a larger number of students than usual was present.

Moving toward the bench, she scanned the crowd, finding familiar faces. Piper's parents, Elmo and Ellen Roberts were there. Elmo was the Bay's police chief, while Ellen taught drama and choir at the high school. Sitting three rows in front of them were Jack and Lark Larson, Layne's parents. That surprised her since they kept to themselves a lot, especially since Layne had graduated years ago. Mila had spoken to her mom about Mrs. Larson, asking about her recent behavior. Mom said that Lark had not been in Coastal Charms for a few months but when she did come in to shop, she would keep an eye on her and report back to Mila. That alone seemed worrisome to her since Lark Larson had always been a frequent customer at her mom's boutique.

When she updated Layne on their last FaceTime call, her friend had merely shrugged, seeming a bit distracted herself. Mila sensed things were still not going well with Jeremy, and she and Piper had texted about that after their call ended. Piper said they needed to stay out of it and let Layne make the decision to stay in or end the relationship without their input. Knowing how stubborn Layne could be, Mila had agreed.

She also saw the town's librarian and its mayor before turning her attention to the court. Her girls were undergoing warmups, led by their two senior captains.

Glancing to the clock, she saw there were two minutes until the first game began, so she walked along the sidelines, approaching the Blue Devils' coach.

"You like your team this year, Coach?" she asked, her manner friendly.

The woman smiled enigmatically. "Let's just say they're better than last year's, and you know we took district and then went deep into the playoffs."

"We earned a district title, too. I see that happening again," Mila said with confidence.

"You've got a young squad, Coach."

"Young—and hungry," she replied, smiling before she turned and retreated to her own bench.

Play began, and the first game was close. The Pirates won fifteen to thirteen, and Mila breathed a sigh of relief, happy her players had taken the first game. The two teams switched sides, and she felt a tap on her shoulder. Turning, she saw it was Carson.

"They look good. Especially Annie Morgan and Fiona Garrison."

"I think so, too. How is Lily enjoying her first volleyball game?"

He chuckled. "She may only be four, but she's acting as if she's an expert. I'm surprised she's not down here, asking for a whistle to be placed around her neck so she could help coach. She's telling me all about middle blockers and opposite hitters and really sounds like she knows what she's talking about."

Mila laughed. "See you after the match. We still on for Backyard Bites?"

"You bet."

As the scoreboard was reset, she watched where Carson went to sit, seeing that he was with Lily and her entire family. Gina caught Mila's attention and blew her a kiss. She pretended to catch it and blow it back, delighting her niece.

Her team lost focus during the second game, losing by five points. They came roaring back, however, in the final game of the match, defeating their opponents fifteen to seven. The gym erupted when the last point was scored, and satisfaction washed over her.

The band director was always good about having a few band kids play at the volleyball games. Today, two trumpets, a trombone, and two drummers were present. They had kept the spirits of the crowd high throughout the game, as had the cheerleaders who had turned out for the match.

Her players lined up, walking past the other team and shaking hands. Mila fell in at the end of the line. She told a few of the other players, "Good game," as she passed them and then reached their coach.

"You do have a good team, Coach Perry."

Grinning, she said, "Told ya so."

She had the players stop and line up on the sidelines while the small ensemble played the school song, the crowd singing along. Once the last note finished, they broke into the school fight song, and her players did an easy lap around the court, soaking in the cheers before they headed back to the locker room.

"You did a nice job out there," she told her team. "At least during the first and third game. We totally lost concentration during that second game, and that's got to be shut down. Now. Don't let anything during a game distract you. No thinking of geometry tests to pass. What you'll wear on the first day of school come Monday. Which guy you're going to make out with at a party."

The team groaned at her last remark.

"I'll see you at practice Monday."

Mila had locked her purse in her car and kept her keys in her pocket, so she walked out to her Jeep now, finding Carson leaning against it. Warmth filled her as he stepped to her and gave her a lingering kiss.

"Need a ride, Coach?" she asked.

"Actually, I do. Lily and I bummed a ride with your parents. She wanted to go with Gina and Bobby now. I told them we'd meet them at Backyard Bites."

"Climb in, Handsome."

On the way to the waterfront restaurant, they did a post-mortem, something that ran in every coach's blood. She gave him insight into a couple of players and some particular plays, while he commented on the teamwork he had seen on the floor.

"Annie is really a dominant player. And I liked what I saw of Belinda, too. They'll be the backbone of your team, this year and next year."

"No one has earned a college scholarship in volleyball since I've been coaching here, but I think that possibility exists this year. If not this year, then definitely next."

They reached the restaurant, which was owned and operated by Betty Chastain. Her husband Ben owned the Pelican Porch, the bar located next door. Their son had left the Bay years ago. The last Mila had heard, Tyler was a chef in New Orleans.

Once inside, she spotted her family. Carson took her hand in his and weaved through the crowd, reaching the large table.

Everyone clapped as they arrived, and she took a bow.

"Undefeated, Sis."

"I don't know how long that streak will last, but I'll ride the wave and enjoy it while it does," she told her brother. "Glad you were able to make it today, Michael."

"I traded a shift with a fellow fireman so I could be here for your first home game. I'm glad I was. I'm proud of you, Mila."

She had always appreciated her older brother's support.

"I've already ordered nachos and calamari for the table," Dad said. "Everybody be ready when the server returns so we can place our orders."

Lily sat between Mila and Carson, and she looked up now, asking, "What should I get, Mila?"

"I think you'd really like the popcorn shrimp. They're tiny little shrimp, and you can dip them in tartar sauce, cocktail sauce, or ketchup. Or just eat them plain."

"I like tartar sauce," Bobby said.

"I like ketchup better," Gina told everyone.

"We'll get a couple of sauces and see which you like best, Peanut," Carson told his daughter, rubbing her back affectionately.

The appetizers arrived, and they placed their orders, with Dad telling the server not to rush the next round of food.

Ninety minutes later, dinner concluded, and Gina asked Cecily, "Can Lily sleep over? Please?"

This was a regular occurrence. The three children had become very tight, being thrown together so much over the summer. Lily even kept a toothbrush at Michael's house and would borrow PJs from Gina sometimes.

"It's up to Mr. Carson," Cecily said. "Why don't you ask him?"

Gina gave Carson a sweet look. "Can Lily please come stay, Mr. Carson?"

"That's a great idea, Gina. To show my appreciation, I'll

come and pick up you three kids and take you to the diner for breakfast tomorrow morning."

"Can we get the pancakes with faces?" Bobby asked eagerly.

"Plan on it, Bobby."

The three children clapped in glee, and Dad flagged down the server, taking care of the bill. She saw Carson try to slip him some money, but Dad refused.

"You can pick up the bill next time," Bill Perry said.

They left Backyard Bites, heading for their cars, and she and Carson went around the corner to where they had parked. He opened her door and closed it behind her before coming around and taking his place in the passenger seat.

"I was hoping this very thing would happen," he said, his voice husky. "Because I have plans for us tonight, Mila Perry."

A shiver danced along her spine. "What kind of plans?"

"The kind that have us with no clothes on and in bed together. If you think the time is right."

His words surprised her. He had been the one who had insisted they take it slowly, and they had. While things had heated up several times, one or both of them had always kept their head and cooled it down.

She realized he was waiting for an answer from her, and it meant a great deal to her that he was including her in this very important decision and not taking anything for granted.

"I can't think of a better way to finish off summer."

"Then let's set the mood."

He got out of the car and came back around, helping her from the Jeep.

"Let's go next door and have drinks in a classy place like adults."

"You're on," she said eagerly.

Carson threaded his fingers through hers and led her inside Pelican Porch. He asked the hostess for a booth in the back. Once Mila slid in, he sat next to her, his arm going around her.

Their server appeared, and they ordered. She asked for a mojito, while he requested a dirty martini.

When their drinks arrived, he clinked his glass against hers. "To a new chapter."

They sipped on the drinks, music low in the background, and talked a bit about school starting on Monday. Carson had attended professional development sessions for new hires, and they both had gone to required meetings this past week for all district employees. They discussed some of the challenges ahead during the coming year, and she shared the first unit her students would be studying.

"I always wanted to teach history, but I never got the chance," he told her. "I taught world geography. Freshman were a bit of a hot mess, but they were pretty darn lovable once I got to know them."

"Said no freshman parent ever," she joked.

The server asked if they wanted another round, but Mila looked at Carson and shook her head. He asked for the check and they left, strolling hand-in-hand back to her car. Anticipation began building inside her, and she was eager to see what coupling with Carson would be like.

"My place—or yours?" she asked.

"Who's got the bigger bed?" he countered.

"Mine is a full. How about yours?"

"King. I win." He lifted their joined hands and said, "We'll both win," kissing her fingers tenderly.

She drove to his house and pulled into the driveway. "Am I staying the entire night? Are we ready for your neighbors to talk?"

"I think all of the Bay knows we're dating." His gaze met

hers. "And tonight we're taking our relationship to an entirely new level."

hers. "And tonight we're taking our relationship to an entirely new level."

Chapter Sixteen

Carson had not told Mila that he loved her, but she felt his love for her in every glance. Every touch. With each small gesture that set him apart from every man she had ever known. She knew it would be hard for him to form those words, especially since he had spoken them to another woman in a different place and time.

She had only told Mark that she loved him, and she now saw how immature her love for him had been. Thankfully, she had grown up a lot since that relationship ended. She knew herself better and was more confident in who she was as a person and professional. While she hoped Carson would one day be able to say those words to her, she wasn't expecting them from him tonight. She also felt strongly that he would need to be the one who spoke of love between them and not her because if she said something first, she didn't want him to feel pressured to repeat it back to her before he was ready to do so.

They went inside the house, and he took her hand, leading her into the kitchen. On the counter stood a beautiful arrangement of snapdragons and morning glories. Tears stun her eyes. She had once mentioned those were her favorite flowers, just another sign of how well he listened to what she had to say—and remembering it.

He took her hands in his. "These flowers are for you. I've never been much of a flower giver, but I wanted you to have a visible sign of my feelings for you."

"They're beautiful, Carson. My favorites."

He swallowed, squeezing her fingers. "You know me well enough after all this time, Mila. I wouldn't take a step like this lightly. I have always seen a future for us. Together. With Lily. And other children." He paused, his gaze searching hers. "I thought it would be hard to say this to you. Now that we're in the moment, though, it's easy because I'm speaking from my heart. I love you, Mila. I have felt a strong connection with you from the moment we met."

He leaned in and kissed her softly, a reassuring kiss.

"I love you, too, Carson. I never want to compete with your memories of Angie. She was your wife. The mother of your child. The most important person in your life. Even though I never knew her, I feel her essence is captured in Lily. Because of that, I know she would want you to be happy. Move on with your life. To hold those memories you have of her dear, but to also let go enough to find happiness and fulfillment again."

Mila smiled at him. "You make me so very happy, Carson. You make my heart sing. I've loved you for what seems like a long time, and I feel that love growing deeper every day."

"Thank you for understanding about Angie. I know it can't be easy for you. She'll always be a part of me. Lily is her legacy to the world. I never thought about remarrying. I never considered my future in the long run before I came to Driftwood Bay. I was more of a put one foot in front of the other and take things one step at a time and try to survive kind of guy. That changed when I met you. You've brought laughter and sunshine into my life."

Carson smiled at her. "Into both mine and Lily's lives. I can't imagine living a single day without you in it, Mila. I just want you to know before I made love to you that the ghosts of the past are gone. When I kiss you—touch you—it's *you* I'm with. When I make love to you, *you* will be the person I see and love. This is a new beginning."

"For both of us," she added softly.

He brushed his lips against hers slowly, and her body responded. Her heart began to pound rapidly, and her insides began to glow.

The kiss went from tame to torrid, their passion for one another rising. Her body and blood heated with desire. Soon, they were frantically tearing clothes from one another, needing flesh to touch flesh.

They didn't even make it to the bedroom. Carson pushed her against the wall in the hallway, his large body pinning hers to it, his kisses hot and passionate. His fingers found her wrists and raised them above her head as he devoured her mouth with his. Her breasts swelled, the nipples coming alive as they brushed against his chest.

He tore his mouth from hers. "I can't wait. I need you so much."

"Take me. Now. I'm forever yours."

She had told him before that she had been on the pill since college, wanting to regulate her irregular periods because of sports, so there was no need for a condom. His hand moved between her legs, pushing a finger inside her. She moaned at the intimate touch, and he stroked her deeply. Moments later, her orgasm came, shattering her. She cried out, riding his hand as he murmured encouragingly, his lips buried against her throat.

When she climaxed, her body shuddered violently, and she felt as if she might be someone else. She grew limp and would have slid to the floor if he hadn't kept her on her feet.

With a wicked grin on his face, he said, "My turn."

Before she could even catch her breath, he had pushed into her, filling her. Not only her body.

But her soul...

He kissed her ravenously as he thrust into her again and again. She had never had an orgasm during sex, but the familiar sensation began building within her, and her cries joined his shouts of triumph as he pumped into her.

She cradled his face in her hands and pulled him to her, kissing him with every bit of love welling inside her. Their bodies remained as one, physical love blending with emotional love.

He broke the kiss, and they both panted, their bodies slick with sweat.

"I'm sorry," he got out.

"What for?" she asked. "That was incredible. *You're* incredible."

"You were perfect yourself," he praised, kissing her again. He chuckled. "I imagined our first time together a lot. I mean, a lot. But I never thought it would be like this. I'm sorry we didn't make it to the bed."

"I'm not. Beds are highly overrated."

They both laughed and kissed again for a long time. Need already burned brightly inside her again. She had liked having sex with Mark and Sam, but what had just happened between her and Carson was mind-blowing.

She knew it was because they shared a rich, abiding love.

He eased from her. "I wish I could go for round two now, but I need a little time to recover. I could use something cold to drink. How about you?"

"Absolutely."

Lacing their fingers together, Carson led Mila back to the kitchen. She had always been a little self-conscious being naked in front of her partners, but she padded alongside him feeling sexy and confident. Even beautiful. All because of this incredible man.

He retrieved two bottles of water from the fridge, and they both downed the contents rapidly.

She saw the heat return in his eyes.

"I'd like to take you to bed now. I want to explore your every curve."

Smiling mischievously, Mila said, "Only if you let me return the favor."

Carson led her to his bedroom, pulling back the covers. Then he swept her off her feet and kissed her once before placing her gently on the bed. He climbed next to her. Good to his word, his lips and hands explored her body in painstaking detail. Already, she was ravenous for his touch and wanted him inside her again.

She pushed him from her so that he was on his back, and Mila did her own, very thorough research of his athletic, muscular frame. Just as she had envisioned that first day at the beach, she ran her tongue along his perfectly-shaped calf. Everything about him was absolute perfection.

Her tongue slid up his leg, then all the way up the hard wall of his chest. She let the tip of her tongue encircle his nipple then teased it, flicking it back and forth against it. He growled, capturing her in his arms and holding her close. A deep sense of contentment poured through her.

"Think you've recovered enough?" she asked, her hand slipping to his cock and squeezing it.

"Keep doing that, and I'll be inside you in ten seconds."

His hands captured her waist, and he lifted her so that she straddled him. She stroked his cock now, and it sprang to life, hard and thick. Her fingers massaged it sensually until it grew large. Then Mila slipped it inside her and rode him with abandon. Neither of them was quiet during this bout of lovemaking, and when they both climaxed at the same time, he roared in triumph.

Exhausted, she collapsed against his chest, her cheek nestled against his beating heart.

Carson stroked her back up and down. "If I would have known how good it would be between us, I don't think I would've held out for so long."

She lifted her head, their gazes meeting. "I'm glad we waited as long as we did. That we took our time. Tonight was special because we've built a strong friendship. We also trust one another."

He smoothed her hair. "You're right. We waited for a reason. We waited for our love to grow. And I know it will continue to grow stronger every day."

Mila lowered her head back to his chest, reveling in the feel of his hard, naked body against hers. She had never experienced such peace after lovemaking. Such contentment.

Eventually, he leaned down and drew the sheet over them, turning on his side. They now faced one another, and she shook her head.

"No can do. I can't fall asleep unless I'm on my left side."

"Then turn around," he encouraged.

She did so, and his arms went fast about her, drawing her back into his chest. Mila had never felt more cherished than in this moment.

As she drifted off to sleep, one thing was emblazoned in her mind.

Carson Andrews was her forever person.

Chapter Seventeen

Basketball practice had started three days ago, and already Carson was impressed with Miss Debra's son. Caleb Connors might only be a sophomore, but he had an incredible work ethic and was already emerging as the team's leader. While several other players looked good in practice, Caleb already appeared to be in mid-season form.

On the other hand, the team's previous star from the past two years, senior Drake Duncan, was a slacker in the classroom and on the court, at least during these early practices. Jackson had told Carson that Drake waltzed through life, only turning on the steam when it was game time. His assistant said that Sam had put up with Drake's half-baked efforts in practice only because the boy was the most talented player on the team.

Carson had a very different philosophy.

He was going to bench Drake—unless the senior got his rear in gear.

It would cause a stir. He also knew Drake's mom, Marge, would be a force he would have to reckon with. Carson would do what he needed to do, however, to ensure team unity.

He went to the front office, heading down a narrow hall to where staff mailboxes were located. He tried to stop by at least once a day to pick up his mail, not wanting it to stack up and miss something important.

"Coach Andrews?" a voice called.

Turning, he saw Edith Smith approaching. Edith taught senior English and had been Mila's English teacher. Mila said Edith was tough but fair and even made Shakespeare interesting to the most bored student.

"Hey, Edith. How is your year going?"

"Splendidly." She frowned. "Except for Drake Duncan, that is. Do you have a moment to discuss Mr. Duncan?"

Mentally sighing, Carson nodded. He glanced at the empty conference room across from the mailboxes. "Let's step in here."

They did so, and he closed the door to guarantee them privacy.

"I am a sports fan, Coach Andrews, but academics always come first for me. I know my course is not necessarily every student's priority, but a passing grade is required to compete in UIL athletic events—and Mr. Duncan is teetering on the threshold of failure. He passed the first grading period with a seventy-one."

He nodded. "I reviewed all players' first report cards, Edith. Even those outside basketball. I want to always have a handle on where players stand and have relevant conversations with their coaches to make sure grades are being kept up. Where is Duncan now, grade-wise?" he asked, knowing that tomorrow, they would be halfway through the second six-weeks grading period.

"He sits on a sixty-five right now. Duncan turns in no daily work. He told me it wasn't worth his time since it's a smaller percentage of his grade. Said he doesn't want to waste time on it."

Carson grimaced. "Duncan said this to your face?"

Edith nodded. "He did. He'll score a high grade on a test and then coast along. I think instead of AI, he has his girlfriend write his essays, but I haven't been able to prove that. Occasionally, he will shine on a project, but as far as group work goes, he contributes nothing. I just wanted to keep you informed, especially since he's the team captain this year."

"Thank you for speaking with me, Edith. I'll be talking to Duncan today."

His stomach churning, he left the office area. Conflict with a student was a part of the job, and many coaches dealt with players who only concentrated on the playing field and let the classroom portion of their lives slide. The fact that Duncan was capable of excelling and chose not to do so really got to him. He also didn't like how the senior could be serving as a leader and chose not to.

He saw Mila approaching from the other end of the hall, and his heart grew lighter. Just catching sight of her made his step lighter.

"Hey, you," she said, stopping to chat a moment.

"Ready for tonight's final district games?" he asked.

Volleyball season was nearing its end. Mila's varsity team was guaranteed to win district no matter how they fared in tonight's match. After a short pause at the end of October, the playoffs would dominate the month of November, with bi-district, area, regional quarterfinals and semifinals, and finally state taking place just before the Thanksgiving break.

On the other hand, basketball was just gearing up for him, with his team's first scrimmage early next week. They would complete play by mid-February, and then the playoffs would occur over the next three weeks. He wasn't ready to make any predictions as to where his team would wind up, especially with the Drake Duncan problem to deal with.

Mila smiled. "The girls are pumped, especially since they'll end district play at home. The fact that it's a bye week for football means that we should really draw the fans tonight. Are you ready for Bayfest tomorrow?"

She referred to the annual community fall festival, full of food trucks, craft booths, children's activities, and contests. They'd made plans to take Lily to it, along with Michael's family, and make a morning and afternoon of it. Dotty had promised to sit with the three kids tomorrow night so that the four adults could enjoy the bonfire held at the beach, along with a free concert.

"I'm looking forward to it. Bayfest will be the last bit of fun I get in before kicking things into high gear with basketball."

"Then I guess I'll see you tonight in the gym."

Carson longed to give her a quick kiss, but they went out of their way to keep things professional on school grounds. The most he had ever done was kiss her cheek after a volleyball match and hold hands with her at one of the home football games.

"I'm off to practice soon. Seems I'll be having a talk with Drake Duncan. Edith just gave me a heads up that he's failing her class right now."

Mila shrugged. "Drake is a hard nut to crack. He's talented, but he's lazy. At least that's my take after having him in class last year. I hope he won't prove to be too much of a problem to you, Carson."

"Talk later."

He returned to the field house, flipping through his mail, and then he and Jackson went over what they would be working on during practice today. Carson subscribed to legendary college basketball coach John Wooden's philosophy. Wooden said he and his assistants oftentimes spent more time planning a practice than the actual practice lasted. He liked being prepared and kept notes of each practice, both on the individual and team drills. It helped him refresh his memory and kept the focus on what needed to be taught and emphasized during the next practice.

"I'm going to need you to handle things for a bit during practice while Drake and I have a little chat," he informed his assistant.

Jackson swore under his breath. "Is he failing a class right now? That's his usual pattern from the last two years, coming into the start of the season teetering on the edge. It's almost as if he's playing a game of chicken and wants to see how close to another car he can drive before he actually crashes."

"Edith's senior English class, for one. There may be others."

Jackson shook his head dismissively. "Drake always pulls out of his nosedive. He will this time."

"I hope so. Because I plan on benching him," Carson informed his assistant. "He won't be playing in the first scrimmage next week."

A low whistle came from the younger man. "You are a brave one. I'll give you that. And hell hath no fury like Marge Duncan coming down on you. You do know that she'll be here minutes after you give Drake that piece of news. It's like she knows everything that goes on everywhere. And when it comes to her precious baby?"

"He's not a baby. He'll be eighteen next week. Drake needs to toe the line—or he's out."

Jackson looked stunned. "You'd kick him off the team?"

"Actions have consequences. Either Drake will improve his

attitude, both in the classroom and at practice, or the Drift-wood Bay Pirates will no longer need him on the team."

"I'm glad you're the boss and not me." Jackson grinned. "Of course, I could make a heckuva lot of money selling tickets to the show. You and Drake. You and Marge." Then he sobered. "I'll back you all the way, Carson. It's about time someone took a stand with Drake."

"Thanks."

"And you also have the backing of the AD. Must be nice," his assistant said, teasing Carson about his dual role in the district.

"See you in the gym in a few."

He went down the hall, stopping at Jon Earl's doorway. The football coach looked up from the play he was mapping.

"I'm going to be benching Drake Duncan. He won't play in next Tuesday's scrimmage. We'll go from there. Just wanted you to know when the earth shook, that's the reason why."

Jon Earl cackled. "You are one brave sumbitch, Coach. Marge'll have your head." The older man paused. "It's long overdue, though. Sam turned a blind eye and let Drake get away with murder. If I were still the AD, I'd tell you that I'd back your move. As it is, you don't need my approval. Good luck to you."

"Thanks."

He left the field house and crossed the parking lot, entering the doors that led into the gym. At this early point in the season, he spent about half of practice time on individual fundamentals and the other half on team skills. After stretching for ten minutes, every practice began with dribbling, ball-handling, and shooting skills. Then he moved on to scripted plays.

Jackson was already there, and the team was coming out onto the court from the dressing room. Drake was the last to arrive. Usually, the team captain led stretching exercises, but so far, Carson had rotated players to head the session.

"Tim, you're up," he said, and the junior center moved to face the two lines of players.

"Packard in the house," hollered Caleb, clapping enthusiastically, his enthusiasm spreading through the ranks of the other players.

Carson watched Tim, nodding with satisfaction, liking the quiet leadership the athlete displayed.

Once the stretching portion was done, they started with full-court dribble moves, followed by fast-break drills. He liked to follow those with a three-man weave, alternating five and three passes, and then break the team into trios for two-on-one competitive drills.

It was at that point that he nodded to Jackson. "It's yours."

His assistant nodded and blew the whistle, indicating for the trios to move to various spots in the gym. Carson went to where Drake stood, his attention focused on his hand as he studied his fingernails, clearly bored.

"You're with me, Drake," he said, motioning for the student to come with him. It took everything Carson had not to turn and confirm the athlete followed him. It would be humiliating if Drake had stayed put and would reflect on his authority in a negative fashion.

He exited the gym and went into the empty locker room. Taking a seat on the bench, he saw Drake entering, eyeing him warily.

"Sit," he said, not bothering with the niceties of inviting the player to take a seat.

"I'll stand."

Carson studied him a long moment. "Sit. Not a request."

Thankfully, Drake did as asked.

"I had an interesting conversation with Mrs. Smith today," he began.

Drake rolled his eyes as only a teenager could. "What did that bitch have to say? Nothing good about me, I'll bet."

"No swearing," he said firmly. "You know that. We've been over that as a team. You're to conduct yourself in a manner that reflects well on our team and this school."

The boy simply stared at him.

"You're failing her class, Drake."

He shrugged. "British lit sucks. She acts like Shakespeare is God's gift to mankind."

"Many literary scholars would agree with her," he said. "It's not all Shakespeare, though."

"It's boring. That's what it is. *Paradise Lost. Gulliver's Travels.* Who cares about shit like that?"

He ignored the cursing. "You better—because you have to be passing to play."

"I'll do what I need to do," he said, glancing up as if counting ceiling tiles were more interesting than talking with his coach.

"The best players lead by example, Drake. Great leaders work harder than others. And from what you've shown me so far, you're not a great player—and you have zero work ethic."

Drake's eyes dropped, and he now glared at Carson. "I'm not some rah-rah cheerleader. It's not my job to rally the team. That's on you, Coach. I'm the best player out there. I have the best free throw and three-point percentage on the team. I can maneuver around anyone. Dribble with each hand equally well. When it's clutch time, the boys know to always get me the ball. I've got ice in my veins. I'll win it for us every time."

"That's not enough."

The player looked confused. "What do you mean? I'm the cream of the crop. All-District as a sophomore and junior.

They're predicting I'll be named Player of the Year for our district. I've already had scholarship offers."

"You haven't played a minute under me—and that's what counts, Drake. You're the last out of the locker room. You go through drills with your head elsewhere. When you get the ball, you're a typical ball hog and never pass to anyone else. That's not being a team player."

Another eye roll. "Oh, I get it. This is the *There's no 'I' in Team* talk. I'm supposed to go along to get along. Pass the ball even when I've got the shot. Well, I don't need any of that, Coach. My reputation is solid. The boys know they can count on me."

Carson gazed at the teenager steadily. "I don't know that. You haven't shown me that I can count on you. You could be so much more than you're showing now, Drake. You're a smart, smart guy, both academically and as an athlete. Give your best in the classroom and on the court. Show me just how talented you are. You can be a tremendous leader and take this team deep into the playoffs."

Drake sat there. Not taking in what Carson had said, merely sitting as if he tolerated his coach's presence. Carson stared back, not saying a word.

Finally, Drake said, "Are we done?"

"First, you need to apologize to Mrs. Smith. You were incredibly rude, telling her that you didn't want to waste your time on daily assignments."

"They're stupid. And that's only twenty percent of my grade. I can make it up in other ways."

His gaze and voice level, Carson said, "I will be checking with Mrs. Smith—and all of your teachers—on a daily basis. The reports I receive from them better reflect that you are doing your work. Living up to your potential. Acting in a polite fashion. And as far as practice goes, I want you to treat it as the most important part of your day. Show me you're in, all in, going forward."

"Or else?" Drake asked, defiance in his tone. "What are you going to do, kick me off the team?"

"Only you can do that. For now, I'm letting you know that you'll be sitting out the scrimmage next Tuesday. Riding the bench."

"You can't do that," the teenager shouted. "I'm the star player."

Carson stood. "And I'm the head coach and AD. You're oozing BA, Drake. Bad Attitude. I want you to go back to the gym and turn things around so that you and this team can have the year you're meant to have."

Drake shot to his feet. "I'm supposed to go out there and smile and work my ass off—and *still* not play?"

"That's exactly what I want you to do. Show me you love basketball. Your teammates. Show me you can be the leader we all know lies within you. Be the example that every guy on the team will follow and want to emulate."

"You're crazy. My mom will make mincemeat of you," Drake warned.

"Marge doesn't play for me, Drake. *You* do. And if you want to be a part of this team, you'll start acting like a team member."

"Go fuck yourself, Coach."

Drake stormed from the locker room. Carson couldn't say that he was surprised, but he would stick to what he said. Drake needed to be a team player.

Else he wasn't going to be on this team at all.

He returned from the locker room, seeing Jackson had half the players working on one-on-one in the lane, while the other half was doing two-on-two stop seams. Joining his assistant, he folded his arms and watched for a full minute before Jackson broke the silence.

"I see Drake didn't return with you. Is he off the team?"

"That's up for Drake to decide."

Carson took over practice after that. He could see the boys watching him, looking at one another questioningly. He ended the final drill and asked them to go and sit in the bleachers.

"A good practice today. Everyone looked sharp." He paused, looking across the group of teens. "And I know you're all wondering where Drake is."

No one spoke.

"Over the years, my philosophy of basketball has come down to a few things. First, I believe in the basics. Fundamentals such as dribbling, passing, rebounding, and shooting are important. If you know the fundamentals, it doesn't matter what offense I run. You'll be a good shooting team, and you'll score and win games because of that preparation."

He waited a moment, seeing a few teens nodding in agreement.

"Second, I believe in everyone being his best. Those are the kinds of teams who come together and gel. They may not have a superstar, but every player contributes. Every player has a role on the team and embraces it. I like a player who wants to grow on and off the court into being the best person he can be. All of you have tremendous potential within you. Some have more physical talent than others, but everyone here can put in the time and sweat and play hard. Play to win."

He gazed out over the group. "Work hard. Play to the best of your ability. Be prepared. Learn the playbook forward and backward. Be generous with the ball when it's called for. Support one another, both as teammates and off the court. If you do those things, you'll be proud of yourself and proud of whatever we accomplish together this year."

Carson took a deep breath. "Drake will need to decide if he wants to be a part of this team or not. I won't tolerate laziness in practice or the classroom. No one player is above any other. That's what being a team is all about. Together, you can accomplish so much more than you can on your own. Any questions?"

Again, no one spoke. It disappointed him a little, but he knew they must be shell-shocked with the idea that the most talented athlete on the team might not be playing alongside them this year.

"Okay, then. Hit the showers. Take some time to relax and enjoy Bayfest this weekend. And when you show up on Monday for practice, give me your all. Pirates on three."

Suddenly, players scampered from the bleachers, eager looks on their faces. Carson thrust out his hand, and it was covered by a stack of other hands.

"One, two, three," he shouted, his players hollering "Pirates!"

As he stepped away, surprisingly the players remained huddled together, causing him to wonder what was going on. Then they broke up, the majority of them leaving the gym, and he caught several smiling at him. Tim and Caleb stayed behind, lingering after the other players had gone.

"You need to talk with me?" he asked.

Caleb nodded to Tim, who said, "We're here to talk for the team and say thank you, Coach. Everyone was sick of how Drake never does much of anything and then grabs the ball and all the glory in games. We know he's got talent, but a lot of guys who are just average players on the team have basketball smarts and can execute plays. Good plays. Whether Drake comes back or not, we know we can be a good team. Maybe even a great one."

Carson smiled. "I'm glad to hear that, Tim. You and Caleb

are displaying real leadership on the court. Showing second and third efforts. Leading by example. The other guys notice that. They appreciate it. They'll do the same."

"You may get some blowback, Coach," Caleb said. "Especially if Drake decides to quit the team. But I can tell you now, the team is behind you on this one."

"I hope Drake comes back," Carson told the pair. "He's got mad talent, but he'll need to learn how to be a team player. I'm counting on the two of you to help him over the hurdles."

"We've got your back, Coach. And Drake's if he wants us," Tim promised.

The two players jogged off the court, and Jackson moved toward him.

"Gutsy move. Sounds like it's one the team was hoping you'd make."

"I mean it. If Drake wants to play for the Pirates, he'll need an entire attitude adjustment. I think we have a winning team, Jackson, because these boys have a winning attitude about life."

"I couldn't agree more. See you at Bayfest," his assistant said.

Carson took a seat in the bleachers, reflecting on what had happened over the last hour. He appreciated receiving the support of the team. No matter what happened next, Carson knew he had acted in the best interest of the team as a whole.

He left the gym, not needing to return to his office. He was going to enjoy this last free weekend before the basketball season began and dominated his every waking moment.

As he walked to his car, he saw someone standing by it.

Marge Duncan.

Bracing himself, he headed toward her.

"What the hell do you think you're doing, kicking my baby off the team?"

"He's not a baby, and I didn't kick Drake off the team,

Marge. I've just given him time to think about if he wants to play on this team and be a good teammate to the other players. I'm not going to coddle him simply because he's got natural, athletic ability. He's skating through school, both academically and athletically. I'm asking him to challenge himself and be the man I know he can be."

Drake's mother cursed at him and then said, "I'm going to Bill Perry next. Of course, I doubt you'll even get a slap on the wrist since you're banging his daughter."

"Whoa. Wait right there," Carson said, his blood boiling. He knew he had to rein in his temper and keep a cool head. Not only was he dealing with a parent, but Marge Duncan was also a fellow professional. He didn't want to escalate the situation. He also suspected Marge was the type of woman who would be recording this conversation. In Texas, a person could legally record a conversation without informing others if he or she were a party to that conversation.

"Do you deny it?" Marge demanded.

"My private life and relationship with Mila Perry have nothing to do with regard to my discussion about your son."

"How can I even get satisfaction, with you being the district's AD? If Jon Earl were still in charge, I could go to him. He'd straighten you out. Since I don't have that option, it means going over your head and taking things up with Bill." She sniffed. "And you're already like family to him. My poor kid is being left out in the cold. Denied his rights."

"Drake is still on the team, Marge, despite anything he said to you to the contrary. Yes, I'm sitting him for the scrimmage on Tuesday because he's been passive and uninterested in practice this week. He was also rude to Edith Smith. He's failing her class now, and he isn't doing much better in his other ones. As a principal, I would have thought you would have discussed with him the importance of getting a good education and emphasizing how he needs to use his natural gifts to excel, as well as trying to be the best person he can be."

Anger flared in her eyes, and her entire body stiffened. "You don't get to tell me how to parent my own child, Coach Andrews. I've done the best I can with Drake. His dad skedaddled three years ago. Even when he was here, he wasn't around much. I'm the one who stuck around. I'm the one who knows what's best for him. So don't you think you can tell me what to do."

"As an educator and administrator, you know better than anyone, Marge, that if you demand excellence, you'll get it. If you set a low bar, Drake will do what he's doing, just barely enough to scrape by. I'm not judging you as a mom. I understand how rough it can be to be a single parent because I'm one, too. All I'm saying is that you have him at home for the rest of his senior year. Talk to him rationally. Tell him you love him—but you need him to be the best version of himself that he can be, both on and off the court."

She raised her hand, and Carson thought she was going to slap him. Marge seemed to realize what she was about to do, and her hand fell. She took a step back.

"I'm going to Bill Perry with Drake. We'll see what the superintendent says. You can't go sitting my boy for no reason at all."

It was as if she hadn't heard a word he'd said. Carson knew enough to keep his mouth shut at this point.

"I'll make sure Bill knows if I don't get satisfaction, I'll go to the school board. It'll be both of your jobs," she threatened.

Marge wheeled and hurried to her car. Carson got in his own vehicle, his heart racing. While he knew he was well within his rights to bench whomever he wanted to, this was not a great start to his first season. Even if he had the support of his team and assistant coach, the trouble Marge could stir up might divide the community enough to force him out, not to mention dragging Mila's name through the mud.

He took a few deep breaths, trying to compose himself before starting his car and heading to pick up Lily at Happy Hearts. They would grab a quick bite at the diner before heading back to school to watch the volleyball game.

The confrontation with Marge was not something he would share with Mila. At least not right away. She needed to focus on tonight's match.

Carson just hoped things wouldn't get ugly.

Chapter Eighteen

Mila was in high spirits as she brushed her teeth and readied herself for Bayfest. Last night, her varsity team had swept their opponents and would be headed to the play-offs. They had honored Fiona Garrison and Deirdre Echols in a senior night presentation. Both captains had played solidly all season, and she knew their experience in previous playoff matches would benefit the entire team.

As she had expected, both Belinda Carter and Annie Morgan had come on strong throughout the season for the Pirates. She anticipated that the pair would land on the all-district team, and it wouldn't surprise her if Annie, though only a sophomore, were named as player of the year. Despite her youth, Annie had a maturity about her and was a calming presence for the team. She detected no jealousies amongst her athletes and had high hopes the Pirates would go several rounds into the playoffs.

She only hoped Carson would enjoy coaching his team this season. Mila had overheard Fiona telling Belinda that Drake Duncan was probably failing English at the moment, which

Carson had already shared with Mila. Belinda had then shared that she was dating Tim Packard, the starting center on the basketball team, and Tim was worried about all the negativity Drake was bringing with him. As a former player, Mila knew how those energy vampires could drain a team's spirits. She wanted to talk to Carson about it, but she decided it wasn't her business to meddle. Carson was a terrific coach, and he would deal with Drake in his own way.

She checked her weather app, seeing the day was going to be cool but sunny, and dressed in a long-sleeved tunic and jeans. Since there was no wind to speak of, she decided to leave her hair down and brushed it until it shone before pulling it away from her face with a headband.

Her phone dinged, and she saw it was a text from Carson. He and Lily were leaving the house and would pick her up in a few minutes. They were going to meet Michael and the kids at Bayfest. Cecily wouldn't be joining them since she was working a seven-to-three shift at the hospital. The four of them did have plans to grab dinner and attend the bonfire tonight, though, as well as stay for the concert. Thankfully, Dotty had agreed to keep all three kids at Michael's house, which meant Mila would be staying over with Carson.

She hadn't wanted to sleep over when Lily was home since occasionally Lily would come and get in bed with Carson if she'd had a bad dream. Neither she nor Carson were ready to explain to the little girl about adults having their own sleep-overs. Heaven forbid that Lily walked in on them making love.

Still, Mila couldn't help but wonder what their future path would be like. They loved one another. She assumed at some point, they would become engaged and eventually marry. Carson had even asked her input into the house plans Sullivan Shepherd had drawn up. They weren't quite complete because Hillary still hadn't found a piece of property for Carson to buy and build on. He was getting antsy to do so, wanting to have his new home completed well before Pete and his wife returned from his sabbatical in Australia.

Grabbing her keys, she locked the door and left her apartment, going to wait in the parking lot. Just as she arrived, Carson's car pulled up, and Mila opened the passenger door and climbed in. Carson leaned over and gave her a quick kiss.

"Hi, Mila," cried Lily. "We're going to a pumpkin patch!"

"I see you're wearing your *Frozen* dress. You look so pretty."

Since Bayfest was held the last Saturday of October each year, Halloween was right around the corner. Many children would be wearing their costumes to the community festival today.

"And I see Binky is also wearing a costume." She leaned back and scratched under his neck. "You look terrific, Binky. You make for a very good dinosaur."

"He's a stegosaurus," Lily corrected.

The beagle wore a dark gray body suit with a foam headpiece and foam plates sticking up along his spine.

Both Lily and Bobby were into dinosaurs. Bobby had a set of plastic ones they played with all the time. It amazed her how they knew the difference between a T-Rex, brachiosaurus, and triceratops. When she was four, she probably hadn't even known what a dinosaur was.

"We're entering Binky in a contest," Lily said. "Right, Daddy?"

"We are, Peanut, but there'll be a lot of dogs in it. Binky might not win."

"That's okay. Miss Andi says you don't have to win. You just have to try hard." Lily glanced at her dog. "Try to look like a stegosaurus, Binky."

She and Carson laughed, and Mila asked, "What are you looking forward to today?"

His fingers found hers. "Just spending a nice day with my two girls."

"Mila isn't a girl, Daddy. She's a lady," Lily corrected, and they both stifled their laughter.

They found a parking spot and left the car. Carson had Binky's leash in hand, while Mila held Lily's hand.

"Michael told us to meet them at the pumpkin patch."

"Pumpkins, pumpkins," Lily called out in a sing-song voice.

She spied her brother and waved. Gina came running toward them and hugged Lily, giggling.

"Ready to see the pumpkin patch, kids?" Michael asked.

They took the kids through the large section of pumpkins, taking a few pictures along the way. Once they worked their way from start to finish, they went to the flatbed truck giving hayrides next to the patch. Mila stayed behind so that she could snap a few photos of the kids. She also grabbed a schedule of events and glanced over it before folding and slipping it into her back pocket.

The others returned, and Gina begged to go to the petting zoo next. That took a good half hour to walk through. The kids got to pet goats, sheep, pigs, rabbits, and baby chicks and ducks.

"I love goats," Lily said happily, skipping ahead as she held hands with Gina.

"She's as happy as I've ever seen her," Carson said. "Coming to Driftwood Bay was definitely the right move. For both of us." He gave Mila a heated glance.

"Calm down, Romeo," she teased. "We need to take Binky over to his contest now. According to the schedule, judging is about to start."

They corralled the girls and went to where about two dozen dogs were gathered. She saw dogs dressed cleverly as a Fed Ex worker, a policeman, a clown, and a spider. Three were pirates, which didn't surprise her.

"Where did people get these ideas and costumes?" she wondered aloud.

"Amazon," Carson said. "That's what I did. I found an insane number of costumes for pets."

The judges assembled, including Dr. Dickey, George Crumby, and Denise Mayfield, who owned and ran Seaside Sweets Bakery. After much deliberation, prizes were awarded, with a schnauzer dressed as Franken Pup crowned the overall winner. The runner-up was Wonder Pup, a terrier wearing a Wonder Woman outfit.

"I'm sorry you didn't win, Binky," Lily said sadly, petting her beagle.

Carson pulled a few treats from his pocket. "Binky is a winner to us," he said, giving the pet the treats.

They hit the food trucks for some snacks. Mila got freshly-squeezed lemonade and split a funnel cake with Lily, while Carson snagged a corny dog.

"Let's take the kids over to the children's area," Michael suggested.

That took up the next hour. The kids did sand art and played simple games, catching plastic fish with a pole and tossing balls into a ring. Bobby won a prize and claimed a stuffed shark. Mila took his picture with it and texted it to Cec.

They wandered over to watch some of the polka dancing, and she convinced Carson and Michael to enter the pumpkin carving contest. Twenty minutes later, Michael's pumpkin looked like a typical jack-o'-lantern, but Carson's pumpkin turned out with the goofiest face she had ever seen. It won him first prize, which was a twenty-dollar coupon to the s'more pit.

"Guess we need to go spend this," he told their group, and they headed for a large firepit on the outskirts of the festival.

When they arrived and he presented the coupon, all three children were given a plastic bag containing two graham crackers, a marshmallow, and a chocolate bar broken into pieces. The guys helped skewer the marshmallows, and each adult supervised one child as they placed the skewers into the fire, rotating them to get a golden-brown color. Once the marshmallows were perfected, they went to tables which had been set up with paper plates and built their s'mores. Soon, the kids wore smears of chocolate on their faces, and a community volunteer came by, handing out wet wipes to help clean the messy faces.

Michael suggested they head to the ride area, where typical carnival rides had been brought in. A small Ferris wheel. A giant fun slide. A bounce house. He had already bought coupons for the kids.

"After that, we can get some lunch in them," her brother said.

They ate at the food truck area, getting street tacos for the adults and hot dogs and fries for the kids. Live performances were in the area next to where they were sitting, and they got to hear several singers and a few musicians as they ate.

"Now what?" Lily asked.

"Let's walk around and see the booths," Mila said.

They went to a different area of Bayfest, where vendors had stalls set up. Carson bought Mila a scented candle of cinnamon spice and Lily a book and pinecone birdfeeder. Other booths displayed wreaths which had been decorated for Halloween, Thanksgiving, and Christmas and jars where names could be painted on to personalize them. Carson also bought a sack of kettle corn.

"I've never had it," he admitted. "Something tells me I'm really going to like it."

Lily yawned, and he looked to Michael, who was already carrying Gina. Mila saw her niece's head rested on Michael's shoulder, and she was fast asleep.

"Time to go," Carson announced.

"No," Bobby and Lily protested weakly, but it was obvious that the kids were worn out from their day at Bayfest.

They headed back to their cars, making plans to meet again at seven tonight by the lobster roll truck.

"That's Cecily's favorite thing to eat at Bayfest," Michael said. "We can grab some rolls and beer. Listen to some music. Then there's the bonfire."

"We'll see you later," Carson said, putting Lily in her car seat and lifting a tired Binky to sit beside her before driving to Mila's apartment.

"I'll be back around six-thirty to pick you up. I figure it'll take us a while to find a place to park."

"Sounds good." She leaned over and kissed him.

Once home, she scanned her email, seeing she had one from the UIL. It had the pairings for the first round of the playoffs. Her Pirates would play the Marlins next Tuesday night in Corpus. She shot a quick text message to her team to let them know and then got in a few hours of reading for the latest course she was taking. She also wrote three pages of a paper which would be due in two weeks, wanting to get as much of it out of the way as possible before playing hooky with Carson tonight.

Checking the weather again, she saw the temps were dropping, so she changed into a cable knit sweater in soft pink, brushing her teeth again and applying a lipstick in a similar color. She texted some of the pictures she had taken today to

Cecily and then saw Carson's text come in, saying he was about to pull up. She went out to meet him.

"Lily okay?" she asked as she got into the car.

"She actually took a nap. She hasn't done that in forever."

"We did a lot today. Hey, I probably could've used a nap."

"Same." He grinned. "Of course, if we would've been together, I doubt much napping would have occurred."

Mila warmed under his heated gaze. "It's nice Dotty took all the kids tonight. I know Cecily said she's looking forward to alone time with Michael."

They met her brother and sister-in-law at the food truck and got in line. She liked how this food truck owner melted butter and mixed it with a lemony mayonnaise before spreading it inside the split, buttery bun. The lobster meat was always tender, seasoned with kosher salt and pepper and mixed with minced chives and celery.

"Get me two," she told Carson. "And some salt and vinegar kettle chips. Cec and I will go get in line for beers and meet up with you."

Ten minutes later, they were sitting at a table, not much conversation going on. Everyone was savoring their lobster rolls.

"I've gotten some great, fresh seafood in the Bay, but these are out of this world," Carson said.

"I'd like to try lobster rolls in New England," Mila mused. "Maybe spend a few weeks one summer driving up and down the coast, vlogging about the search for the perfect lobster roll. And maybe the right bowl of clam chowder to go along with it."

"That sounds good, but I'd rather do a queso vlog," Michael said. "I think taking a tour of Texas and tasting queso and writing about it would be my idea of heaven."

They finished their beers and wandered over to where a

makeshift pavilion had been set up. Ellen Roberts was singing, her voice low and sultry.

"You said Ellen is your friend Piper's mom?" Carson asked.

"Yes. Piper got Ellen's musical talent and acting chops," Mila said.

"I know you miss Piper like crazy," Cecily said.

"At least, I FaceTime with her and Layne a couple of times a month, but Piper is always on the road in some traveling production. Sometimes, it's a musical. Other times, it's a play. She's never in one place for very long."

"I would hate that kind of life," Carson said. "Always on the road. Not having anywhere to call home." He paused. "Speaking of home, Hillary called me this afternoon."

"She found something?" Mila asked eagerly.

"Sort of. The people at the end of the street I'm on now have decided to sell. The green house on my side of the street."

She wrinkled her nose. "That eyesore? I can't believe it's still standing. It looks like it's ready to fall down any minute. I thought you wanted to build using plans from Sullivan."

"They can't get much of anything for the house. It hasn't been lived in for years. It would take a small fortune to bring it up to code. They're willing to sell the house and the land it's on. I called Sullivan, and he came over. We walked down to it. It's a good-sized lot. On the corner, so it has a little more room than other houses on the block." He paused. "We're going to raze the house and clear the property. That way, we're starting from scratch."

Mila smiled. "That's great news, Carson. When will the work start?"

"Now that Sullivan knows the dimensions of the property, he's going to fine tune what he's drawn up. I'll need to approve it, but in the meantime, Hillary recommended someone who could come in and bulldoze the house and cart away the rubble."

Mila looked around. "It looks like people are heading down to the beach for the bonfire. Cec, want to hit the restroom with me before we go that way?"

"You bet. Do you guys want to meet us at the beach?"

"Sure, babe." Michael leaned over and kissed his wife. "See you soon."

Mila and Cecily made their way through the crowd, stopping at the Porta Potty area.

"Meet back here," Cec told her.

Mila went into one, taking a deep breath before she stepped inside. Portable toilets were not her thing, and she breathed through her mouth, hurrying to finish up. As she stepped outside, she moved to where they were supposed to meet.

Suddenly, someone grabbed her elbow, spinning her around. Mila saw it was Marge Duncan, the middle school principal.

And she looked ready to spew anger like an erupting volcano.

"Did he tell you?" Marge demanded.

Confused, Mila shook her head. "I'm not sure what you're talking about, Marge. Who?"

"That worthless boyfriend of yours. He removed Duncan from the basketball team. My boy *lives* for basketball."

It surprised her that Carson had made such a major move so early in the season, much less not tell her about it. She saw Marge wanted to pick a fight now, and Mila wasn't about to fall for that. The principal had a reputation for being feisty and not backing down. Never compromising and meeting someone halfway.

Especially when it came to her spoiled son.

"That doesn't concern me," she said coolly.

"Well, it could," Marge whined, and Mila caught the scent of the woman's breath, heavily laced with alcohol.

Mila glanced around and saw they were attracting a crowd. A few people even held cell phones up, and she assumed they were being filmed. "Would you like to talk about this in private?" she asked, hoping to keep the situation from blowing up.

"No, I would not!" Marge shouted. "Your idiot fuck buddy benched my kid for no reason."

"Carson wouldn't do that," she said, her own stubbornness rising. "Speak to him. There are two sides to every story, Marge. Not just Drake's."

The older woman pushed Mila's shoulder hard, causing her to stumble back a few steps. "Drake wouldn't lie to me. He's a good boy. He's the only player on that team with any talent, and everyone knows it. It's obvious Carson Andrews has no clue how to recognize talent when he sees it, much less know what to do with it."

"Don't touch me again," warned Mila as the principal closed the gap between them.

"What are you going to do, go tell your daddy on me?" Marge asked belligerently. "I already talked to Bill about this. He said there's nothing for him to do. That it's a coaching decision." The woman glared at her. "But Bill knows his daughter is in the sack with Andrews. He was always going to take his side."

Marge swayed a moment, and Mila reached out, catching her elbow to try and steady her.

"Get your hands off me!" Marge yelled.

Then she spit in Mila's face.

Stunned, she blinked, lifting her arm and wiping the spittle away. The crowd gathered had grown considerably larger. Cecily hurried up.

"Come on, honey. Let's go."

"Yeah. Run away. Go play house with your loser boyfriend. He's never going to marry you. He's just using you, Mila. But don't think I'm stopping now. I'm going over Bill's head. I'll go to the school board. Even the damn UIL. Somebody is going to listen and be impartial. My Drake is going to play this year. Your asshole boyfriend is history."

Cecily grabbed Mila's wrist, tugging her away. Thankfully, the crowd parted, allowing them to escape Marge's wrath.

"What was that all about?" Cec asked.

"I don't know," she said truthfully. "But I obviously need to talk to Carson right away."

Chapter Nineteen

Tonight was the night Carson would ask Mila to marry him.

Some might have said it was too soon to act. That they had only known each other five months, but he knew her heart. Her soul. She was his other half. She was good not only for him, but also Lily. He thought of it from her point of view, going into a marriage with a man who had a child, but she had shown nothing but love for Lily. And him. He knew they had built a firm foundation and were ready to take the next step in their relationship. One which would be permanent.

"How have you liked Bayfest?" Michael asked.

"It's been a perfect day," he told his friend and soon-to-be brother-in-law. "Driftwood Bay is a very welcoming place."

Not only had he forged a friendship with this firefighter, but he was also enjoying getting to know Keaton and Sullivan. Carson felt he fit in this town.

A large crowd had gathered on the beach, waiting for the bonfire to be lit. The wood which had been assembled was a good height and would burn for hours. He could see asking Mila to marry him as they stood alongside it, watching the flames lick the night sky.

"The lines must be long at the Porta Potty," Michael commented. "I thought the girls would be back by now. Wait, there they are."

Carson turned, immediately sensing something was wrong with Mila.

Something very wrong.

He broke away from Michael and jogged to meet her. Cecily had a hold of Mila's arm, and she looked white as a ghost. His eyes cut to Cecily, who shook her head, and he knew not to bring up anything here. Whatever Mila needed to say would demand privacy.

Her gaze met his. "Take me home."

Without question, Cecily relinquished her hold, and Carson wrapped an arm about Mila's shoulders, leading her away from the laughter on the beach. Though the air was only a bit cool, her teeth began to chatter noisily, and he stopped.

"Keep going," she said, her head down as she began walking faster, leaving him behind.

He caught up to her and noticed others eyeing them with interest as they passed. His gut told him something terrible had happened in the short amount of time they had been apart.

They reached his car, and he helped her inside it. He came around and climbed behind the wheel and looked at her.

She stared straight ahead and merely said, "Drive."

Carson left the parking lot and didn't press her to speak. When they reached her apartment, he cut the engine, and they faced one another.

"Something happened," she said quietly. "With Marge Duncan."

He winced. "What did she say to make you so upset?"

She finally turned to face him. "Why didn't you tell me you'd kicked Drake off the team? I thought we shared everything with one another."

Marge had gotten into Mila's head.

"First of all, Drake is still on the team, despite whatever he told his mom. I had already mentioned to you he was lackluster in practice and how Edith said he was failing her class."

"What else?" she demanded.

Carson swallowed. "I pulled him aside at practice yesterday and told him that he needed an attitude adjustment. That he needed to realize he was on a team and not the only player who counted. I didn't cut him from the team. I merely told him he'd sit out Tuesday night's scrimmage to give himself time to think about things."

Her gaze met his. "That's a really big deal. Drake is a big deal."

"He may be talented, but there are a lot of hard-working young men on this team. Drake stormed out of practice, and I let the players know what had happened. They were supportive of what I'd done, Mila. They're tired of his prima donna act."

He raked his fingers through his hair, frustration building within him.

"Marge confronted me after practice. I'm sure Drake called her right away, giving her a distorted version of what happened between us. She demanded that I put him back on the team. Said she was going to your dad. I'm sorry she dragged you into this."

Her mouth trembled. "I was blindsided, Carson. I don't understand why you didn't tell me any of this. It's not as if we never talk shop."

"When was I supposed to talk to you about it?" he asked,

his temper flaring. "I picked up Lily. Fed her. We went straight to your game. I wasn't about to march over to the bench and give you a blow-by-blow account of what occurred with Drake, Marge, and me. Not before your match. Then today, we've been at Bayfest the entire time. Yes, I planned to talk to you about this. Get your input to see if I handled things correctly. We just needed alone time for that to occur."

Mila bit her lip. "Marge said she had already talked with Dad. That he said it was a coaching decision, and he wasn't going to get involved in it. She was loud—and I think drunk. She said some pretty nasty things about you. Since she didn't get any satisfaction by talking to Dad, she said she'll go to the school board. Even the UIL governing board if she has to."

Tears welled in Mila's eyes, and Carson reached for her hand. She pulled away, and he suddenly realized how serious this was.

"I worried about two things from the moment we started seeing one another," she told him. "One was trying to compete with Angie. We got over that hurdle. I can accept that you love her and always will. You're a kind, decent man, Carson, and I would expect nothing less of you. Still, it was something which concerned me, but you helped me put those fears to bed."

She fell silent, and he wanted to press her. At the same time, he was trying to give her space.

"My other concern was dating my supervisor. The optics just don't look good to outsiders and whether you admit it or not, Marge has a point. You've become family to my family, especially Dad. I think even though he's a terrific professional, I'm just not sure how objective he would be when it came to you and something like this."

Tears fell down her cheeks, and Mila wiped them away.

"I do not want to endanger your job. Because it's not just

you involved. It's also Lily. You have to put her first. Her—and your career."

"What are you saying?" he asked worriedly.

"We need to take a break. Step back from our relationship and think things through carefully."

Her words gutted him. "No. Why? You can't let a rambling, drunk Marge Duncan drive a wedge between us, Mila."

"It's not just Marge. It's what everyone else will be saying. We need some time apart in order to have a clearer perspective on things. Jon Earl will still be in charge of evaluating my performance this year as far as athletics goes. You'll be expected to come to my playoff games as AD, but I don't believe it's wise to continue seeing each other."

"I strongly disagree. You're letting a disappointed parent's bitterness seep into our private lives."

She looked at him sadly. "A small town constantly has its nose in people's business. Especially public figures such as teachers and coaches."

Mila sighed. "You're everything that I could want in a man, Carson, but there's more than just the two of us to consider. I don't want to torpedo your career. Please respect my feelings, and respect my decision to have us spend some time apart. Things need to be settled regarding Drake. You need to get your season off on a good foot, while I need to keep my head in the game as I lead my players through the playoffs."

Carson saw the pain in her eyes, knowing she was hurting as much as he was. This wasn't easy, but she was being the level-headed, more mature person right now. She was right. Whether he liked it or not, her idea to take a step back from their rela-tionship held merit.

"You know this is right thing to do," she told him. "It will give you a chance to focus on your career and your daughter. I need to concentrate on my team and both the classes I'm teaching and taking."

"How long is this time apart going to last?" he asked evenly, knowing he had to keep the bitterness from his tone.

He was afraid by agreeing to this that he would lose her for good, yet he understood where she was coming from. Too often, perception was viewed as truth. The residents of Driftwood Bay knew he was in a serious relationship with Mila and perceived that the school superintendent would give him unwarranted favor in a sticky situation.

"I respect what you're saying, Mila. What you're trying to do for my career—and us. I'm not happy about it, but until things have been worked out with Drake, I'll agree to put the brakes on us. For now. I don't see this going on for too long. I hope you'll give me a chance again once the dust has settled." He hesitated. "What should I tell Lily? She's used to seeing you often."

"That's up to you. You might tell her I'm busy with these playoff matches. School. If we do decide to continue our relationship down the road, I probably will need to leave the district, though."

"I can't ask you to do that. You were here first. You love what you do."

"And I can't ask you to leave. This is a huge opportunity for you, Carson, to be both a head coach and an AD."

She sighed, her shoulders slumping, looking as if she carried the weight of the world upon them. He knew nothing further would be settled tonight.

"All right. I agree that we'll put a pause on our personal relationship."

"If we start up again, we may have to make some changes," she told him.

The word *if* hung in the air between them, and his throat thickened with emotion.

"Can I at least walk you to your door?"

"That's not a good idea," she said softly.

"Can I at least kiss you goodbye?"

Mila nodded, tears streaming down her face now.

Carson touched his lips to hers, tasting the salt of her tears. He kept the kiss soft. Brief.

She pulled away, regret in her eyes. "No matter what happens, Carson, I've loved every minute of our time together."

"I love you, Mila," he said quietly. "That'll never change."

She opened the car door and closed it behind her, walking briskly to her apartment. Inserting the key, she opened the door and turned, giving him a small wave before disappearing inside.

He sat, stunned by everything that had unfolded during the last half hour. He had thought they would have a romantic night together, ending in a proposal of marriage. Now, he wasn't sure if Mila would even be speaking to him, other than in a professional capacity.

Despondency engulfed him, much as it had when he had learned of Angie's murder. His heart told him this might even be worse. With Angie, she had been gone from his life quickly, leaving a huge hole in his heart. This time, though, it would feel like a living death, with Carson seeing Mila at school almost daily and not being able to touch her. Really talk to her. She had become not only his lover but his best friend, and now everything had been ripped from him. It was going to be next to impossible to function without Mila in his life, but he respected that she was trying to make the best decision for the both of them.

Carson needed to get this situation with the Duncans

straightened out as quickly as possible and not let anything disrupt his focus. That had to be on basketball now. His professional reputation was at stake, and he knew the residents of Driftwood Bay expected big things from his team.

And him.

With a heavy heart, Carson started his car and drove home, not bothering to keep his own tears at bay.

<h1 style="text-align:center">Chapter Twenty</h1>

Mila dragged herself from bed and went into the bathroom. Her eyes were still red and puffy from crying. She had gotten very little sleep, lying awake and replaying everything she had said to Carson.

Had she made a mistake, telling him they needed to stop seeing each other?

She was torn. On one hand, it was the rational thing to do. It had been foolish to think they could skate by, with no one questioning their involvement. Even though they had reported their romance to HR and arranged for Jon Earl to complete her evaluations, the lingering appearance of her receiving favoritism—or him gaining some because of who her father was—had been bound to surface. Marge questioning Carson's decision to bench Drake had not been something quiet. Instead, the principal had been very loud when she told Mila what had happened.

It had hurt, hearing these accusations out of the blue. While she could understand why Carson had waited before he spoke to her, she wished he would have done so earlier. That way, she wouldn't have been hearing about them for the first time in a very public setting. She might have been able to steer her conversation with Marge in a different direction, assuring the principal that Drake had only been told he was sitting out a single scrimmage. Instead of getting ahead of it, Mila felt she had been at a disadvantage from the first word Marge uttered.

The rest of her, the part that thought with her heart and not her head, told her she needed to call Carson immediately. Apologize for her knee-jerk reaction. Show a united front. But it would be hard to unring the bell she had loudly sounded. He might be having doubts about them now. About her love for him. Her commitment to him.

That was the furthest thing from the truth.

Should she call Dad? Or go see him?

Before she could decide, her phone rang, something which rarely occurred. She texted everyone and hardly ever received any calls. When she saw it was Piper calling, her gut lurched. As she answered, worry filled her.

"Piper? Are you okay? Where are you?"

"I'm in Detroit. I'm fine. But I'm calling about you and that video that circulating online. Mom sent it to me."

"What?"

"It's you and Mrs. Duncan, our old algebra teacher. I never liked her. She was always so impatient and never explained things well. She's in your face, complaining about her kid and saying mean things about Carson."

A sick feeling washed over her. If Piper's mom had seen it, how many others had? This was the kind of thing that could blow up and go viral.

"That was from last night. Just before the bonfire at Bayfest," Mila said, her voice dull. "Carson benched her son, but Marge is on a mission of vengeance, thinking Drake got kicked off the team."

"Carson didn't tell you about this?" Piper asked. "Because you sure look surprised."

"It just happened before my last district game Friday night. He didn't want to tell me and have me thinking about that instead of my players," she defended.

"I get that," Piper said. "But man, you should've known. Benching a player is a huge deal, especially when his mom is a mover and shaker in the district."

"I know. We broke up over it."

"You what? No, that's wrong, Mila. I can tell just from FaceTiming with you guys that you're crazy about each other."

"Well, it's not a permanent breakup. At least I don't think it is." She choked up. "I just told him we needed to take a step back and let things cool off and play out."

"What did your dad say?"

"I was about to go over and see him."

"Then I'll let you go. If it's okay, I'll call Layne and tell her about it. We're supposed to FaceTime tomorrow morning. Maybe you'll have some good news for us by then."

"I hope so."

Dejected, she hung up. Knowing she shouldn't, Mila picked up her phone and found the video. It hurt watching it, seeing it replayed again, knowing it was all over the internet. There probably wasn't a single person in Driftwood Bay who hadn't seen it. Then she saw more popping up and forced herself to put her phone down, telling herself not to go down that hellish rabbit hole.

Her phone rang again, and she jumped. Then she saw it was Dad calling.

"Hi, honey. I assume you've seen the videos."

"I just did. Piper called and told me about it."

"I'd like to talk with you and Carson about this situation. Could you two come over now?"

"I'm not with Carson. We… we sort of broke up."

Her dad was quiet a moment. "I see. Well, I still need to talk with you both. Would you rather I do that separately?"

"No. Things are civil between us, Dad. And I'm hoping it's not a permanent split."

"Okay. Can you be here in half an hour?"

Since it was Sunday morning, that meant Dad was missing church over this, something he never did. That let her know just how serious things were.

"Yes. I'll see you then."

"I'll call Carson and ask him to come over, as well."

Mila stripped off her clothes and took a lightning-fast shower. She dressed quickly and downed a bottle of water, her stomach too queasy to eat anything. It only took her five minutes to reach her parents' house. She didn't see Carson's car and wondered if Dad had gotten in touch with him.

At the door, Mom gave her a big hug. "Oh, baby. Come in. I know you're upset. Dad told me that you and Carson aren't together any more. Is it because of the videos? Marge?"

Mila came inside and walked straight to the kitchen, where Dad sat at the table, wearing a dress shirt and tie. His suit jacket hung on the chair behind him. She took a seat and then looked at her mom.

"I thought because of what was happening, it might be better if Carson and I didn't see one another for a while. I've always been a little uncomfortable dating my boss. Now, with Marge's accusations, I thought removing our relationship from the equation might help streamline things."

Mom took her hand and squeezed it. "I know you're hurting. That you love him."

Tears filled her eyes. "I saw a future with him," she admitted. "Now, I don't know what he thinks of me. Of us."

Dad spoke up. "The school board is convening at noon

today. I wanted to speak to both you and Carson before that happens. They may want to talk to you both."

She looked down at her sweatshirt and jeans. "I can't go like this."

"You can borrow something from me," Mom volunteered.

The doorbell rang, and her stomach flipped over twice, knowing Carson had arrived. Mom left the kitchen to answer it.

Dad said, "It's going to be okay, honey."

Bleakly, she said, "I hope so," doubt filling her.

Carson entered the kitchen and from the looks of it, he had slept even worse than she had. His gaze immediately went to her, and she gave him a weak smile. He took a seat and reached for her hand.

This time, Mila didn't pull away.

Mom asked, "Would you like me to leave since this is official school business?"

"No, Laura. Stay. I think the kids could use a friendly face."

Mom took a seat.

"Carson, you probably know that Marge Duncan came to see me late Friday afternoon. I need you to start at the beginning. Recap everything from the time practice started Friday. And if you don't mind, I'll record you."

Dad placed his cell phone on the table and pressed the record button. He gave the time and date and noted everyone present before nodding at Carson.

"Actually, I'd like to speak about how things got started before yesterday's practice, Dr. Perry," Carson said formally. "Involving a conversation I had with Edith Smith, then my practice planning session with Jackson Rudd, who is my assistant."

For the next quarter-hour, Carson walked them through the events of two days ago, first detailing his conversations with

Drake's English teacher and the team's assistant coach. Next, he talked about practice and how he had called Drake aside, speaking to him in private. Mila was pleased at Carson's recall of the details of their conversation. He emphasized Drake was not asked to leave the team, voluntarily or otherwise.

"I told Drake that he needed to be more of a team player. That he had leadership potential, but he needed to behave as a leader and not a loner. I did inform him that he would be sitting on the bench for our first scrimmage this upcoming Tuesday. I wanted to give him time to process our conversation and what I'm asking of him. I also wanted him to make some changes in his poor attitude. I told him the only way he was off the team was if he left it of his own accord."

Dad, who hadn't interrupted Carson once, nodded and asked, "What about the other players? What were they told regarding Drake's absence from practice?"

"Drake voluntarily left practice. I never asked him to do that. I returned to the gym, having let Jackson run things during my short absence. We finished practice, and then I called the team together. I told them Drake was still on the team, but that I wanted him to think carefully of his role. I emphasized that every player, whether a starter or not, contributes to the team and that no one player is above the team or the rules. They're a sharp group, Dr. Perry. Already, I see how these players work hard and work well together. They understood my decision about benching Drake for the opening scrimmage, and no one seemed to have a problem with that. In fact, two players stayed after practice and thanked me for taking the action."

"Who are those players?"

Carson hesitated. "I'm not certain I want to mention them by name. They spoke to me in confidence."

"I see," Dad said. "Now, let's move on to your conversation

with Marge Duncan. I believe it occurred Friday after practice had ended."

Again, Carson methodically went through what he and Marge had discussed in the parking lot and her unhappiness with the outcome of their conversation.

"Mrs. Duncan said she was going to speak to you regarding Drake not starting or playing in the scrimmage. My impression was that she thought Drake was no longer on the team. Though I tried to correct that, she wasn't in a mood to listen to what I had to say. I can't speak as to what Drake told his mother, but I was very clear with him that he was still a Pirate for as long as he wished to be."

"Do you have anything to add, Coach Andrews?"

"No, sir."

"Then I would like to move along and speak with Mila Perry, whom I mentioned as being present at the beginning of this recording." Dad looked to her. "Ms. Perry, would you please recall your conversation with Marge Duncan last night and elaborate on it?"

She sat up a little straighter. "Yes, Dr. Perry. I spoke with Mrs. Duncan at Bayfest last night, shortly before the bonfire was to be lit."

Dad gave her the chance to recount the entire conversation before he asked, "Did you notice anything unusual about Mrs. Duncan's behavior?"

Mila knew what he meant. "Besides being openly hostile, Mrs. Duncan was extremely loud. I smelled alcohol on her breath, which may have caused her to speak more loudly than seemed appropriate."

"But you never witnessed her consuming any alcoholic beverage?"

"No, sir. I did not. Mrs. Duncan was standing very close to

me at times, however, and I did pick up the scent. I believe there are several videos which show our conversation."

"Yes, I have seen some of them," Dad said. "Anything else you wish to share, Ms. Perry?"

"No, Dr. Perry. I'm happy to talk with the school board if necessary."

Dad tapped his phone, ending the recording. "You both did extremely well. You were articulate. You provided clear details. I'll be playing this for the school board."

"Is this about Carson benching Drake, or is it about Marge being drunk and disorderly in public?" she asked.

"Possibly both," Dad said cryptically. He glanced at his watch. "I'm going to head over to admin now. If you don't mind making yourselves available, I think it would be a good idea if you waited outside while the board meets in closed session."

"I want to go home and change," Carson said. "If I'm going to appear before the board, I want to be dressed more appropriately. I also need to make arrangements regarding Lily. I called Cecily on my way over here and explained I couldn't pick up Lily just yet. Since it sounds as if I might be tied up this afternoon, I need to figure out what to do with her."

"I'll have Michael and Cecily bring the kids over here," Mom said. "I'll feed them lunch, and we can watch a movie together."

Carson said, "I appreciate you helping out, Laura."

"I'll go home and change, as well," Mila said. "What about Marge?"

"I've already notified her that the board is meeting," Dad said. "She'll also be there at noon."

She hated that they would have to see Marge. The foyer outside the boardroom was small.

Carson finally released her hand and rose, offering Dad his

hand. "Thank you for hearing my side of the story, Dr. P. I know you went out on a limb, backing me and telling Marge it was a coaching decision."

"I still feel it is, Carson. A superintendent has no business becoming involved in coaching decisions."

"Is my job on the line?" Carson asked, causing Mila to hold her breath.

"If I have anything to say, you'll be staying on," Dad confirmed. "However, I can't guarantee anything. It's up to the board."

Carson nodded. "I understand. And whatever the outcome, I want to thank you for having faith in me to do the jobs you hired me to do. I appreciate your belief in me more than I can ever convey."

Mila walked out with Carson, saying, "You really were good in there. I know if the school board calls you in, it'll be nerve-wracking, but just do what you did when you were explaining everything to Dad. It's going to work out, Carson. I know it will."

They stopped at her car.

"I hope so," he said. His gaze searched her face, and then he said, "I'll see you in the boardroom."

Mila drove home and changed into a shirt, pants, and navy blazer. She pulled her hair from its ponytail and brushed it thoroughly, adding earrings and a spritz of perfume. Gazing at herself in the mirror, she freshened her lipstick, thinking she looked polished and professional. She knew every board member personally, but this was going to be a different situation than their usual light, breezy conversations before a game or in the grocery store. Though she wasn't certain if they would ask to speak to her, she wanted to be prepared for whatever came.

She drove to admin, seeing the parking lot was full, and

crossed the street to park at the high school. When she moved to the front doors, she saw at least fifty people milling about outside.

Sandy stood holding the door open, waving her inside.

"Your dad is in with the board right now," the secretary informed her. "Everyone was here by eleven-thirty, so they went ahead and started in closed session. Come wait with the others in the conference room."

Sandy led the way, and Mila entered, seeing the seats around the conference room were filled. Mae from HR. George, their principal. Jon Earl. Carson was seated at one end of the table, while Marge and Drake were at the opposite end of the table. Mila seated herself next to George, who nodded briefly.

"I'll be back," Sandy told the group.

And so the wait began.

Chapter Twenty-One

Carson shouldn't have been surprised to see a crowd gathering outside the school administration building when he arrived. News spread like a California wildfire in a small town, as he'd learned during his months living in Driftwood Bay. The fact that the school board was meeting—on a Sunday—would have got the gossip mill churning fast. He recognized some of the faces in the crowd as he was admitted by Sandy, including a few of his players. Caleb smiled encouragingly and gave Carson a thumbs up.

Now, they sat in the conference room, waiting to see what the board had discussed behind closed doors. He wasn't apprehensive. In fact, he was confident in the decision he had made to bench Drake. The teenager sat sullenly at the far end of the table next to his mother, his eyes downcast. Carson didn't think the board had called them together because of his decision regarding a single player. Most likely, it was to discuss Marge Duncan's public outburst at Bayfest last night. He was on the periphery of that.

He had seen the most popular video circulating on social

media which entailed most of the confrontation. Keaton had texted him early this morning as he drank a cup of coffee, asking to come over. He had made another cup for his friend, who asked if Carson knew about Marge getting in Mila's face last night. When he said Mila had told him about the incident, Keaton asked if Carson had seen any video of it. He took out his phone and pulled up one of several circulating online.

It had sickened him, seeing Mila being verbally attacked in that manner. It was even worse than she had described. He now understood why she had been as upset as she was and why she wanted to protect him professionally by pausing their relationship. Carson and Keaton had been discussing what to do when he received the call to come to the Perrys' house and discuss the matter. That had led to being called before the board now.

Sandy reappeared. "If everyone will please follow me, we're all—"

"Everyone is going?" Marge interrupted. "I thought there would be an expectation of privacy."

Looking flustered, Sandy replied, "You'll have to take that up with Mr. Hopewell. As the school board's president, he's calling the shots."

Marge harrumphed as everyone came to their feet and moved to the next room. Carson sat with Mila in the first row on one side of the aisle, while Marge and Drake took chairs on the other side. Jon Earl sat behind them, with Mae and George to the football coach's left.

The board members sat in a semicircle at the front of the room. Hank Hopewell, Carson's barber, was in the center. His nameplate identified him as the president. To his right sat Hillary, Carson's realtor, and a man whose nameplate said Jack Larson. He wondered if Jack might be related to Layne, Mila's childhood friend. On Hank's left were Neville Wagner from the Driftwood Diner and a woman named Pat Mayfield. While he didn't know her, he knew the name. Mayfield Charters ran boats for tourists and locals for deep sea fishing and dives. Dr. Perry sat off to the side, while Sandy moved to a table to act as stenographer for the proceedings.

Hank called the meeting to order. Immediately, Marge rose to her feet to protest.

"Sit down, Marge," the barber said. "I know what you're going to say. I'll tell you now that you're a public figure—and a social media star by now—so we're going to proceed as planned."

Carson watched the principal reluctantly take her seat again.

Hank cleared his throat. "We are here today to deal with one issue, and it's all over the internet, as most of you know. In case anyone hasn't seen it, we're going to replay a version now."

He sensed Mila tensing next to him and slipped his hand around hers. Thankfully, she didn't pull away.

The room was incredibly quiet as Sandy picked up a remote and clicked it toward the screen. Then last night's scene between Mila and Marge unfolded. Carson couldn't help it and glanced to Marge, who sat stone-faced. Drake looked as if he wanted to crawl into a hole.

"Play the second version, Sandy," Hank instructed, and they saw one which had a little more of the conversation, only from a different angle.

"I think that's enough," the president said.

Immediately, Sandy turned off the video and poised her fingers above the keys again.

Hank looked directly at Marge now. "We're here today because of you, Marge. And don't talk when I'm trying to," the barber warned. "You made a spectacle of yourself at Bayfest last night. As a public school employee—a principal, no less—you are charged with being your best self at all times. You know that, Marge. You're a leader. A damned good one. The middle school has a fine reputation and exemplary test scores. Very few disciplinary actions need to be taken because you run a tight ship. Kids behave. And they learn on your watch."

He frowned. "But you were not the representative of Driftwood Bay Independent School District that you needed to be last night. What have you got to say for yourself?"

Defiance laced Marge's tone as she said, "My son was removed from the basketball team by Carson Andrews. He did not even notify me. I had to seek him out, and he would not listen to reason when I tried to speak with him about the issue. Since he is also the district's athletic director, I felt I had no recourse but to take my concerns to Dr. Perry. As our superintendent, I expected Dr. Perry to be fair." She paused, taking time to glance at Mila and Carson. "But his daughter is sleeping with Andrews, and Dr. Perry said it was a coaching call, something he would not get involved in."

Marge came to her feet now. "I tell you, Carson Andrews has had it out for my boy. And he knows he can do whatever he wants because he's got the backing of the superintendent. Dr. Perry is biased in favor of Andrews. No one will listen to me."

"Please have a seat," Hank suggested. He turned his attention to Carson. "Coach Andrews, the board is not going to become involved in a personnel decision you made regarding your basketball team. You are well within your rights to dismiss a player if you have due cause. Will you please elaborate on your decision, however, as it may have factored into Mrs. Duncan's mindset and behavior?"

Carson rose. "Drake Duncan was never removed from the team," he began.

"Are you calling me a liar?" Marge demanded, her face red

with anger. "How's he supposed to get a scholarship if you don't let him play?"

"I don't believe you have all the facts, ma'am," he replied.

He returned his attention to the board, explaining how Drake's grades were subpar and even failing in his English class. How his English teacher was concerned not only with Drake's grades but also his attitude, and had made Carson aware of both.

"I took Drake aside at practice on Friday while the other players were involved in drills. We went to the locker room and had a frank discussion." He paused, looking at the teenager. "I believe Drake is a gifted athlete who is not living up to his full potential. That was what our discussion was about. At no time did I tell Drake he was dismissed from the team. I did make him aware that he was going to ride the bench during next Tuesday's first scrimmage of the year. I wanted to shake him up. Make him know how serious the situation is. Help him to become the player—and leader—I know he can be."

He saw several board members nodding, and Jack Larson said, "Dr. Perry played the interview tape which detailed more of your conversation with Drake." He looked at the player. "I think we need to hear from Drake."

Carson sat, and Mila's fingers found his, squeezing them.

All eyes were on the teenager now. He shook his head, and Carson thought he might actually cry. Then Drake turned to his mom.

"I'm sorry, Mom. Coach is telling the truth. I've been a real asshole to him and everyone on the team."

Marge looked stunned by her son's admission.

"I'm not blaming you, but after Dad left? You let me get away with murder. I think you were trying to make it up to me, having a lousy dad who didn't give a... who didn't care about either of us. I just turned off all my feelings. I don't care about my classes. I may be the best player on the basketball team, but I'm a lousy teammate."

Drake paused, visibly swallowing. "I was mad because Coach was the first person trying to hold me accountable. None of my teachers pushed me, asking me to try harder, except for Mrs. Smith. The other coaches always let me skate by with a bad attitude because I win games for them and make them look good."

He glanced across the aisle to Carson. "You're the first to call me out on my bullshit." Drake looked sheepish. "Sorry, Coach. I shouldn't have lied to Mom about being kicked off the team. I thought she would just chew you out, and you'd cave. Like everyone else does. That you'd let me play on Tuesday. But I don't want to start. I want to ride the bench and see how the team plays. They make me look good, and it's my turn to do the same for them."

Drake looked to the board. "I'm the one to blame. Mom was just trying to stick up for me. Don't punish her for what I did." He sat, wiping his eyes.

Hank looked to the other board members. "HR was informed about the relationship between Coach Andrews and Coach Perry. Dr. Perry was acting on good faith in his AD, not getting involved when Mrs. Duncan came to him with a complaint regarding playing time for her son." He looked to Marge. "There still is the matter of you appearing to be drunk in public." He looked to the other board members.

Pat Mayfield spoke up. "Marge wasn't arrested on a DUI. If she had been, the board would certainly need to take disciplinary action. We would suspend or even vote in favor of termination, because that charge would reflect poorly on our district. Without an arrest, we have no evidence of her blood alcohol level."

"But we do have the video of her ugly confrontation,"

Neville pointed out. "Whether an arrest was made or not, that video has gone viral. I think Marge needs to be held accountable in some manner."

"But I—"

"Drake, please be quiet," Hank cautioned the teenager. "Whether you believe you hold some responsibility or not, your mother is an adult, and her actions were her own. She knows public educators are held to a higher standard than others." Looking at both sides, he said, "What do you wish to do, board members?"

"I'm in favor of a reprimand," Hillary recommended. "A formal warning."

The rest of the board members nodded in agreement, and Hank asked, "What kind? We can issue an inscribed, which goes on the public record, or a non-inscribed. That means the reprimand would remain private."

"Non-inscribed," Jack voiced. "While the video isn't pretty, Pat is right. No formal charges were filed. Marge just looks like an idiot. But I don't think it should keep her from her job."

"What if we issued the reprimand and a three-day suspension with loss of pay?" Neville countered. "That way, the public will know something was addressed."

All the board members began nodding, and Hank said, "Let's take a vote."

Carson watched as the unanimous vote occurred. Marge was told the suspension would be effective starting Monday, and that she could not be on any school grounds until she had served the entire suspension. That meant she wouldn't be allowed to attend the Tuesday night scrimmage.

"I think we're done here," Hank said. "Meeting adjourned." He banged a gavel, and the board members filed out, leaving through a back door.

Jon Earl leaned forward, squeezing Carson's shoulder.

"Stick to your guns, son. You may actually make a player—and leader—out of Drake Duncan."

The others exited the boardroom, leaving Mila and him.

And Marge and Drake Duncan.

The four of them rose, and Marge spoke first. "I'll apologize to you both. I let things get out of hand. You've both been professionals, and I've been anything but."

"You're a mom," Carson said. "A single parent. I know what that's like, having to make all the decisions on your own. You bear the burden of all the worries. Yes, you lashed out. Didn't have all the facts. But deep down, your heart was in the right place. I get that."

Drake spoke up. "You can ground me forever, Mom. I deserve it."

His mother frowned at him. "We will definitely be talking about that at home. I hope this is a wake-up call to you, Drake. Colleges will be looking at your grades. They don't want to issue a scholarship to a player who can't make grades at the university level. You're no good to them if you flunk out."

"They'll also be looking for a team leader," Carson added. "You have the talent. Now, you need to add the drive and discipline, as well as being one member of the team."

An earnest expression crossed Drake's face, and determination filled the young man's eyes. "I can do it, Coach. I want to show everyone I can be a better player. A better student. A better person."

"Good." Carson extended his hand, and Drake shook it. Marge did as well.

"See you at practice tomorrow," he said, and Drake grinned.

Mother and son left the boardroom. He turned to Mila.

"Thanks for being here today."

"I didn't do anything. The board never asked me a question."

"They listened to your interview. And you were here, by my side." He hesitated. "I hope that's somewhere you still want to be."

Tears filled her eyes. "I just wanted to do what was best for you and Lily, Carson. I thought if we weren't a couple, your professional reputation wouldn't take such a beating."

"The board acknowledged that they know we are. It's all I want, Mila. To love you. To be together forever. To be a family." He searched her eyes. "I was going to ask you to marry me at the bonfire last night. Because you are my future."

His reward was a radiant smile. "I want to share all my tomorrows with you, Carson."

"Then let's make it official."

Carson dropped to his knees. Taking her hands in his, he asked, "Will you marry me, Mila? Make us a family of three—and hopefully add to it?"

"Yes!" she cried, pulling on his hands and bringing him to his feet.

The kiss they shared was one filled with the promises of all their tomorrows.

"Let's go tell your folks that we're ready to put a ring on it."

They left the boardroom, hand-in-hand. When they emerged from the building, he saw a crowd still gathered. Everyone broke out in applause, and his players surrounded them.

"We know everything is okay, Coach," Caleb said. "Drake told us he'd be at practice Monday, and we'll see a new guy."

"He pulled us over and talked to us," Tim added. "He apologized for being such a...jerk." Tim blushed. "My word. Not his."

"I think we're going to have a terrific basketball team this year," Carson told the players. He thrust out his hand. "Pirates on three."

Quickly, hands stacked atop hands, and he said, "One. Two. Three."

"Pirates!" reverberated through the air, not only from the players, but from the rest of the crowd surrounding them.

Carson looked around, knowing not only had he found a home with Mila, but he'd discovered a professional home in Driftwood Bay.

He pulled Mila to him, giving her a kiss, which caused the crowd to applaud again.

Breaking it, he asked, "Can we get married right away? I don't think I can wait. I'm ready to start forever with you right now."

She beamed at him. "I have a feeling I'll be saying this for years to come. Let's check our sports schedules and see when there's an open window to hold a wedding."

"You're on."

Carson kissed her again, eager to start the next chapter of his life with the woman he loved.

Chapter Twenty-Two

Only one time worked out in which to hold their wedding, and that would be during the week of Thanksgiving break. The volleyball playoffs would run through the weekend before that school vacation began, with the final matches for state titles held Friday and Saturday. Because Mila couldn't predict how far her team would go, she didn't want to leave anything to chance and have the wedding on a weekend before the playoffs concluded.

It was a good thing—because the Pirates made it to the final match.

No sports team in Driftwood Bay had ever contended for a state title, so the town was thrilled to send off the Pirates to Houston, where the match would take place. George Crumby gave permission for a send-off pep rally to take place in the high school's football stadium, and many residents of the Bay turned out for it. When it ended, students and citizens alike lined the sidewalk as Mila and her team boarded the bus bound for Houston. They would arrive mid-afternoon after a five-hour drive and stay overnight in a hotel. Carson had worked with her on the budget as athletic director, and he had brought Lily with him to Houston.

Her parents would also be in attendance and had led the caravan of fans departing the Bay. The hotel where the team was staying had a block of rooms available, and several moms had helped with chaperoning the girls as they played at a Topgolf the previous afternoon and then had a team dinner following that outing.

This morning, Mila had the team eat brunch. Their match would take place at two, and she didn't want anyone sluggish from lunch. The hotel had set aside a small dining room so players and their families could eat together. A few of the players had given speeches, and Mila was touched by what had been said.

Now, she looked across the locker room at this close-knit group of young ladies. She would miss the seniors who would be graduating and was excited that Fiona had been offered a volleyball scholarship to Sam Houston State in Huntsville. Even though Deirdre hadn't been given the same opportunity, the two best friends had decided to room together, with Fiona majoring in accounting and Deirdre in education.

She addressed her athletes now, smiling the entire time.

"This has been a dream season for me, thanks to every player on this team. A team is defined as a number of people associated together in work or an activity. Our activity was playing volleyball, and every member on our roster definitely put in the work. Some of you contributed in big ways. Some in smaller ones. But it took everyone present in this room to get us to state."

Mila paused. "State. Let that word resonate through you. We made it to state. From that very first practice back in August until now, we have achieved what very few teams ever do. And while I want that state title so bad I can taste it, no matter what today's outcome is, we are winners. You are at the top of your game. We've peaked at the perfect time."

Grinning, she added, "Now it's time to go and kick Townbluff's butt!"

Her team cheered, and they left the locker room, spirits high. They went through the usual warmup routine, and Mila kept her eye on their opponents. The Townbluff Trojans had won three previous state championships, two a decade ago, and the other one last year. They were eager to win back-to-back titles, but her gut told her that her Pirates would prevail. Both teams were comparable physically, but this team from Driftwood Bay was closer than any she had ever coached or played for.

The pre-game clock wound down, and she called her players over. As they huddled about her, she said, "This is it. Your time to shine. It's your title to claim. Don't let the Trojans snatch it from you. Pirates on three."

"Pirates!" yelled her girls.

While the larger division schools in Texas had to win three games out of five to be crowned state champions, as smaller schools, Driftwood Bay and the Townbluff Trojans would compete in a best two out of three. Mila had stressed how important it was to take that first game decisively, and her players came through, winning fifteen to nine.

As they switched sides, she finally glanced into the crowd and spied Carson. He gave her a thumbs up, and she smiled at him. She couldn't help but glance down at the diamond solitaire she now wore on her left hand. Her fiancé had insisted upon an engagement ring. Though Mila had never worn any jewelry other than small gold studs in her ears, she liked wearing this ring.

The second game was dog-eat-dog, with the Trojans eking out a victory, seventeen to fifteen. Mila couldn't fault the play of her team. She called them to her before the final game got underway.

"You made them earn every point the hard way that game," she praised. "No matter what unfolds next, win or lose, you are champions in my book."

"We're going to suck the life out of them," Annie declared. "They're never going to forget this day—or the Driftwood Bay Pirates."

The sophomore's words stirred the team, and they took the court again, a visible energy vibrating through them. When the Pirates led five to three, Annie took charge. The next five points were all kills, and Townbluff seemed stunned. Leading by seven points now, Mila could taste victory. She called a timeout, though.

Surrounded by her players, she said, "Don't ease up. Don't give an inch. Don't get cocky. Confidence is one thing, but don't get reckless. Stay calm. Stay focused." She paused. "And go bring back a state title."

Her girls did exactly that.

When the last point was scored, sealing the title, her team began jumping up and down, falling into one another's arms. The court was flooded by their fans. Mila found every girl, hugging them tightly, telling them each something different as she acknowledged their contribution to the team's success.

Then Carson was there, kissing her, Lily clinging to her leg. Mila scooped up the little girl and kissed her cheek.

"We won, Lily!" she cried. "We won!"

"I'm gonna play volleyball. I'm going to win state," the little girl declared.

Mila beamed at her soon-to-be daughter. "I'm sure you will."

Carson kissed her again, and then her parents were congratulating her, as well as so many others who had made the drive from the Bay. An official claimed her attention, and Mila gathered her team for the trophy presentation. She accepted the award, and her eyes swept across the bleachers crowded with fans.

"I have never seen such selflessness and camaraderie as I do with these young ladies. They are the epitome of a team in every sense of the word. I accept this honor on their behalf—and for the town of Driftwood Bay!"

Rousing cheers sounded, and Mila knew when she looked back on the highlights of her life, this would certainly be one of them.

"You look beautiful," Layne said, her smile wide.

Mila hugged her friend. "I'm so glad you could make it to the wedding. I'm just sorry Piper isn't here."

"Well, it was hard for her to get away, especially on short notice. I mean, she's playing Roxie Hart in *Chicago*—and she's actually *in* Chicago doing so."

"I'm happy for her. I can't wait for her to meet Carson in person."

"She'll love him. Same as I do. You picked a really good one, Mila. And you get to be a mom right away."

"I worried about what Lily is supposed to call me. Carson said that she called Angie Mama. She really was so young when she lost her mom, but Carson is good about showing her pictures and telling her stories and showing her videos of her and Angie together."

"So, what is she going to call you?" Layne asked.

"She's been calling me Miss Mila, but the three of us talked about it. We decided on Mommy. We plan on having kids, and it would be odd for them to hear their sister call me Miss Mila. I'm good with Mommy."

"You'll be a wonderful parent to her, Mila," her friend assured her. "And I can tell how you've made her a part of you. Lily and Carson are lucky to have you."

"Just like I'm lucky to have them."

Her mom entered the locker room. "Everything is ready. We're just waiting for the bride."

While neither Mila nor Carson had wanted a large wedding, especially on such short notice, they were going to have what most likely would be the largest wedding Driftwood Bay had ever seen. Everyone had wanted to attend the ceremony. Her volleyball team and students. His basketball players. Coaches and teachers. People in town. Finally, they had asked George if they could simply hold their wedding in the boys' gymnasium since it seated so many. Their principal had agreed to their request, and the reception would follow in the cafeteria, where it was to be a potluck. Mila had already gone down earlier and seen so many covered dishes, as well as the wedding cake, which had been provided by Seaside Sweets Bakery.

With her volleyball season completed, Carson's basketball schedule had a small break in his over Thanksgiving. His boys would be playing in a tournament over their Christmas break, so getting married at Thanksgiving made sense. They didn't want to interrupt Thanksgiving Day itself or the weekend after, so they were getting married on a Tuesday afternoon.

"Let's do this," Layne said, leading Mila and her mom from the locker room, where she'd gotten ready, to the gym.

She clutched her bouquet as Mom kissed her cheek. Dad appeared, offering his arm to Mila. Layne opened the door and signaled to the orchestra teacher, and his strings students began playing.

Cecily smiled at Mila and then nudged Bobby, who was

serving as their ring bearer. He walked across the gym to where Carson and Michael awaited with the officiant at center court. Lily and Gina followed, carrying baskets filled with rose petals. They scattered them along the floor and then stood next to Bobby. Cecily had slipped into the gym and walked close to the bleachers. She now signaled to the children, and they joined her, sitting with Mila's mom in the front row.

Then Layne moved across the gym to the center, turning and smiling widely. The orchestra ended their tune and then broke out in *Here Comes the Bride*. Dad guided Mila along the rose-strewn way. A lump formed in her throat as she made eye contact with her groom, looking steadily at him the entire way.

The wedding itself passed quickly. Mila vaguely remembered repeating her vows and Carson placing a wedding band on her finger. She did the same for him, and they were suddenly kissing in front of everyone, now man and wife. Thunderous applause echoed throughout the gym, and her husband broke the kiss, smiling broadly.

"We did it. We're husband and wife."

She returned his smile. "We are. This is the best moment of my life, Carson."

"I hope we have many more best moments to come," he replied, kissing her again, much to everyone's delight.

Then he tucked her hand into the crook of his arm and led Mila to the cafeteria. Lily ran from the bleachers and joined them. They each took her hand and went as a family, and her heart swelled with joy, knowing she was the wife of this wonderful man and would be raising Lily as her daughter.

The next two hours were also a blur, filled with greeting guests and sampling various dishes. They cut into their wedding cake and fed one another a bite of it. Since they were on school grounds, no champagne was allowed, but they toasted one another with a delicious punch.

When it came time to leave, everyone present lined the halls of the school, all the way out to Carson's car, which his basketball team had decorated with shoe polish and cowbells and streamers. Lily ran to them, and they both kissed her, telling her they would see her tomorrow. She would be staying with Michael and Cecily tonight in order to give the newlyweds some private time.

Carson helped her into the car, and they both waved as he drove from the school's parking lot back to their house. Julie Shannon, the middle school coach Mila had hired back during the summer, was taking over her apartment lease, leaving the single room she had been renting. She was not only taking over the apartment but also Mila's furniture. They had decided they would shop for new furniture together for the house, which had broken ground last week. Carson would go to Houston and retrieve a few pieces that had sentimental value to him, but he would sell the rest, giving them a fresh start as a couple.

He carried her over the threshold and into the house, placing Mila on her feet and giving her a heady kiss.

"I'm thirsty," she told him. "I need something to drink."

In the kitchen, they found a beautiful bouquet of flowers on the table and a note. She opened and read it aloud.

> *Hey, Newlyweds!*
> *The flowers are for the beautiful bride. Champagne is chilling in the fridge. Chocolates are by the bed. Congratulations!*
> *Love,*
> *Keaton & Sullivan*

"That was so thoughtful of them," she said.

"They're turning out to be terrific friends. I'll uncork the champagne."

He did so, pouring it into juice glasses since he'd never seen any flutes in the cupboards.

"To my wife—and a life filled with experiences large and small. I can't wait to go on this adventure with you, Mila. I love you with all my heart."

Carson clinked his glass against hers, and they sipped the cold champagne.

"I think this is even better than a state title," she declared.

"Hmm. Let me win one before I agree with you," he teased.

Her husband took her in his arms again. "This is the life. Our life. In our town. I thank the heavens that the stars aligned, bringing me to Driftwood Bay—and you."

As they kissed, Mila knew wherever Carson was, that would be home.

Epilogue

FOURTEEN YEARS LATER...

Carson took his duffel bag and Mila's weekender and placed them in the back of his SUV. As he returned to the house, he heard the microwave ding, letting him know the breakfast burritos were ready. He retrieved them and went to stand at the bottom of the stairs.

"Jess! Henry! Come on down with your things. Time to go."

Moments later, the two scrambled down the stairs, both wearing backpacks, and he added, "And don't forgot your toothbrush."

Henry froze, flashing a sheepish grin, and turned to run up the stairs again. Jess gave Carson a smile, and his heart turned over, thinking how much she resembled pictures of Mila at this same age. At twelve, Jessica Andrews was already five-nine and the star of her volleyball team. She also enjoyed singing in the school choir and idolized her older sister.

He handed her a burrito wrapped in a paper towel.

Henry, who was ten, came bounding down the stairs again. His son had his father's dark brown hair and eyes and was the leading scorer on his soccer team. Henry was also mad for drumming and enjoyed fishing, something Carson had taken up over the years, living so close to the coast.

He gave his son the second burrito and said, "Make sure both your water bottles are filled."

They went out to the SUV, with his daughter reminding him, "Don't forget. We're picking up Grammy and Gramps."

"I wouldn't forget," Carson said, not admitting that he had forgotten they were supposed to stop for Mila's parents on the way to the pep rally.

This was the first time Driftwood Bay's volleyball team had been in the state finals since the year Mila took them to the championship. She would be riding the bus with the team, not as its coach but as a chaperone, with her family following.

He pulled into the Perrys' driveway, where Bill and Laura stood waiting with small suitcases. Carson got out and took their luggage, placing it in the back of the vehicle. Bill had retired as the Bay's school superintendent four years ago. While Laura still owned Coastal Charm Boutique, she had hired a manager to take on the day-to-day running of the store. She and Bill had taken up golfing, which they thoroughly enjoyed, and they were also beginning to do some traveling. For a week each summer, they took all five grandkids on vacation with them. This past summer, they had visited Yellowstone, and the kids were already clamoring to return next year.

Carson parked near the field house and looked over his shoulder. "Why don't you head to the football stadium for the pep rally? Be sure to sit on the north side since Mila will be calling soon for all students, and they'll sit on the south side."

The kids left their backpacks in the car, and he locked it, heading to his office in the field house and making a cup of coffee. Drake Duncan breezed in and greeted him.

His former, troubled star player had turned his life around, putting up the best numbers any athlete had ever seen before or since in the Driftwood Bay basketball program during his senior year. Drake had won a scholarship to TCU. He had injured his knee his sophomore year and sat out most of that season, getting a medical wavier and saving his year of eligibility. After five years, he earned his degree in education but remained undrafted by the pros. Fortunately, he was invited to a tryout with the Celtics. Drake spent three years in Boston, coming off the bench as their sixth man. Later, he was traded to Miami, where he spent another two seasons in that same role.

Now, Drake had come home to the Bay and had been Carson's assistant coach for the past four years. After this upcoming season was completed, he would encourage Drake to accept a head coach offer and push him from the nest. Drake was ready. It was time for him to run his own program.

"Don't worry about practice, Carson. I don't think any players are actually going to be there, not with Mila giving an excused absence to students who are attending the match. Are you excited about going to San Antonio? I think half the town is heading up the road to see the Pirates play."

Drake would be one of the few exceptions. His wife had given birth to their first child less than a month ago, so they would be staying in Driftwood Bay, watching on TV.

Mila's voice came over the PA system, greeting the student body and dismissing seniors to report to the stadium. He knew the volleyball team, band, cheerleaders, and drill team would already be present.

"Let's head over," he told Drake.

The pep rally celebrated the school's volleyball team, and the last speaker was Julie, who had taken over the program several years ago when Mila had stepped off the court and out of the classroom into her first administrative position with the district. Two years ago, his wife had been named head principal at Driftwood Bay High School, and Carson couldn't be prouder of all her accomplishments.

As the band played the school fight song to conclude the pep rally, students and fans streamed from the stands, lining the entire way to the bus the team would take to San Antonio. It gave him a sense of déjà vu, thinking back to Mila's coaching days.

When the team moved past where he stood, his daughter stopped and gave him a big hug.

She pulled away and he looked at her, tears in his eyes, thrilled by the young woman she had become. True to her word, Lily had played volleyball and was now the setter for her team, the playmaker who set up offensive plays for her team-mates. Lily had two scholarship offers to play in college, and they would sit down and deliberate that choice once state concluded.

"Good luck, honey. See you there."

Gina also stopped for a quick hug. His niece was a junior and served as the manager of the volleyball team. She and Lily were still close friends after all these years. Bobby was the school's mascot and gave Carson a wave as he went to the bus, dressed in his pirate uniform.

Once the team was settled on the bus, students and fans alike began dispersing to their own cars to caravan the three hours north. Carson had told everyone to meet him at the car, and he was the last to arrive. He unlocked the doors and everyone piled in. Both his kids slipped on earbuds. Jess said she was going to watch a movie, and Henry began playing a video game.

He settled into an easy conversation with his in-laws, thinking how lucky he was that they lived closed by and had a hand in helping to raise their grandchildren.

They reached San Antonio after one stop for drinks and

the restroom. Since it was too early to check into their hotel, they went for a lunch of Mexican food on the Riverwalk before going to the market to browse. They also included a stop at the famous Mi Terra bakery. Then they returned to the car and went to their hotel.

Carson texted Mila that they had arrived and gave her the room number he and the kids would be staying in. As a chaperone for the team, her room would be in close proximity to the players.

He couldn't wait for tomorrow's finals, hoping his daughter would lead her team to victory.

THE CROWD WAS ELECTRIC, the Driftwood Bay cheerleaders leading their fans in chants. When the Pirates emerged from the locker room, the noise became deafening. As Mila walked to the bleachers, she searched the crowd, finding Carson. She joined her family in the stands.

"They're ready," she said, confidence in her voice. "Gina told me she really doesn't remember the last time we were at state, but Lily has a clear recollection of it. Julie is definitely the right coach to be leading this team. I'm so glad we hired her all those years ago."

Driftwood Bay won the first game of the match in a very close game, fifteen to thirteen. They lost the second game by an identical score.

Everything came down to the final game. A state title hung in the balance.

Carson watched as Lily came up to serve, something she had excelled in since her days playing at the Y in elementary school. She didn't have her sister's height, but her serve was powerful. Even overwhelming, at times. The Pirates ran off four points in a row under Lily's hand, and he sensed their opponents deflating. Ten minutes later, he watched Lily set what could be the game-winning point. Sue, her best friend and an outstanding outside hitter, leaped high into the air, slamming the ball over the net for a kill—and the victory.

The stands erupted in joy for Pirates fans, and Carson watched as his daughter ran from player to player, embracing them.

He leaned over to Mila. "It's hard to believe that our girl is a senior and leaving the nest soon."

She smiled. "She still has a good chunk of the year to go before we drop her at college. Let's savor every sweet moment of this senior year."

They watched as Lily turned, searching the stands for them. She never knew where they sat during her matches, preferring to concentrate on what happened on the floor. When she spotted them, her face lit in a radiant smile, and she dashed across the court, running into the bleachers and throwing her arms around them both. Then she hugged her brother, sister, and grandparents and turned back to her parents.

"We did it!" she cried. "We did it. We're state champs!" Then Lily looked to Mila. "I told you. When I was four years old. I knew I would be back here and help win a championship." She swallowed. "Thanks, Mom. You've been the best role model ever."

As Lily hurried back to the floor to join her teammates, Carson embraced this milestone. His arm went about Mila's waist, pulling her close to him.

"We've done a good job with that one, haven't we?" he said.

"Angie would be so proud," Mila said, always wanting to acknowledge his first wife's presence in their lives.

"I love you, Mila Andrews. More than I'll ever be able to show you."

Tears misted her eyes. "You show me—and tell me—every day, Carson. You'll always be the man I love."

He kissed her, the kiss speaking of all the years they had already spent together.

And the wonderful ones yet to come.

Also by Alexa Aston

COASTAL DREAMS

Second Chance on the Shore

The Art of Healing

Crafting Love

Tides of Trust

THE STRONGS OF SHADOW CREST

The Duke's Unexpected Love

The Perks of Loving a Viscount

Falling for the Marquess

The Captain and the Duchess

Courtship at Shadowcrest

The Marquess' Quest for Love

The Duke's Guide to Winning a Lady

CAPTIVATING KISSES

An Unexpected Kiss

An Impulsive Kiss

An Innocent Kiss

An Unforeseen Kiss

An Enchanting Kiss

An Urgent Kiss

An Unforgettable Kiss

A Promising Kiss

A Possessive Kiss

An Irresistible Kiss

HEARTS IN HAWTHORNE

Heartstrings and Helmets

Heartbeat Harmony

Agent of the Heart

Hearts and Hooves

Hoops and Hearts

LOST CREEK, TEXAS HILL COUNTRY

The Perfect Blend

Painted Melodies

Script of Love

Love in Every Bite

Whispered Melodies

SUGAR SPRINGS

Shadows of the Past

Learning to Trust Again

A Perfect Match

A Fresh Start

Recipe for Love

MAPLE COVE

Another Chance at Love

A New Beginning

Coming Home

The Lyrics of Love

Finding Home

HOLLYWOOD NAME GAME

Hollywood Heartbreaker

Hollywood Flirt

Hollywood Player

Hollywood Double

Hollywood Enigma

LAWMEN OF THE WEST

Runaway Hearts

Blind Faith

Love and the Lawman

Ballad Beauty

SAGEBRUSH BRIDES

A Game of Chance

Written in the Cards

Outlaw Muse

KNIGHTS OF REDEMPTION

A Bit of Heaven on Earth

A Knight for Kallen

SUDDENLY A DUKE

Portrait of the Duke

Music for the Duke

Polishing the Duke

Designs on the Duke

Fashioning the Duke

Love Blooms with the Duke

Training the Duke

Investigating the Duke

SECOND SONS OF LONDON

Educated by the Earl

Debating with the Duke

Empowered by the Earl

Made for the Marquess

Dubious about the Duke

Valued by the Viscount

Meant for the Marquess

DUKES DONE WRONG

Discouraging the Duke

Deflecting the Duke

Disrupting the Duke

Delighting the Duke

Destiny with a Duke

DUKES OF DISTINCTION

Duke of Renown

Duke of Charm

Duke of Disrepute

Duke of Arrogance

Duke of Honor

SOLDIERS AND SOULMATES

To Heal an Earl

To Tame a Rogue

To Trust a Duke

To Save a Love

To Win a Widow

THE ST. CLAIRS

Devoted to the Duke

Midnight with the Marquess

Embracing the Earl

Defending the Duke

Suddenly a St. Clair

STANDALONE ROMANTIC THRILLERS

Leave Yesterday Behind

Illusions of Death

About the Author

USA Today and Amazon Top 100 bestselling author Alexa Aston lives with her husband in a Dallas suburb, where she eats her fair share of dark chocolate and plots out stories while she walks every morning. She enjoys travel, sports, and binge-watching—and never misses an episode of *Survivor*.

Alexa brings her characters to life in steamy historicals, contemporary romances, and romantic suspense novels that resonate with passion, intensity, and heart.

Keep up with Alexa
Visit her website
Newsletter Sign-Up

More ways to connect with Alexa

A small press bound by the belief that every voice matters.

Sign up for our newsletter to learn about new releases and more.
https://oliver-heberbooks.com/subscribe/

Follow us on social media:

facebook.com/oliverheberbooks

instagram.com/oliverheberbooks

amazon.com/oliverheberbooks

youtube.com/@OliverHeberBooksPublisher